HARRIET RUTLAND
KNOCK, MURDERER, KNOCK!

Harriet Rutland was the pen-name of Olive Shimwell. She was born Olive Seers in 1901, the daughter of a prosperous Birmingham builder and decorator.

Little is known of the author's early life but in 1926 she married microbiologist John Shimwell, with whom she moved to a small village near Cork in Ireland. This setting, transplanted to Devon, inspired her first mystery novel *Knock, Murderer, Knock!* which was published in 1938. The second of Harriet Rutland's mysteries, *Bleeding Hooks*, came out in 1940, and the third and last, *Blue Murder*, was published in November 1942. All three novels are remarkable for their black comedy, innovative plots, and pin-sharp portraits of human behaviour, especially concerning relationships between men and women.

Olive and John were divorced in the early forties, and Olive remained single for the rest of her life, without apparently publishing anything further. She died in Newton Abbot in 1962.

Also by Harriet Rutland

Bleeding Hooks
Blue Murder

HARRIET RUTLAND

KNOCK, MURDERER, KNOCK!

With an introduction
by Curtis Evans

DEAN STREET PRESS

"In the tea-room, and hovering round the card-tables, were a vast number of queer old ladies, and decrepit old gentlemen, discussing all the small talk and scandal of the day, with a relish and gusto which sufficiently bespoke the intensity of the pleasure they derived from the occupation."

MR. PICKWICK, at Bath.

INTRODUCTION

Until my research into the life of Harriet Rutland, occasioned by the welcome reprinting by Dean Street Press of her three classic detective novels, little was known about her beyond the fact that "Harriet Rutland" was a pseudonym concealing the name of one Olive Shimwell. In 2009 I queried whether anyone knew anything about Olive Shimwell, and even leading mystery genre scholar Allen J. Hubin pronounced himself stumped. Happily, we now know something about the life of the elusive Olive Shimwell, author of three of the most unjustly neglected English mysteries from the Golden Age of detective fiction, now back in print after more than seventy years.

In 1926, in Harborne, a prosperous suburb of Birmingham (in England's West Midlands), schoolteacher Olive Maude Seers (1901-1962), daughter of prominent Birmingham builder and decorator Joseph Seers, wed John Lester Shimwell (1901-1964), grandson of a monumental stonemason and himself a brewing microbiologist who a few years previously had received a degree in biochemistry from the University of Birmingham. John Shimwell worked for Mitchells and Butlers Brewery in Smethwick, another Birmingham suburb, but in 1931 he and Olive moved to Ireland, where he became the Head Brewer for Beamish and Crawford, a company headquartered in Cork, Ireland's second largest city. The Shimwells would remain in Ireland until the outbreak of the Second World War, when John accepted a position as the head of the yeast research laboratory at the Whitbread Brewery in London.

During the near decade they spent in Ireland the Shimwells resided at least part of the time not in Cork proper but at Hillside Cottage in St. Ann's Hill, a tiny nearby community that in 1930 boasted a post and telegraph office, a railway station (four trains to and from Cork daily), several shops, thirteen desirable residences and, last but not least, St. Ann's Hill Hydropathic Establishment, opened by pioneering hydropathist Dr. Richard Barter in 1843 and still in operation throughout the 1930s, when the Shimwells dwelt in the vicinity. The Hydro, promoted "as a residence for invalids and accommodation for tourists to the region," boasted, in addition to its hydrotherapy facilities, eighty bedrooms, a circulating library, a reading room, a theatre, a billiard room, tennis courts, a nine-hole golf course and "an American bowling alley" (see Tarquin Blake's *Abandoned Ireland*website).

When, sometime around 1937, Olive Shimwell decided to try her hand at mystery writing, surely nothing was more natural, given her years of residence at St. Ann's Hill, than for the author to stage her first "Harriet Rutland" murder extravaganza--published in England in 1938 under the title *Knock, Murderer, Knock!*--at a hydro hotel. *Knock, Murderer, Knock!* succeeds splendidly not only as a clever puzzle but as an acerbically amusing satirical portrayal of genteel hotel society. In *A Catalogue of Crime* the authoritative genre critics Jacques Barzun and Wendell Hertig Taylor compare *Knock, Murderer, Knock!*, which they pronounce "shows a good intelligence at work," to Leo Bruce's classic 1962 mystery *Nothing Like Blood*, but I was also reminded of John Rhode's nearly exactly contemporaneous 1939 detective novel *Death on Sunday*, wherein the author draws commensurately acid pen portraits of his hoity-toity guest house subjects, though not quite with Rutland's remarkable literary flair.

Although Shimwell took care to cloak her true identity behind her Harriet Rutland pseudonym, she also adopted the additional obscuring course of transferring the locale of her imaginary hotel, Presteignton Hydro, to Devon, England. (Presteignton may be based on Paignton, a real Devon town located near Torquay, home of Agatha Christie, just as the novel's fictional Newton St. Mary may be based on Newton Abbot, the Devon town where Olive Shimwell moved after her divorce from John in the mid-1940s and where she would pass away in 1962.) Given her withering portrayal of many of the characters in *Knock, Murderer, Knock!,* Shimwell's evasive actions seem reasonably prudent.

Among the ghastly gallery readers will find at Presteignton Hydro are Mrs. Napier, a batty exhibitionist who pretends she is too frail to walk ("She's down again, miss."); blind and blunt Miss Brendon ("Senna pods were good enough for my mother, they ought to be good enough for me. I've had no action for six days!") and her loyal maid Ada Rogers ("Oh, no, miss... Two days, miss, it is, and time yet."); proudly pious Miss Astill ("Psalms and a sermon once a week are what everyone needs, I say."); painfully proper Mrs. Marston ("I'm no believer in letting youth have its fling. It's only asking for trouble these days, especially with girls."); and snobbish and imperious Lady Warme, who, to her secret shame, worked in her father's shop as a girl and married a man who owed both his fortune and his title to his widely-used Patent Cornflour.

The favorite form of recreation for these good ladies is indulging in censorious gossip about other Hydro inmates, especially young and pretty Miss Blake and handsome Sir Humphrey Chervil. Shimwell handles with facility a large cast of characters at Presteignton Hydro that includes, in addition to those individuals mentioned above, the hydro owner, Dr. Williams, and his secretary, nurse, housekeeper, and young daughter; Mrs. Marston's husband, two teenage daughters and the Marston chauffeur; a couple of retired military men, crossword-loving Admiral Unwin and knitting hobbyist Colonel Simcox; and the aspiring mystery writer Mrs. Dawson and her young son Bobby.

In a memorable bit of genre parody, Mrs. Dawson ("that blasted woman thriller-writer" another character derisively terms her) views everything that occurs around her at the Hydro as potential material for her books. "[T]here have to be several murders in the book," pronounces Mrs. Dawson on the fine art of mystery writing. "Two or three, at least. The reading public nowadays is never satisfied with only one murder."

When murder strikes most viciously at the Presteignton Hydro, it is up to stolid Inspector Palk, with the help of Sergeant Jago, to untangle the horrid affair; but after a second decidedly unnatural death takes place it becomes clear that the good inspector is in over his head. Fortunately, at this point it appears that an amateur detective is in the offing, quite eager to lend Inspector Palk a hand. Has this person turned up in time to prevent the third murder that, according to Mrs. Dawson, the Golden Age reading public demanded in its mysteries?

A strikingly assured performance for a first-time mystery writer, *Knock, Murderer, Knock!* compares so favorably with the work of Shimwell's great British Crime Queen contemporaries--Agatha Christie, Dorothy L. Sayers, Margery Allingham and Ngaio Marsh--that one might justly dub Harriet Rutland an heir presumptive. In addition to its beautifully designed clue puzzle, the debut Rutland novel has witty writing, a memorable setting, finely drawn characters, moments of shock, poignancy and romance and lashings of literary allusions. The novel's title alludes to a line in Macbeth and it opens with an apt epigraph from Charles Dickens' *The Pickwick Papers*, while throughout the text there are references to classic literature. My favorite example is when the incorrigible Miss Blake, asked to read aloud to the ladies of the Hydro while they perform their needlework, chooses scandalous passages from Aldous Huxley's *Brave New World*, provoking this exchange with Lady Warme:

> "Of all the low, immoral books. But I'm not surprised. That is just the kind of literature I imagined you would choose. I don't wonder that the youth of today is corrupt, with that kind of dirt lying on every library shelf for young hands to reach."
>
> Miss Blake corrected her with a smile.

"Not every shelf, Lady Warme. It was banned in the Irish Free State, or Eire, as they call it now."

"I'm very glad to hear it. It's about the only decent thing I've ever heard about the Irish."

Knock, Murderer, Knock! was published in England in late 1938 and the United States early the following year. It was warmly received in both countries, with the *Saturday Review*, for example, pronouncing the novel an "exceptional" book; yet until now it had never been reprinted and had dropped almost entirely from public consciousness. As indicated above, Barzun and Taylor took favorable note of Rutland's debut novel in 1971, but as far as I know no one mentioned the novel in the internet age until I included it on my list of 150 Favorite Golden Age British Detective Novels, posted at the website *Mystery*File* in 2010. Since then, *Knock, Murderer, Knock!* has been lavishly praised by vintage crime fiction blogger John Norris, who wrote of the novel: "A hardcore mystery fan couldn't ask for a more literate and witty refresher in the genuine traditional mystery." I concur. It is a great pleasure for me to have the chance to welcome Harriet Rutland into the ranks of revived classic mystery writers, as I can scarcely think of an individual more deserving of revival.

Curtis Evans

CHAPTER I

Mrs Napier walked slowly to the middle of the terrace, noted the oncoming car, looked round to make sure that she was fully observed, crossed her legs deliberately, and fell heavily on to the red gravel drive.

"Just look at that old hag!" exclaimed Admiral Urwin, chuckling.

"A bloomin' acrobat, that's what she is," muttered Matthews, the chauffeur, who had just managed to bring the car to a standstill in front of her.

Amy Ford, the chambermaid of the front corridor, leaned from an upper-window to shake a duster, and retired, convulsed with laughter, to call, "Molly, come here, do; she's fallen down again. If that isn't the fifth time this morning!" She jumped quickly back to her work as she heard the housekeeper's sharp voice behind her: "Slacking as usual, Amy Ford!"

"She's down again, miss," commented Ada Rogers, Miss Brendon's personal maid, drawing the curtain back from the bedroom window.

"Who? Who?" croaked her bedridden mistress, looking like an ill-fated owl.

"Why, Mrs. Napier, to be sure, miss. She did ought to be in a loony home, that she ought, but they do say that her family's that fond of her that they couldn't abide to let her go."

"That woman ought not to be allowed to reside in the Hydro," said Lady Warme indignantly. "She's a public nuisance."

"But she's grand copy, poor thing," replied Mrs. Dawson, taking out her little red notebook.

Miss Blake lifted her mascara-lidded blue eyes to Sir Humphrey Chervil, Baronet, who was affixing the orange-and-black striped canopy of her deck-chair over her head, and shrugged her smooth, bare shoulders.

"It must be terrible to grow old," she said, with a little assumed shudder. "If I ever thought that I should grow like that woman, I'd kill myself."

"You never will," Sir Humphrey assured her, gazing with admiration at her stream-lined figure in its skin-tight sunbathing frock. "You're a sight for the gods in that get-up, and whom the gods love, die young."

The little group of people on the croquet lawn looked up towards the terrace.

"There she goes again!" exclaimed Winnie Marston.

"Who? Tishy?" asked her younger sister, Millie, laughing.

"Hush, girls. It's unkind of you to take any notice of poor Mrs. Napier," said their mother. "She's not quite –"

"They're all 'not quite'," wheezed Mr. Marston asthmatically. "How I ever keep sane myself in this god-damned hole, I don't know!"

Colonel Simcox looked up from his deck-chair, snorted, and buried himself again in his newspaper.

"My God!" ejaculated Dr. Williams, who was standing with his secretary, Miss Lewis, regarding the little scene from his surgery window. "One day I shall commit a murder in this place."

"The silly old fool!" said Nurse Hawkins, savagely stamping out a forbidden cigarette. "Now I suppose I shall have to go and pick her up."

Mrs. Napier lay still in an agony of mind.

"No one is coming to help me," she thought. "I shall have to get up by myself, then they'll all laugh at me. No one knows what I suffer. Nobody understands. They wouldn't leave me here if they did. It's unkind of them, cruel. They know I can't get up... Perhaps no one saw me. Perhaps I chose the wrong moment, when they were all looking the other way. But this chauffeur person saw me. He's looking at me now; looking at me in a way that no man should look at a woman. I shall scream..."

Miss Astill, a thin woman wearing an old-fashioned dress which had originally been black in colour, but now looked rust-brown in the morning sunlight, walked jerkily forward and spoke to the recumbent figure on the gravel.

"What's the matter, Mrs. Napier?" she asked softly. "Why don't you get up?"

Mrs. Napier rolled her eyes upwards and made a few movements with her body like a wounded bird.

"I'm dying!" she gasped. "Poisoned! My enemies have had their revenge; they know that I have the King's shoe. Oh, nobody knows what I go through in this dreadful place."

"God knows, dear," soothed Miss Astill. "You must have faith. He will take care of you."

Two firm arms tightened around Mrs. Napier and raised her to her feet before she had realized what had happened. She clung hysterically to Miss Astill's bony frame as Nurse Hawkins came running up to them.

"What's happened to you, Mrs. Napier?" asked the nurse.

"Happened?" Mrs. Napier glared at her through her thick-lensed, gold-framed spectacles. "I've been lying here for hours. I might have died for all that you care. You all hate me. I'd far better be dead. I pray that you will never be like me."

"Amen to that!" exclaimed Nurse Hawkins fervently. Then, in softer tones, she added: "There, you'll soon feel better now. Let me see if you can walk to the nearest pillar. Ups-a-daisy! Don't fall down again; left, right, left, right. I'll go and fetch the bath-chair for you."

The thought of the bath-chair acted like a spur, and Mrs. Napier began to walk slowly, still crossing her legs one over the other, to the pillars which supported the open, glass-covered verandah which ran round the south front of the Hydro. There she left her.

"That dreadful nurse!" said Mrs. Napier. "She neglects me so. I think I shall have to go away from here. Nobody cares about me." She began to whimper.

"Oh no, you can't mean that," protested Miss Astill in her gentle, ladylike voice. "Nurse Hawkins is very trying, we know, but you must have patience with her. She has all the faults of an unbeliever. But you must never think of leaving the Hydro. Where else would you ever find such comfort and peace, and anyone so thoughtful as the dear, kind doctor? The one fear of my life is that I might have to live somewhere else. You surely could not deliberately choose to go away. Besides, we should all miss you so much."

Mrs. Napier smiled.

"Perhaps I spoke hastily," she said. "If you want me to stay, of course, I will. You are always so kind."

"That's right," replied Miss Astill with an encouraging smile. "Now I must leave you. I am going to take my morning exercise along the shrubbery path." She jerked herself away.

Mrs. Napier began dusting down the front of her shapeless brown woollen cardigan suit with a large silk handkerchief. A burst of laughter from the croquet lawn arrested her attention, and she looked up.

"Those horrid Marstons," she thought. She could never make up her mind which of the four she hated the most; the supercilious mother, the bad-tempered father, or the two stupid, giggling girls. What did any of them know about suffering like hers?

Another laugh. Mrs. Napier glared suspiciously at them.

Were they laughing at her? No, it was at Mr. Marston, who was driving all the croquet balls off the edge of the lawn because he was annoyed at losing the game. And his language! Really, she could not stay and listen to it.

She made two steps, crabwise, holding on to the nearest pillar, then relaxed as she saw that they were not going to play any more. As they walked away Mr. Marston's loud voice could be heard discussing, like any bridge-player, every wrong stroke which had been made during the whole course of the game, both by his partner and by his opponents.

Mrs. Napier looked beyond the croquet lawn to the grassy edge of the bright-red cliff, and across the sunlit sweep of Devonshire Bay to the opposite arm of land from which the distant, vast expanse of Dartmoor rose in a dim purple haze. The thought of the moors soothed her. As she stood there on the terrace gazing across towards them, a deep peace enfolded her, and she forgot the troubles of the morning. It was thus that the moors had looked down with unchanging brows on the troubles of countless generations, so big were they, so calm, so remote.

She remembered the time when they had not been so remote to her. Thirty-five years ago she and Mortimer had spent their honeymoon on those same moors, and had tramped for hours among the tors. She in a short plaid cape and long tweed skirt, and he in ulster and deerstalker, with a half-plate camera strapped to his back. What fun that camera had brought to them! How often had they been turned away and refused food and shelter because some worthy farmer's wife had mistaken it for a pedlar's pack or for part of the equipment of the scorned tinker folk.

They had never been content to tramp the easier, wooded paths which skirted the edge of the moor. Each day had seen the conquest of yet another of the highest tors, and they had dared the long road which swept down to the little grey village of Widdicombe, only to shoot up again to an equal height on the other side in a gigantic switchback. In those days she had skipped along the crisp loamy undergrowth as actively as a goat, often running to the top of a rise before Mortimer, and calling, in the high-pitched voice he had loved, upon all the new beauties of form and colour which lay before her eyes.

Now she could no longer run, or even walk, and she pretended that she was happier for it. Such joys as she and Mortimer had experienced had vanished, she said, with the charabanc, whose noisy, motley crowds of boisterous holidaymakers so often disturbed the peace of the country. But in her heart she knew that she envied them, just as she envied the straight, lissom limbs of Miss Blake and Winnie Marston, who could still tramp the red turf of the moors while she had to be wheeled about in a bath-chair.

The rolling sound of the great Chinese gong from the entrance hall of the Hydro cut across her mind. It imbued the scattered figures in the grounds and on the terrace with a sudden, single purpose. They passed through the double swing-doors, leaving the brown-clad figure of Mrs. Napier alone.

She remained there until the cheerful rattle of knives and forks echoed through the open dining-room windows, then, looking round furtively to make sure that no one was in sight, she walked steadily towards the front doors into the Hydro.

CHAPTER II

Presteignton Hydro is a rambling greystone building set on the cliff above a private beach in Devonshire Bay. To reach it by road you must drive along the whole sleepy length of Excester and swing round to the right, taking the road which leads direct to Newton St. Mary with its chief hotel, "The Angel and Child," dairy, police-station, and bank, all standing within a few hundred yards of the circular, covered, old stone market stalls against which half of the people of Britain and the United States must have been photographed at one time or another. If you are not already familiar with the district you are not likely to happen upon Presteignton by accident, for in this part of the county the high Devon hedges with their wealth of wild flowers have not given place to non-skid motor roads and pseudo-thatched cottage garages. In spite of the shining black-and-yellow sign on the main road advertising Presteignton Hydro as an A.A. hotel (in the book it boasts two modest stars), only one person in a thousand ever breaks his journey to turn up the hill, for thirty miles ahead of him lie the red-roofed bungalows and wooden huts which mark the beach at Tormouth, and here he can park his car on the front and open up his luncheon basket without further expense.

But for all its unassuming airs, Presteignton was in existence long before the more popular Tormouth, and Presteignton Hydro had been built in an age when people visited hydropathic establishments more for the sake of fashion than of health, in a leisurely age when rooms were booked by letter a month or more in advance, and the telegrams which made the lives of hotel proprietors so erratic in these uncertain days were unknown. The old weather-beaten oak board, bearing directions to ostlers and still fixed for sentiment's sake to the corner of the palatial stables, now mostly converted into lock-up garages, bears testimony to this. But these days have long since vanished from Presteignton just as they have vanished from Matlock and Bath, and although the position of Presteignton Hydro ought to have secured for it the patronage of younger generations, set, as it is, on the high, red cliff looking across the whole vast sweep of the bay, it remained too conservative to attract them. While other hotels were adding squash rackets courts, artificially coloured swimming-pools, and even small golf-courses, the building and grounds of Presteignton Hydro remained unaltered, except for the addition of a sun-lounge, and still retained old-fashioned wash-stands with their attendant cold water and slop pails, while its more progressive rivals boasted fitted wash-basins with running H. & C.

If it had been an ordinary hotel it would long since have fallen into oblivion, but whereas the rest of the hotel remained unaltered through the years, the equipment for the baths and treatment rooms had been kept surprisingly up to date, chiefly because few doctors stayed longer than two years, and each one as he arrived demanded some new machine with which he could try out his own pet theory. It thus catered for patients who suffered from some bodily infirmity requiring periodic treatment, for which the resident doctor and nurse were responsible. In addition, it suited people who steadfastly set their faces against all progress and change, and as such people as these are greater in number than is generally supposed, the Hydro was by no means deserted. Locally known as THE Hydro, the once fashionable meeting-place and matrimonial bureau had become a hotel for middle-aged or elderly people who had either sold their homes or passed them on to their grown-up children, and sought greater comfort combined with less expense in the Hydro's special residential terms.

It was not, therefore, surprising that the advent of anyone so young and attractive as Miss Blake, followed some weeks later by that of Sir Humphrey Chervil, presumably a rich bachelor, had occasioned a wave of curiosity in the Hydro which, even after several months, had scarcely died away, but still gave rise to interested speculations as to the reason for such a prolonged visit.

"The poor lady, 'tis languishing for love she is," sighed the Irish chambermaid, Molly, who spoke in terms of cheap novelettes when off duty.

"Love! Your mind's for ever running on love!" returned the more practical-minded Amy. "She's been going the pace more like at night-clubs and cocktail parties. I've seen folks like her in the society papers when I've been doing out the library. She'll come to a bad end, you mark my words."

"'Tis love, I'm telling you," persisted Molly. "I'm reading a gorgeous sixpenny now where the beautiful heiress is after being carried off by the wicked Sir Jasper, with a look of unearthly pallor on her face. She's just like Miss Blake on the cover."

But there was no lack of colour on Miss Blake's carefully made-up cheeks as she strolled downstairs at ten o'clock one Sunday morning and walked out on to the terrace. She wore a brilliant cerise-and-white ensemble, evidently not intended for church-going, and had a "neat, unhurried, bite-your-thread" look which she might have learned in the United States if she had ever been there.

Colonel Simcox, who had been awaiting her appearance ever since breakfast, hurried after, her, carrying three balls of different-coloured wools and four knitting-needles.

"I was just looking for you, Miss Blake," he said. "You know you promised to help me with my new socks. What I want to know is, what am I expected to do with the red and green wools when I knit the blue? It says here..." He pulled a crumpled page of instructions from his pocket, dropping a ball of wool as he did so. Miss Blake stooped to pick it up. "Thank you. It says: K.1. red, P.2. blue, K.6. green. But what in the name of goodness happens to the other two colours when I 'K' the red?"

"It sounds like a new form of billiards," smiled Miss Blake. "You know, you'll have Miss Astill on your track if you start knitting on Sundays."

"It's very irritating, dammit... I beg your pardon, but these books are most annoying, they leave the important part out altogether. Written by a woman, I've no doubt."

"Now, Colonel, don't be so cross," returned Miss Blake. "If you will choose such a complicated design, you must expect to find it difficult. I'm sure I couldn't manage to knit with three balls of wool at once. I can't think what you are worrying about, all the same. It seems quite easy to see what to do. You just leave the colours you are not knitting in little loops behind, I should think."

"I can't do that, it would look such a mess. My God! What a mess it would look."

"But no one would see the inside of the socks."

"No, but I can't do things like that. You women don't care, you're held up by safety-pins half the time."

Miss Blake laughed.

"Not nowadays, Colonel," she objected, but the Colonel did not seem to hear.

"Perhaps I'm old-fashioned," he went on, "but I have to have my things just right. I'm an old bachelor and very particular about my clothes. It's my belief that most married men look untidy because they rely on their wives to mend their clothes for them, and most women have no idea how to do it. Here, let me have another look."

He took the booklet from her and muttered under his breath as he read it, his forehead so wrinkled that his eyeglass fell with a tinkle against the black button of his morning coat, which he wore in deference to its being Sunday.

Admiral Urwin hobbled towards them between his two walking-sticks, carrying a folded paper underneath his arm.

"Ah, there you are, Miss Blake. I've been looking for you everywhere. I've a new crossword puzzle for you in today's *Observer*. It seems even more difficult than usual. I can't think of a word... of a word of... let me see... twelve letters, meaning... twenty-four across, I think it is – yes, twenty-four across. Pom, pom, E, pom, A, pom, T..."

The Colonel snorted.

"That old fool and his crosswords," he muttered to Miss Blake. "What a hobby for the Senior Service! Senile Service is more like it if he's any example. Oh, damn! I've dropped a stitch. Can you pick it up for me?"

Miss Blake sat down on the nearest green wooden seat, the Colonel seated himself on her left, and the Admiral subsided at her right with his usual grunts and clattering of sticks. He took a silver propelling pencil from his pocket and carefully adjusted the lead, then applied himself to the puzzle.

"Now then, Colonel," he said breezily, "this is in your line. A weapon of three letters, beginning with G."

The Colonel snorted again.

"Gun, I suppose," said the Admiral in answer to his own question. "G-U – no, it isn't. That's funny."

"Very funny, sir," said the Colonel in biting tones.

"Gat," suggested Miss Blake.

"Gat? Never heard of it," said the Admiral.

"Short for gatling, sir," remarked the Colonel.

"Never thought of that," said the Admiral. "Clever of you both. 'The gatling's jammed and the Colonel dead' – I beg your pardon, Colonel."

The Colonel snorted.

"There's the stitch," said Miss Blake sweetly, handing back the Colonel's knitting. "Now don't drop any more."

"Gat is right. Now, Colonel, perhaps you can do this one. A word of fifteen letters –"

"I do not like crossword puzzles, sir. I refuse to assist you with them. In my opinion it is an old man's game, sir."

"It's more dignified than knitting socks, anyway," retorted the Admiral. "That's an old woman's game. There are enough old women in the Hydro, God knows; why don't you leave the knitting to them?"

Miss Blake sat quite still, looking like Tenniel's illustration of Alice between the two queens. She looked up as footsteps crunched towards them on the gravel and saw Sir Humphrey, dressed in a Harris tweed sports suit with leather buttons, making his way to the seat on which she was sitting. He halted in front of them and exchanged a few conventional remarks with the two men, then spoke expressly to Miss Blake.

"Would you care to come for a walk?" he asked. "It's a glorious morning."

"Thanks, I'd love to," she replied, and, rising to her feet, looked down with a smile at the Admiral and Colonel as if she were sorry to leave them. She and Sir Humphrey walked away like two children who share a secret.

The Admiral chuckled.

"That looks like a match," he remarked, putting away his pencil and taking a heavy gold repeater from his pocket.

"What does?" asked the Colonel, without raising his eyes from his laborious knitting.

"Why, Miss Blake and the baronet, of course."

"Stuff and nonsense!" exploded the Colonel. "Just because a man asks a girl to go for a walk with him, you think they're going to get married. I've no patience with you. You're as bad as all the other old women gossips in this place."

"Well, there's no need for you to get so crochety about it. Anyone would think that you were after the girl yourself." He leaned across and nudged the Colonel in the ribs.

"Keep your offensive remarks to yourself, sir," replied the Colonel.

Admiral Urwin looked carefully at the Colonel's crimsoned face, fumbled under the seat for his sticks, and levered himself to his feet.

"If I'm not wanted, I can go," he said. "So that's why you wanted to know whether I thought you'd look younger without your moustache, eh?" He stood between his two sticks, shaking with laughter. "Well, they do say there's no fool like an old fool. If you're going to church this morning you'd better get ready."

He limped off, still chuckling.

Colonel Simcox tried to continue with his knitting, dropped five stitches in as many seconds, drove a needle into his finger, then, with an oath, thrust needles and wool into his pocket, and strode off in the same direction as the Admiral, pulling savagely at his moustache.

He was worried about this new turn of events. He had never disguised from himself the fact that he was deliberately fostering his friendship with Miss Blake in the hope that it might lead to a deeper emotion, however much he had disguised it from everyone else. His intentions were, of course, honourable. By his code, the intentions of a retired colonel who had passed through Sandhurst and served three sovereigns with honour in many countries, could be nothing else, but he had been content to drift along and to monopolize her company unchallenged. Sir Humphrey had never deliberately sought out Miss Blake's company before in all the weeks that he had been at the Hydro. With his entry into the lists as a rival for Miss Blake's favour, the Colonel was confronted with the necessity for making some sort of declaration, and never since the Major's daughter had refused him behind the palms at a regimental dance in his subaltern's days in Malta had he ever proposed to a woman.

He made his way up to his bedroom and walked over to the mirror of his dressing-table, still fingering his moustache.

He wondered whether he would really look younger without it. After all, there was no sense in looking older than one's years in these days.

He took a coloured silk handkerchief from the neat pile in the left-hand top drawer and held the end across his upper lip, but somehow it only contrived to make him look like a stage pirate, and he folded it into its careful creases and returned it to its exact former position.

He could not imagine himself without his moustache. Even in his subaltern days he had worn one, very long, with pomaded ends. The ladies used to like them like that, and they had certainly looked very smart with the old dress uniforms. During the Great War he had altered it to a shaggy toothbrush, and had worn it in that shape ever since.

He frowned at his reflection in the mirror, shook his head at himself, and went to get his top hat out of its hatter's box ready for church.

In the meantime, Miss Blake and Sir Humphrey had passed along the whole length of the terrace and turned down the path leading through the little pine wood to the sea. Had they wished to create a scandal in the Hydro they could not have chosen a safer path nor a better time, since all, except such patients as Mrs. Napier and Miss Brendon, were grouped outside the front porch, ready to set out for church.

"I only hope she doesn't get hold of him," murmured Mrs. Dawson, who, as a widow on the right side of forty, had great hopes of getting hold of Sir Humphrey herself. "It's obvious that she thinks of nothing but attracting men."

"And it's a downright pity that a few more women in this place aren't the same," said Mr. Marston, regarding the circle of badly dressed women who were standing on the porch.

"I have never met a man with sufficient intelligence to realize that beauty is only skin-deep," remarked Miss Astill.

"Obviously," returned Mr. Marston, gazing pointedly at her tattered toque, faded costume, grey cotton gloves, and low-heeled black shoes.

"Hush, Charles!" said his wife.

"I wouldn't mind so much," put in Lady Warme, "if they were not going through the woods. There are so many other walks that are more open, but just as pretty, that it does look as if..."

"It does, indeed," agreed Miss Astill, her colour heightening at the unspoken thought. "They ought to go to church in any case. I don't believe in all this modern talk about worshipping God in nature and seeing heaven in a butterfly's wing. My poor dear father used to see that I went to church regularly every Sunday and went himself, though he had to be wheeled there in a bath-chair. And how he suffered! I know, for I nursed him for years. Psalms and a sermon once a week are what everyone needs, I say."

"I can't think what you are all making such a fuss about," said Mr. Marston. "Why can't they go for a walk if they want to? I bet any one of you ladies would jump at the chance if Sir Humphrey ever asked you, which he's not likely to do as long as Miss Blake is here. It's far too nice a morning to sit in church, and I don't suppose that they will misconduct themselves in broad daylight, if that's what you are all thinking."

"Charles! How can you be so coarse in front of the girls? As if anyone had suggested such a thing!" exclaimed his wife.

"How very vulgar!" said Lady Warme. "But still, as you have suggested it, it is a fact that Miss Blake is to be changed into an upstairs bedroom tomorrow."

Her voice held a triumphant note, and Mr. Marston turned away with a snort of disgust.

"You don't mean to say...?" queried Miss Astill, her voice trembling with suppressed emotion.

"Indeed, I do. You may depend that the doctor knows more about them than we do. Of course, he says that he requires her bedroom for Mrs. Napier because it is on the ground floor, and Mrs. Napier can no longer walk upstairs, but I shouldn't be surprised if –"

"Neither should I." Mrs. Dawson added her voice to the discussion. "After all, what could be easier than for him to stroll out on to the terrace for a smoke and just walk into her room through the french window?"

"Oh, but I can't believe that," said Mrs. Marston, fearful lest Winnie and Millie should pay too much attention to the conversation.

"Nonsense! She would get him inside on some pretext or other," continued Mrs. Dawson. "It wouldn't be his fault. I blame her entirely."

"I don't know so much about that," boomed Lady Warme, in her deep voice. "You never know with a man. I wouldn't be surprised at anything."

"I hardly think that even a girl like her would have the cheek to do such things right under our very noses," protested Mrs. Marston half-heartedly.

"Dear Mrs. Marston, you are far too warm-hearted to think badly of anyone," returned Lady Warme. "I can believe anything of girls nowadays, anything. I'm sure I don't know what they are coming to with their bare backs and shorts. They leave absolutely nothing to the imagination. Now, in my young days –"

"Good God!" exclaimed Mr. Marston, as he joined them again. "Haven't you finished tearing them to pieces yet? You'll all be late for church. It's half past ten by the wireless, ten to eleven by the Hydro clock, and five past by my watch!"

CHAPTER III

For every one rule made by Dr. Williams there were three made by the residents themselves, but whereas his were printed on neat cards and hung about the Hydro, theirs were enforced by a kind of concerted freezing-out process, the technique of which was known to them alone. Thus the window tables in the dining-room became allotted to guests by virtue of their length of residence in the Hydro. If any stranger wandered towards one of them in the mistaken presumption that each table was alike with its bottle of Vichy or Evian, its old-fashioned cruet, its medicine-bottle and its box of digestive tablets, he would be greeted with a silence charged with such unmistakable emotion that, after casting several defiant glances through the window, he would turn and seat himself at one of the ill-lit tables in the less attractive part of the room.

By this same silent means it had become an unwritten law that after luncheon those ladies who did not take an afternoon nap should congregate in the lounge, and that the men should drift into the reading-room. The fact that Miss Blake walked towards the reading-room after luncheon one day with a laughing glance over her shoulder at the pursuing Admiral did not, therefore, escape comment.

"So it's the Admiral's turn now," remarked Winnie, as she, her mother and sister, Miss Astill and Lady Warme, wandered by mutual consent towards one of the card-tables in the lounge and cut for partners. "She's only got to look twice at a man and he simply grovels. It's technique, that's what it is. I wish I knew how she does it."

Miss Astill leaned across from her chair opposite, and patted her soft young hand so that the rings she wore on her own bony hand clicked loosely together.

"Don't ever wish that," she said seriously. "You are just the kind of girl we all like to see here. You're so unspoiled. It would be quite wicked to wish to be any different."

Mrs. Marston smiled as she shuffled the cards.

"So kind of you to say so, Miss Astill," she said, complacently. "I'm sure Charles and I have always tried to do our duty in bringing the girls up well. I'm no believer in letting youth have its fling. It's only asking for trouble these days, especially with girls."

"'Spare the rod and spoil the child' was a good maxim in my young days," nodded Miss Astill, "and it holds good today just the same." She glanced through her cards. "I suppose we are playing for halfpenny stakes as usual. My dear father would be horrified if he could see his little Eppie playing cards for money, but I'm afraid I'm a terrible gambler. Always ready to have my little flutter, you know."

Winnie Marston restrained herself with difficulty from grimacing. There was, she thought, something definitely sick-making about these old women when they grew coquettish and facetious, and their sly jokes seemed infinitely more dirty than the latest Stock Exchange joke from robuster lips. She and Millie lived under a constant strain among them in their endeavour to laugh in the right places and to hide their laughter in the wrong ones.

"One diamond," called Lady Warme firmly, and the game started and continued smoothly, until a diversion was created by the entrance of Mrs. Napier with Nurse Hawkins.

As soon as she saw the assembled women in the lounge she leaned heavily upon the nurse, and nothing would induce her feet to point in the right direction, so that both double doors had to be opened before she could be guided into the room. No chair would content her but the one in which Mrs. Dawson was sitting, and she proceeded to annex it by falling first over the back and then the arm of it, till Mrs. Dawson, in response to the appeal in Nurse Hawkins' eyes, got up and moved to a neighbouring one. With a muttered, "Always neglects me. No pity," Mrs. Napier settled herself in comfort and dusted down her dress with her large silk handkerchief.

Nurse Hawkins stuffed a cushion none too gently behind her patient's head, and glanced swiftly round the room.

Miss Astill smiled icily.

"If you're looking for Miss Blake," she remarked, "she's in the reading-room with Admiral Urwin. You'll have to take care or your nose will be put out of joint."

Winnie made a half-suppressed sound of remonstrance and, looking up, was startled to see the expression of vindictive hatred which momentarily replaced the impersonal professional look on Nurse Hawkins' face. So suddenly was it obliterated that Winnie afterwards could not say with any certainty that she had not imagined it.

Nurse Hawkins opened her mouth as if to reply, then checked herself, and having assured herself that Mrs. Napier was already interested in the book which Mrs. Dawson was showing her, moved out of the lounge with heightened colour and head held high.

"And is she jealous!" exclaimed Winnie's film-struck sister Millie. "Why, she looked as if she could have strangled Miss Blake!"

"I must say it serves her right," remarked Lady Warme. "She's been setting her nurse's cap at the Admiral for months. She ought to have more sense than to try and catch a sailor: they have had too much experience for any woman, even a nurse."

"You don't think there's anything wrong between them, do you?" asked Miss Astill anxiously.

Lady Warme snorted.

"Certainly not," she replied, "but I don't doubt that Nurse Hawkins wishes there were. These nurses are all alike, always looking for a husband. I've seen two of them married off to rich old patients here myself. I don't believe that the doctor pays the nurses at all; he lets them come on prospects, like head waiters at those big London restaurants."

"But it's so silly of her to be jealous," meditated Winnie. "Miss Blake isn't likely to prefer the Admiral to Sir Humphrey, even though the old man is a damned good sort."

"Winnie!" exclaimed her mother.

"Sorry, Mother. Though he's such a jolly good sort, I meant. After all, she is the only good-looking woman in this place..." The last word ended on a squeal of pain as Mrs. Marston's foot gave her ankles a vicious little kick.

But no one present had taken her words personally.

"Oh, do you really think so?" said Miss Astill. "I always think that the doctor's secretary has such a pretty little face."

"Miss Lewis is a great deal too pretty to be secretary to a young widower like Dr. Williams, if you ask my opinion," said Lady Warme. "Nurse Hawkins isn't the only woman with her eye on the main chance, by any means."

Miss Astill looked pained.

"But I'm sure the doctor..." she began.

Lady Warme and Mrs. Marston laughed with each other significantly.

"Oh, we all know what you think of the doctor," they chorused, and Miss Astill glanced coyly downwards.

"You don't really believe that Miss Blake could prefer the Admiral to Sir Humphrey, do you?" asked Millie, looking reflectively at her buffer-polished nails.

Lady Warme snorted at her cards.

"I should say that Sir Humphrey has found out that she is nothing but a common adventuress," she replied. "You only have to look at her to see what she is, while Sir Humphrey is a real gentleman."

Mrs. Dawson joined in the conversation.

"Has it ever occurred to any of you," she remarked, "that we really know nothing about Sir Humphrey Chervil? You'll find no mention of his name in either *Burke* or *Debrett*. It always seems a strange trait in the human character that we inquire so closely whether the Smiths or Browns of this world come from

Yorkshire or Gloucestershire but are willing to take any title at its face value."

Lady Warme swung round in her chair.

"That remark is in extremely bad taste, Mrs. Dawson," she said, and ice could almost be heard clinking in her voice. "As for not finding his name in the peerage, I would remind you that the copies of *Debrett* and *Burke* in the library are twenty-five years old, and many eminent people have been elevated to titles since they were printed. My own name is not in those particular copies, but I hope that you will not question my right to a title on that account."

Mrs. Dawson grimaced and returned to her book.

"Dear Lady Warme," purred Miss Astill, "of course we all know who you are –"

"Warme's Patent Cornflour," whispered Mrs. Napier, but luckily her voice did not carry beyond Mrs. Dawson's ears.

"– and it's the same with Sir Humphrey, as we all know. Such charming manners, and manners maketh man! I'm sure Sir Humphrey is an only son, and owns some stately home of England. Besides, his name is quite familiar to me. I may have seen his photograph in one of those society periodicals *In the Royal Enclosure at Ascot* or something like that."

"He certainly goes out of his way to be pleasant to all of us," agreed Mrs. Marston, who had not given up hope that one of her daughters might become Lady Chervil.

"Indeed, yes," continued Miss Astill. "Very pleasant. He's been advising me about a little affair of business; so kind of him. I'm sure I don't see why he should waste time on me."

She smiled self-consciously, and Winnie looked at her sharply. Surely Miss Astill didn't imagine that Sir Humphrey was interested in her? These old maids!

Mrs. Dawson made a pencilled note on a piece of paper and abandoned her book temporarily. She glanced at Mrs. Napier's nodding head, then sat for a moment watching the four at the card-table, wondering for the hundredth time how they could all talk so incessantly without losing touch with their game.

Miss Astill rose from her chair.

"If you'll excuse me – such a delightful game – but I must really get on with the altar-cloth for the dear Vicar." She gathered up her tapestry work-bag and went to sit beside Mrs. Dawson.

Lady Warme turned to Miss Blake, who had just entered the lounge.

"Oh, Miss Blake, would you care...?" She indicated the chair which Miss Astill had just vacated.

"Thanks very much, but I never play cards." Miss Blake smiled vaguely at them all, sat down, and, opening her book, began to read.

The three card-players got up and arranged themselves near the fire, and soon there was no sound except the clicking of knitting-needles or scissors.

Miss Astill threaded her needle with a strand of scarlet silk.

How like Miss Blake to walk in and disturb them all, she thought. The Hydro was a different place nowadays. Miss Blake had no consideration for the feelings of others, but strolled about in clothes which showed a really indelicate amount of limbs. She had such an arrogant way of walking, too, swinging her legs from the hips so that she really looked quite indecent from behind. She made no secret of the fact that she only cared for the company of men, however old they were, and that story about her and Sir Humphrey, about her enticing him into her bedroom, she meant – the very thought made her blush – well, really, you never knew how it all might end. So far as she could ascertain, Miss Blake had left the doctor alone, but you never knew what she might do next. Surely something ought to be done about it.

"I wish you would read to us, Miss Blake," she said aloud. "We are all busy with our needlework and it would help to pass the afternoon more pleasantly."

"It would be like our schooldays when we took it in turns to read *John Halifax, Gentleman*, in the sewing hour," said Lady Warme.

As soon as she had said this she looked around furtively.

Perhaps that was a book unknown to the others, she thought. Even though it was so many years since she had married John Warme, she was still afraid lest she should make a reference to something which might associate her with the old life, when, the eldest of a swarm of wet-nosed children, she had taken her thick slices of bread and jam to St. Chad's Elementary School and had returned to help behind the counter of the little grocer's shop which had proved such a gold-mine to her parents.

But Mrs. Marston's next words reassured her: "Such a sweet story, I always think," for Mrs. Marston, she knew, had been "finished" at Ascot.

"I don't mind reading to you if you would really like it," said Miss Blake, stretching herself in her chair

"Just like a cat," remarked Millie in an undertone.

"– but let me fetch another book. I don't think you'll like this one."

"Too modern for us, I suppose," replied Lady Warme, while Miss Astill leaned forward and read the title.

"*Brave New World*. I don't think I've ever heard of it. Is it a new book?"

"I'm afraid not," replied Miss Blake indulgently. "It must be at least four years old."

"The last book I saw you with was the one with the rude title," said Mrs. Marston. "*In All My Nakedness*, I think it was called."

"*Without My Cloak*," corrected Miss Blake. "You wouldn't call me naked just because I took off my coat, would you?"

"Yes, I should," came a booming whisper from Mrs. Napier, who had apparently been asleep through the rest of the conversation. "Some of the frocks she wears under that thing she calls a house-coat are no bigger than vests."

Miss Blake remained unperturbed, but without further protest she turned over the pages of the book until she came to Lenina's attempted seduction of the savage.

Her clear young voice floated pleasantly through the lounge. She was aware of altar-cloth, scarf, socks, and sewing being dropped, but although she expected to be stopped every minute, she was allowed to read on to the end of the chapter.

"Shall I go on?" she asked.

Lady Warme rose from her chair, with crimsoned face, and drew herself up to her full height.

"You ought to be ashamed of yourself," she said. "Of all the low, immoral books. But I'm not surprised. That is just the kind of literature I imagined you would choose. I don't wonder that the youth of today is corrupt, with that kind of dirt lying on every library shelf for young hands to reach."

Miss Blake corrected her with a smile.

"Not every shelf, Lady Warme. It was banned in the Irish Free State, or Eire, as they call it now."

"I'm very glad to hear it. It's about the only decent thing Eve heard about the Irish," replied Lady Warme, with dignity. "But I know you are only trying to be flippant."

"But," persisted Miss Blake, her eyes twinkling, "what kind of literature would you like me to read?"

"I have no desire to enter into a literary discussion with you," replied Lady Warme. "There are plenty of classics in the English language if you want to improve your mind."

"Shakespeare, for instance?"

"Shakespeare is, of course, the master."

Lady Warme stooped to pick up the gaudy-coloured scarf she was knitting out of odd pieces of wool for the lepers.

Miss Blake turned a few pages and read again:

"But virtue, as it never will be woo'd
Though lewdness court it in a shape of heaven:

So lust, though to a radiant angel link'd,
Will sate itself in a celestial bed,
And prey on garbage."

Mrs. Dawson's hearty laugh rang through the lounge.

"I don't blame you, Miss Blake," she said. "They're always baiting you, and she asked for it."

Lady Warme ignored this interruption.

"Miss Blake," she said, "I order you to stop reading. You are insulting me and these others ladies with that – that incestuous book. I shall complain to the doctor."

"But," protested Miss Blake, "that was Shakespeare."

Lady Warme, now white with passion, blundered out of the room.

For a few minutes there was silence, then Mrs. Dawson came across the lounge.

"Good for you," she said. "I couldn't have routed the old girl better myself."

"Really, Miss Blake," came a protest in Miss Astill's most indignant tones. "You had no business to offend poor dear Lady Warme with that disgusting book."

"I wonder that you dared read it aloud," said Millie.

"Dear Lady Warme, she was very much upset," boomed Mrs. Napier.

"I hope it won't bring on one of her attacks."

"But she really did ask for it."

"I know it's very wrong of me, but I can't help smiling at the way she went out. She could hardly see for temper."

"It's a dreadful book, but, of course, very clever."

"A splendid satire on modern times. I shouldn't be in the least surprised if it does come to that at the rate modern young people are going on."

"So dreadful of me, but I can't help laughing. The book, you know. It really is funny."

"The idea of it. All the wrong way round."

"The clothes! If they ever came in as spring fashions!"

"Those zip-fasteners, so convenient!"

"And going into the bathroom like that – wearing only a hat and shoes and socks –"

"Something like our bathing caps and aprons when we go into the baths for treatment –"

"So much more indecent than wearing nothing at all!"

"Oh!"

They all gasped and looked guiltily at each other, as if ashamed of the thoughts they had exposed.

The door opened.

"Thank heavens!" exclaimed Winnie Marston. "Tea!"

CHAPTER IV

The following evening, Lady Warme dressed her buxom figure with unwonted care in a velvet evening gown of a colour only to be described as puce, added eight of her finest rings, one string of real pearls, one string of cultivated ones, and a diamond-and-sapphire brooch. She took out her diamond star and pondered whether to wear it in her hair or not. Poor John had bought it for her to wear at the Lord Mayor's reception in Manchester soon after he had been knighted; he had said it looked so pretty in her hair.

She sighed.

Dear John! He had never to the day of his death noticed her growing stoutness, her unbecoming wrinkles, her greying hair. Lancashire men were hard in business, but very sentimental at heart.

She lifted the star to the crimped waves of her dull, grey hair, but could not delude herself into thinking it becoming, and, sighing again, she fastened it to a narrow band of velvet ribbon which she wore to hide the sagging skin beneath her chin. She knew that the points of the star would prick her throat every time she swallowed, but felt that the occasion merited some display. For, as a typewritten correspondence card fastened to the green baize of the notice-board in the lounge had announced for the past week, there was to be a concert this evening in the drawing-room of the Hydro, to which all guests were bidden.

The organization of concerts was always left to Lady Warme, partly because of her rank ("though whether you can really call her a lady, my dear... Of course, I know he was knighted, but they were flour, you know... Warme's Patent Flour!...") and partly because of the entirely fictitious reputation she possessed in the Hydro because she had once been present at the Scala in Milan for a performance of *The Magic Flute*, and had never ceased to talk about it.

"I never want to hear another opera after that," she would say, somewhat ambiguously, when describing that experience.

She strengthened this reputation by exclaiming, on the few occasions when the wireless in the lounge had not been rendered dumb by some well-meaning attempt to make it work better, "Oh, do switch it off! I can't bear British music after the Italian. Why don't you get Milan?"

And her companions would nod to each other and say: "Dear Lady Warme is so musical."

She went round the Hydro during the week preceding the concert looking like a flustered hen. If anyone stopped to speak to her she soon hurried away, saying: "You really must excuse me. I am so busy. This concert takes up so much of my time. Of course, I am very glad to be able to do it, but really I wish they had asked someone else to arrange it this time." And everyone smiled sympathetically and was not deceived.

"Poor Lady Warme," remarked old Miss Brendon, after she had invited her to tea in order to hear the advance programme, "she used not to get so flustered when she served behind the counter of her father's grocery store as plain Lizzie Parkes. And she was plain, Rogers. I remember seeing her when her father came out to my mother's carriage to take her order. My mother was a different kind of lady."

"Indeed, and she was, miss," agreed Rogers, who had been the Brendons' scullery-maid in those days, and still thought apprehensively of Mrs. Brendon's stern, "Ada! Come here!" when she had left an eye in a potato or cracked a cup.

But on this particular occasion Lady Warme had reason to be flurried. She bustled into the lounge before dinner, wearing an ermine cape over her dress.

"What am I to do?" In her agitation she addressed the first person she saw, who happened to be Miss Blake. "What am I to do? I have no accompanist for tonight. You know that we always have the woman who plays the organ in church...or perhaps you wouldn't know. She plays dreadfully, of course, but I had to ask her, and now she has let me down at the very last minute. So tiresome of her."

"What's wrong with her?" inquired Miss Blake.

"A sick headache. She's in bed. Yes, she really is sick. I went to see her... most unpleasant." She screwed up her face in disgust.

"Well, it's hardly her fault. She didn't let you down on purpose."

"No, poor thing, and of course I'm desperately sorry for her, but if she had only waited till after the concert.... I'm afraid it means postponing it. Of course, I used to play myself, but its many years since I touched the ivory keys, and I shouldn't care to perform in front of my friends here. They all expect far too much from me. I'm afraid it will have to be postponed. Such a thing could never happen in Italy."

She did not explain why.

"Oh, but you mustn't put it off," replied Miss Blake emphatically. "Not after all your trouble. Why, it's taken you days to get it all fixed, and we're all dressed up for the occasion.

Lady Warme allowed a frosty smile to part her lips, and began to wonder whether she had not been a little too severe about Miss Blake. Perhaps all the scandal about her and Sir

Humphrey was not true. She really sounded quite affable and polite now, and, yes, almost respectful towards Lady Warme's rank.

"So I see," she replied, glancing at the lace bertha with which Miss Astill had decorated her black taffeta dress, and at the insignificant blue silk dresses worn by the Marston girls. "Even Miss Astill is in evening dress... at least, I suppose that is what it is meant to be. I can see her elbows and the salt-cellar in her neck. But we have all grown so much smarter since we have had a baronet staying among us, haven't we?" She smiled more graciously. "But really, it's no joking matter," she went on, "I would put on the concert if I possibly could, but whom can I have for accompanist?"

"Me," replied Miss Blake unexpectedly.

"You?" gasped Lady Warme.

"Why not? I was taught well at school, and I suppose I went to as good a school as anyone here."

"Yes, yes, I'm sure you did," returned Lady Warme hastily, as a vision of the fourth standard at St. Chad's Elementary School rose before her eyes. "I wouldn't dream of doubting your word, but I hardly like to trouble you."

"Oh, don't worry about that," replied Miss Blake airily. "I shall enjoy it. I play quite well at sight, and I won't let you down."

"Our organist was to have given us a pianoforte solo." Lady Warme pronounced it "piarnoforty," in accordance with the best B.B.C. standards, though in her young days she had known it more familiarly as "the pianner."

"I can manage that, too."

Lady Warme weakened visibly.

"But you won't play – er – jazz?"

Miss Blake laughed.

"I suppose you won't believe me," she said, "but really I prefer Mendelssohn."

Lady Warme bit her lip in a wave of indecision, then gave a little nod.

"Very well, then," she said. "Nine o'clock in the drawingroom, and – er – thank you."

CHAPTER V

In the daytime the drawing-room at the Hydro was as depressing as only a period room can be, but in the full glare of the electric lights set in the prismatic glass of the tiered chandelier, it took on an air of fusty dignity not unsuited to a formal function. It was decorated in the style which our grandmothers called the French, and which we call Victorian. The walls, which were enamelled white, and could have looked spacious and restful, were compressed and deformed by raised, gilded mouldings which contorted themselves into serpentinous whorls and curlicues. As if this were not adornment enough, they were hung with huge German engravings in ornate gilded frames. In these, Victoria, Queen of England, sat at her coronation, stood at her marriage, reclined with her children, opened the Great Exhibition and posed for *The Secret of England's Greatness* with an open Bible in her hand.

The effect had been slightly spoiled by some Edwardian who had introduced two cosy corner seats, and the period had been completely ruined by Dr. Williams, who had replaced most of the original furniture by a number of modern lounge arm-chairs and a low, deep settee, although he secretly felt that knick-knacks and what-nots made a more fitting background for Hydro chit-chat.

This was the room into which the Hydro residents made their way after dinner in search of the promised concert. They found Miss Blake, wearing a pearl-grey evening gown, with long jade ear-rings and a carved lump of jade swinging on a slender platinum chain as her only ornaments, seated on the hard, round, plush-covered music-stool at the Steck grand piano.

Lady Warme stepped up to the piano, the black tails of her ermine cape all a-quiver, and explained that "owing to the sudden regrettable indisposition of our valued and esteemed accompanist, Miss Blake has kindly undertaken the task at a moment's notice," although she knew such an announcement to be quite unnecessary since she had paused at every table in the dining-room during dinner to spread the news properly.

Miss Blake was far too young and pretty to be popular with the womenfolk in the Hydro, and most of them hoped that they would at last have the opportunity of seeing her make a fool of herself. They were soon disillusioned. She was a pleasing pianist. She attempted nothing either too classic or too elaborate, but played, as solos, tuneful pieces which they all liked so much that they tapped out the rhythm audibly with their feet to show their appreciation. No doubt, they all agreed, she would not have shone in Chopin's *Polonaise in A Minor*, which the organist always played as a solo with such verve and her foot well down on the loud pedal, but her solos were pleasing and her accompaniments were unobtrusively correct.

"We might have known what to expect," murmured Mrs. Dawson. "She has far too good an opinion of herself to undertake anything she is not sure of doing well."

Before the concert began Miss Blake had been handed a sheaf of well-thumbed songs patched with strips of transparent paper, and as Lady Warme had omitted to provide her with a programme she had amused herself while the audience were settling in their seats by guessing to whom the songs belonged. But, like those newspaper competitions which carry large money prizes, the solutions were not at all what one might have been led to expect.

After she had accompanied Millie and Winnie Marston through the duet "Songs of Araby", in which Millie took the

baritone part and Winnie the tenor; after Mrs. Marston had
sung "Drake's Drum" in a tremulous contralto voice; after Miss
Astill had sung "Rose in The Bud" in a perfectly trained
soprano voice, which remained sweet for thirty bars, and by
request as an encore, "that little French thing you sing so well,"
the meaning of which was mercifully obscured from all the
audience; after Colonel Simcox had recited "The quality of
mercy is not strained" in a highly unnatural falsetto, and Mr.
Marston, who had been known to trump his partner's ace and
to revoke twice within one game of whist, had given them a
dolorous monologue in which he compared Life to a Game of
Cards; after all this, Miss Blake felt that the evening could hold
no more surprises for her.

In this, however, she was mistaken.

Just as the concert seemed to have straggled to an end, and
she was wondering whether it was usual to play the National
Anthem, and if so, what key would be most suitable for such a
diverse range of voices, someone called out, "Let's have the
Admiral's song," and everyone took up the words clamorously
with more enthusiasm than any had as yet shown.

Admiral Urwin was hoisted to his feet to the
accompaniment of many creaks and grunts, and hobbled
towards the piano, chuckling with delight.

"Can you play "The Keel Row", and that little Gilbert and
Sullivan thing that goes like this?" he asked, and in a deep bass
voice, which suited him, he hummed:

"Jimmy, jimmy, jimmy, jimmy, back to Spain,
Never, never, never, never, cross the seas again."

He replied to her doubts with a wink and a chuckled: "Well,
never mind. Vamp. You can do that all right, I know," and
without further ado he plunged into a song which possessed as
many verses as a traditional Irish jig, and began something
like this:

"Oh, the Hy-dro, the Hy-dro, the Hy-dro, the Hy-hy-
dro,
Oh, when I'm at the Hy-dro, I'm happy as can be.
We all live at the Hy-dro, the Hy-dro, the Hy-hy-dro,
We all live at the Hy-dro like one big fam-i-ly."

"Change tunes!" yelled the Admiral, sounding very much like the Gryphon explaining the Lobster Quadrille to Alice in Wonderland, and continuing in the same breath:

"And when you see a pretty nurse,"

he leered at Nurse Hawkins, who was sitting at the very back of the room with Miss Lewis, the doctor's secretary, and Ada Rogers:

"You tell the doctor, you're feeling worse;
But never do you feel so ill,
As when you read the doctor's bill;
It gives you such a terrible pain
That you swear you'll never come back again:
You'll never, never, never, never, never, never, never,
never,
Never come back to the Hydro again!"

After everyone had sung these last two lines in chorus for the last time, the audience passed a vote of thanks to the performers, and the performers retaliated by passing a vote of thanks to the audience.

Then they all sang "God Save the King" in the half-defiant, self-conscious manner in which English people do sing their national anthem, and began to move towards the lounge, where cakes and coffee were being served.

Miss Blake remained at the piano, gathering the music together.

"I should like to congratulate you," said a voice behind her. She turned.

"Why, Sir Humphrey, how nice of you. I didn't see you amongst the audience."

Sir Humphrey smiled down at her.

"I came in rather late," he said. "Frankly, I wasn't looking forward to the concert, but when I heard that you were to play, I came straight in. It was well worth going without a drink for an hour and a half just to see your performance."

Miss Blake did not miss the significance of his use of the word "see" instead of "hear," and looked pleased. Sir Humphrey, apparently encouraged, moved closer to her and began speaking earnestly in a low voice.

The audience, who were dispersing slowly, wandering out in little chattering groups, cast many curious glances at them, and the women exchanged knowing looks and raised their eyebrows at each other. Lady Warme waited for ten minutes to attract Miss Blake's attention, then stamped her foot in disgust and went out. The Colonel hovered about the room for a quarter of an hour, screwed his eye-glass in his eye with a vicious twist, and followed the others.

CHAPTER VI

The following morning the housekeeper walked into one of the large attic bedrooms, her heavy footsteps echoing on the uneven boards of the uncarpeted floor, and eyed with disgust the six motionless forms lying in their single black-enamelled beds.

"Will you girls never learn to get out of bed in the mornings?" she shouted. "Six o'clock is the time for you to begin the day. It's a quarter past now, and this is the second time I've called you this morning."

She moved across to the nearest bed and stripped the clothes on to the floor. Amy Ford, thus rudely awakened from a deep sleep, stared at the housekeeper with red-rimmed, baleful eyes. Her face, seen under such conditions, had none of the prettiness which it assumed under her Tudor-patterned starched morning cap or her afternoon frill. She looked unhealthy and bad-tempered.

"I wasn't in bed till after one o'clock this morning, miss," she said in a grudging attempt to excuse her laziness. "I had to put the lights out in the drawing-room."

"That's nothing to do with it," retorted the housekeeper sharply, "and it's a waste of time to make excuses to me, as you ought to know well enough by now. I have the same trouble with you girls every morning. Now get out of bed, all of you, before I move out of this room."

The beds creaked with the unwilling movements of their occupants. The housekeeper moved towards the small flat windows.

"Faugh!" she exclaimed with exaggerated emphasis. "Why will you always sleep with the windows fastened? I don't wonder that you get spots on your faces." She flung each window up to its fullest extent, letting the chilly autumn draught into the room, then she gazed around, and, satisfied that all the girls were at last out of bed, she walked out, slamming the ill-fitting door behind her.

The girls gazed vindictively after her, and Amy put out a none-too-clean tongue at the closed door.

"I could murder that woman!" she exclaimed. "She treats us like muck. For God's sake, shut the blasted windows!"

"Ah, hold your tongue now, Amy," said Molly O'Shea, a little black-haired girl from County Cork. "Sure, 'tis bad luck to be saying that word and the blessed name of Almighty God in the same breath. And well you know that 'tis at six o'clock we should be rising, as she's after saying."

Amy muttered coarser blasphemy under her breath, but it was too cold to stand there arguing in their cheap cotton nightgowns, and the girls were soon half washed and dressed and going about their several morning duties.

Amy and Molly, who had the task of turning out the drawing-room and writing-room this morning, went downstairs together. They both made their way into the little writing-room, where Amy immediately began to collect a few scattered scraps of paper in the paper-basket.

"And what in the name of heaven do you think you're doing?" demanded Molly. "Isn't it myself did the drawingroom yesterday morning, and it the biggest room? Get you in there yourself now!"

Amy, grumbling as usual, went through the communicating door into the drawing-room. She switched on the light over the piano and walked across to the windows, pulling at the side cords which swung the heavy velvet curtains silently back. She grimaced at the rows of chairs left over from last night's concert, hating the extra work which was entailed by sorting them out and restoring them to their original places.

She was always the one to come in for the extra work, she grumbled to herself, and it was a downright shame, it was. If ever there was a concert or a party in the Hydro you could be sure that she would be the one on duty for that week. She often thought that the whole system of exchanging corridors was specially arranged to pay her out, and what had she ever done to anyone, she would like to know? Nothing!

Last night had just been typical of her luck. She had had to wait up till one o'clock until Sir Humphrey and Miss Blake had gone to bed, and they'd gone together for all that she knew. It was all very fine for Miss Blake to stay up spooning till all hours of the morning, but *she* had to get up at six o'clock, no matter what time she went to bed. And when she tried to get a few extra minutes of sleep, what must that damned housekeeper do but come in and pull all the clothes off her, to say nothing of opening all the windows and trying to give her her death of cold. And as if all this wasn't enough without it being her morning to turn out the room that was all topsyturvy with last night's mess. What did an occasional squint at the concert last night count against this?

Well, one day they'd see, she thought, banging the chairs about. She'd get her ambition of being the one to find out some dreadful scandal in the Hydro before that skinny hussy Rogers nosed it out.

She always went about with her eyes open, and she'd be sure to come across it before long. It would be something really juicy, too, that far surpassed anything the Hydro had ever heard yet. Then she would be famous. Everyone would hang on her words at meal-times in the staff room. She'd be given the best cut off the joint and the largest piece of cake. And as for that old cat of a housekeeper – blast her eyes! – she wouldn't treat her like dirt any more. Not she. She'd come shining up to her more like, her big ears twitching to hear all the details at first hand so that she could pass them on to her friend Ada Rogers, that stuck-up piece who thought she was better class than a mere housemaid because she waited on a blind old lady and didn't wear a cap. She didn't wonder that Miss Brendon had gone nearly blind either, considering the number of years she had been looking at a face like Rogers'. It was a pity that Sir Humphrey and that flashy piece of goods Miss Blake hadn't given her a chance to make up some scandal about them. But though they had been sitting on the settee in the drawing-room till one o'clock in the morning, depriving her of her sleep, Amy knew that she could not hope to invent more scandal about them than had already been invented by all the others in the Hydro.

She made her way over to the fireplace, and seizing the nearer arm of the large high-backed settee which stood in front of the dead embers of the fire, she gave it a vicious pull.

She started back, then began to scream in terror as the slim figure of Miss Blake rolled off the settee to the floor, the subdued light from the single electric bulb over the piano glinting on something like a steel arrow which projected from the back of her head.

CHAPTER VII

Inspector Palk, a broad-shouldered man of about fifty, with only a touch of grey in his hair, looked up from his seat at the table in the centre of the library and glanced inquiringly at the frightened girl standing in front of him.

"Your name is Molly O'Shea?"

"Yes, sir."

The constable who was sitting at a smaller table in the far corner of the room dashed off a series of dots and dashes and curls in his official notebook.

"You were in the writing-room when the housemaid found Miss Blake's body?"

"I was, sir, God help us all!"

"Tell me what you know about it."

"I was after raking out the hearth when I heard a screeching, and Amy rushed into the writing-room, hopping about like a hen on a hot griddle. She caught hold of me and said that the poor young lady was after being killed."

She gulped at the recollection.

"Did you go into the drawing-room to look at the body?"

"I did not, sir. Why would I? I took Amy off to tell the housekeeper."

"Did the housekeeper seem surprised?"

"She did not, sir; but 'twould take an almighty shock to. surprise that one. She shook Amy till the teeth were nearly rattled out of her head and went to see for herself. Then she sent me to fetch the doctor."

"Did you like Miss Blake, Molly?"

"I did indeed, sir. Sure, didn't we all? She was a great lady for the tipping, and she had a smile and a kind word for every one of us. There's many of the others would be expecting you to fetch and carry for them all the day long with never a 'Thank you' at the end of it, but she was never like that. Sure, she didn't deserve to be murdered, the poor young lady."

Palk placed a little gold-and-shagreen petrol-lighter on the table in front of him.

"Have you ever seen this before?" he asked.

Molly looked more frightened than ever.

"No, sir," she whispered.

"Don't you know whom it belongs to?"

"No, indeed. It doesn't belong to me."

"Have you any idea who killed Miss Blake?"

"It wasn't me, sir, but it might be that it was Amy had something to do with it. She did tell me that Miss Blake would come to a bad end, and she has a holy fright of a temper, that one."

Palk dismissed her and sent for Amy, and the women residents decided that he was no gentleman for keeping them waiting while he first gave his attention to the staff.

Amy, pale, trembling, weeping, thoroughly unnerved by her recent experience, was shown into the library. Inspector Palk took one look at her and shouted, "Sit down!" in a voice which any sergeant-major might have envied. She ceased weeping and obeyed. Before she had time to begin again, he hurled a question at her:

"Did you kill Miss Blake?"

"Who? Me?"

This was the last straw on top of all the injustices of the week. Amy promptly forgot to be hysterical and, growing indignant, launched into a tirade against big-footed policemen who tried to frighten confessions out of hard-working servant-girls. Palk noted her rising colour with satisfaction, and cut short her words.

"All right, forget it," he said, and proceeded to question her about the finding of the body. But he elicited no information from her beyond a dramatic description of how Miss Blake had rolled off the settee and what a fright it had given her.

Palk indicated the little petrol-lighter on the table and asked if she knew to whom it belonged, but here again she was of no help.

"How did you know that Miss Blake was going to be murdered?" he startled her by saying next.

Amy stared in amazement, and said again:

"Who? Me? I didn't know, sir, and I never said I did, and anyone who says so is a liar."

"You told Molly that you knew Miss Blake would come to a bad end," said Palk calmly. "What did you mean by that?"

"Oh, that!" replied Amy in tones of relief. "I didn't mean anything, so to speak, if you understand me. Me and Molly was having an argument about what kind of a girl Miss Blake was."

"And what kind was she?"

"I'm sure I don't know," said the flustered girl, "but I did think that she'd perhaps come from London and stayed here for a rest, and when she went back she'd be gadding round drinking at night-clubs or roadhouses, and wouldn't end up as an honest woman. It was only for the sake of argument, as you might say. I always liked Miss Blake."

"You never actually saw Miss Blake drunk, then?" persisted Palk.

"No, I never did, and what's more, nobody else ever did neither. She was very genteel while she was here and I never heard it said that she ever came from London. It was just to contradict that Molly that I said it."

"All right," said Palk again, and was about to dismiss her when she startled him by saying:

"I can tell you who murdered her, if you like."

"Well?" he asked.

"The housekeeper," Amy whispered vindictively. "She's always up first in the mornings, even before us girls, and she'd murder her own mother, I shouldn't wonder."

Mrs. Dukes, the housekeeper, a dark, fluffy-haired, brown-eyed, tight-lipped woman of about forty-five, was sent for. She sat upright in the chair opposite the Inspector with her hands clasped together in the lap of her black dress, her whole attitude denoting disapproval of the proceedings.

Yes, she said, she was always up first in the morning, and a disgraceful thing it was, too, for a woman of her age to have to call young chits of girls who were too lazy to get up when the alarm went off at six o'clock. She'd never been used to doing any such thing before and she was glad that it had been made public at last, because now perhaps the doc-tor would do something about it. If her husband had been alive she wouldn't be working at all, but she'd buried two. Oh, she wasn't grumbling; it was her burden, and she could bear it... No, she knew nothing about Miss Blake's murder. She had indeed scarcely ever seen Miss Blake. Her duties as housekeeper were mainly connected with the maids, and that gave her quite enough to do without her having time to keep an eye on the visitors as well. She knew that Miss Blake always had her breakfast in bed and, in her opinion, it ought not to have been allowed, although meals in bed-rooms were extra. It meant that Miss Blake never got up till nearly luncheon-time, and it was a great mistake. The chambermaid couldn't do out her bedroom at the right time, and it upset the household arrangements all round. She had always been accustomed to working to a regular time-table, but you couldn't expect the maids to keep to it if the visitors set them such bad examples.

Yes, certainly she had been very much surprised when Amy and Molly had come running in to her, shouting at the top of their voices that Miss Blake had been murdered. No, of course she had not shown her feelings in front of the maids; they'd have gone into screaming hysterics if she had. As it was, she had shaken Amy until she had shaken a bit of sense into her, and had gone into the drawing-room to see for herself. Of course, she could see that Miss Blake was dead, and she didn't need to touch her to find out, either. She had stayed in the drawing-room until Dr. Williams came in answer to her message. She had thought it the best thing to do. Molly was the more composed of the two girls, so she had sent her for the doctor, and she had kept Amy outside in the corridor where she could see her through the open door, so that she wouldn't go about scaring the whole Hydro.

She didn't hold with murder, and no one could say that she did. No doubt the Inspector would soon clear it up. If it came to that, she could tell him who might have had a hand in it, herself. Who? Why, that little slut, Amy, of course. Hadn't she found the body? Wasn't she in the drawing-room after everyone else last night and in it again before anyone else this morning? You could never tell what those girls might get up to next!

Inspector Palk, proceeding in his usual way, liked to interview people on the plan of Clock Patience. As long as one person introduced another, they followed, each other in natural sequence; when the sequence was broken, as with the turning up of a king in the card game, he started afresh. The housekeeper's evidence having just returned in a circle to Amy Ford, he had to choose another person to interrogate, and was just running his finger down the typewritten list of names, which the doctor's secretary had provided, of those in the Hydro when the murder was committed, when Sergeant Jago came into the room.

The Inspector looked up.

"Well, did you find it?"

"Yes, sir."

"Good. Where?"

"Everywhere!"

Palk's expression plainly said that this was not the moment to be facetious.

"I sent you to find the knitting-needle which makes a pair with the one we found stabbed into the back of Miss Blake's head," he said.

"Yes, sir, I know. Well, we found one corresponding to it in nearly every bedroom in the Hydro. Some rooms had two or three or more; all of them were of the same size and make, but only two rooms had one single needle apiece. I've brought them all down. They're labelled with the number of the room they were taken from."

Palk looked closely at the various bundles of steel knitting-needles which the sergeant placed on the table before him, some tied with tape, some tied with ribbon, some with string, some with pieces of frayed rag; and all alike in being plain, straight, rustless steel needles without knobs, and without any name or size stamped on them.

"They're all the same size," said the sergeant again. "I tested them in the gauge from the needlework shop. We handled them with gloves very carefully."

"That won't help us much, I'm afraid," said Palk. "There were no finger-prints on the needle which killed Miss Blake." Sergeant Jago made a gesture indicative of extreme disgust. "That's the worst of this craze for detective fiction," he said. "I must say that no one could be more interested in a new thriller than I am, and I get plenty of good ideas from them, too. It's all right for me because it's my job, but it gives the general public too much information about finger-prints and police procedure. It doesn't give us a chance."

Palk shook his head.

"It isn't that," he said. "No one could have got the grip necessary for such a blow on the smooth surface of that needle. There must have been a handle of some kind. I should have thought that you'd have noticed that after reading so many thrillers. I want you to go over the rooms again with a toothcomb looking for it."

"It'll take time," said the sergeant dubiously.

"You've plenty of time. I shan't have finished with these people till the evening; they've all got so much to say. Try the maids' rooms and every nook and corner in the Hydro. It's an old-fashioned house with all kinds of holes and crannies; don't miss any of them. It doesn't matter about leaving everything exactly as you found it; it won't hurt them to know that their rooms have been searched. Look in the bath-rooms and cisterns, hot press, electric-light plant, everything you can think of, if the building possesses it. The very fact that the handle was removed shows that the murderer knew it would be incriminating. The whole damned thing is far too clever for my liking."

He turned again to the little bundles on the table in front of him, with their identifying labels, and looked up the names of the occupants of the bedrooms from the secretary's list.

The first room from which one odd needle had been taken was occupied by Colonel Simcox!

CHAPTER VIII

Colonel Simcox came into the library holding a half-knitted sock in one hand and a ball of wool in the other, while strands of wools of different colours led to each pocket of his faded tweed sports jacket.

"Colonel Simcox?"

"Lieutenant-Colonel retired, sir, and what the blazes d'you want to send for me for when I'm just in the middle of a most intricate pattern? Look at it, sir, look at it! 'K. one red, P. three blue...' Why couldn't you send for me when I was doing the top?"

Palk ignored the question, which he rightly supposed to be a rhetorical one.

"Knitting is not a very usual occupation for a man," he remarked quietly.

The Colonel's face grew red beneath its hardened coat of tan.

"Got to do something to pass the time away here. Better than drinking, even if one could get a drink in this confounded place, which one can't. And why the devil shouldn't men knit if they want to? Women are a damned sight too keen on doing our jobs, even if they have left the Army to us up to now. Why shouldn't we do their jobs for a change? I know a colonel who makes the most beautiful tapestry – the real stuff; and a major who does *petit point* – he's a marquis, too. Surely I can do a bit of knitting if I want to. It's easy to see, sir, that you have never been in the Army."

"I served in the Great War," replied Palk diffidently; "but no doubt you wouldn't think that the same as being a regular trooper."

The Colonel shot a glance at him from beneath his shaggy grey eyebrows.

"What d'you call yourself, sir?" he asked suspiciously, "Major? Captain? General?"

Palk smiled. "No, just Inspector."

Colonel Simcox relaxed.

"Ah, very good. So many of these war titles about these days in this corner of the world. It's damned bad taste, sir, that's what it is. Half of them have never seen that hole, Woolwich, let alone Sandhurst. Good fellows and all that; couldn't have got on without them, but it's damned bad taste."

"May I ask your regiment, Colonel?" asked Palk.

"What's that got to do with it?" He glared angrily at the Inspector, then suddenly changed his tone and said, "Queen's Own," as if he expected this to be challenged.

But Palk went on with his questions without comment. He produced the little shagreen petrol-lighter from his pocket and asked whether the Colonel could give him any information about it.

"Not mine," said the Colonel curtly. "Don't smoke, so nobody would be likely to lend it to me, either. Wait a minute, though. I've an idea I've seen it somewhere before. It might be the Admiral's – no, too dainty for him. No, I can't remember."

Palk did not pursue the subject.

"You know that there has been a murder in the Hydro?" he asked.

"Know it!" The Colonel almost jumped off his chair. "Of course I know it! I'm not likely to forget it either, after being made to sit all morning with all the old hags in the Hydro, penned up like a lot of cattle. Why, dammit, sir –" He broke off abruptly. "Well, well, got to be done, I suppose. Court martial, Inspector, eh? Court martial?"

"That's it, sir. I'd be glad if you would answer a few questions."

"Anything, anything. Glad to help you if I can. A dastardly crime, sir, a dastardly crime, and I hope you get the one who did it. Miss Blake was a lovely girl. Can't understand why anyone should want to murder her. Now, if it had been one of those old hags in the Hydro, I could understand it well enough. I've often wanted to murder some of 'em myself."

"Did you know Miss Blake well?"

Colonel Simcox, who by this time had put down his knitting on the table in front of him, fumbled for his monocle and pushed it with a self-conscious air into his right eye.

"Well – I – I – well, I did. Dammit, I may as well tell you that I was, that is, that Miss Blake and I – well, that I was thinking of making her my wife."

In spite of himself, Palk expressed his surprise as he mentally compared the bowed shoulders and choleric face of the old Colonel to the beautiful figure and features of Miss Blake. And perhaps his mind unconsciously recorded a mark against the murdered woman as he said:

"This must be a terrible blow for you, then, Colonel. I had no idea that Miss Blake was your *fiancée.*"

The Colonel looked flustered, and pulled heavily at his moustache.

"She wasn't my *fiancée,*" he protested.

"But you've just said –"

"I know, I know, but that was only in a manner of speaking. I was very fond of her and she seemed to like me well enough until that tailor's dummy of a baronet started making eyes at her." He glared at Palk. "You don't know what it is to be a bachelor all your life."

"Oh yes, I do," returned Palk with a smile. "I happen to be one myself."

"Oh – ah – well," stammered the Colonel. "You get tired of it, that's all, and I thought – fond of me – beautiful wife – so I meant to ask her. But I never did and now I'm glad I didn't."

"You mean the publicity?"

"No, no, I mean it wouldn't have done. You know that as well as I do. Makes me sound a cad, sir, but the fact is I'm not feeling her death as much as I ought to. You can see it, Inspector. Can't play the distracted lover at my age. Mind you, I'm appalled at the callousness of the brute who did it. Would do all I could to catch him, but I can't help feeling relieved that I'm still unattached. Used to looking after myself for years – knit my own socks... Doddering old fool to be attracted by a girl young enough to be my daughter. No, dammit, you shall have the truth!" He suddenly thumped the table with his fist. "She was young enough to have been my granddaughter, sir!" He sighed. "She was a very charming young lady, and made me feel young again."

Palk, secretly thinking that the Colonel was either very sincere or very clever, asked:

"Have you any idea why Miss Blake came to the Hydro in the first place?"

"Why, yes, she told me herself. Said she spent her whole life going from one hydro to another. I never asked her the reason. A younger man might have done so, but in my day it wasn't considered the thing for a man to discuss bodies with a woman. She always looked healthy enough, but if she came here for treatment the doctor could tell you."

Palk picked up the knitting-needle which the sergeant had found in Colonel Simcox's bedroom. "Do you recognize this?" he asked.

The Colonel looked at it suspiciously.

"No," he said sharply.

"Miss Blake was murdered with a knitting-needle like this," Palk continued, "and this one was found in your room."

The Colonel's face assumed a purplish tinge, and he looked for a moment as if he might be about to fall down in a fit of apoplexy.

"Do you mean to tell me that you've been nosing into my private possessions?" he shouted. "No gentleman —"

Palk interrupted him quietly.

"I'm investigating a case of murder."

The Colonel subsided a little.

"Of course, of course; martial law, martial law. But I tell you that I don't like it, sir, behind my back. Why couldn't you have asked me for my permission? I hope those men of yours haven't broken the top of my new trout rod."

"You can take my word that they have damaged nothing," said Palk, tapping the needle on the table between them.

"Well, I hope I can." The moving steel seemed to mesmerize him and he spoke with an effort. "If you found that in my room, it must be mine, I suppose. You can see that it isn't the same size as my sock needles, but I believe I did buy two like that one some time ago, when the doctor's little girl wanted to show me how to knit garters."

"I didn't know that Dr. Williams had a daughter," remarked Palk.

"Little girl, about nine. Not a bad child, but noisy. All children are a confounded nuisance in a hydro. They ought not to be allowed."

Palk felt like prefixing his next question with the words, "Well, Mr. Grouser, sir," but resisted the temptation.

"Why have you only one knitting-needle left?"

The Colonel looked startled, then got to his feet and jerked his chin forward at the Inspector.

"God bless my soul! You don't think that I murdered her, do you? Whatever for? Just because a younger man with a title cut me out? Don't be a fool, Inspector. You surely don't think that a soldier who has served under three sovereigns in all parts of the British Empire would murder a woman with a knitting-needle, do you? Damned rot, sir, damned rot! I've a perfectly good Service revolver upstairs in my drawer, as I've no doubt you already know. I should have shot her, my good man, I should have shot her. That knitting-needle was a woman's weapon, and I can tell you who used it and stop you wasting your time on people who had nothing to do with it."

"I shall be most interested to hear," replied Palk politely.

"Nurse Hawkins," said the Colonel triumphantly. "I don't like accusing a woman, but it's obvious. Admiral Urwin has been neglecting her lately for Miss Blake, and she's a jealous woman. And now for heaven's sake let me get on with my knitting!"

CHAPTER IX

Continuing the chain of evidence, Palk sent for Nurse Hawkins.

She was a fairly tall woman of about thirty-five, with auburn hair and a figure that was well defined without being plump. She wore a white overall, fastened in Russian style down the left side, with sleeves rolled above her elbows, showing her strong, muscular arms. Her freckled face was pale under her fly-away headdress, but she looked perfectly calm, having the trained nurse's rather callous familiarity with death.

"You don't object to answering a few questions about Miss Blake?" asked Palk, when she was seated in front of him.

"Oh no, poor thing! I'll do all I can to help."

"Did you know her well?"

"I'm afraid not. You see, I'm usually so busy with my patients that unless people need treatment here, I don't come into contact with them much."

"I understand that Miss Blake did have treatment."

"Oh no, not unless the doctor was giving her injections, and even then I should have known of it. Perhaps she was on a diet.

She often spoke to me when I had time off. She seemed a very pleasant young lady, who didn't think herself too classy to talk to a nurse, like some of them I could mention."

She sniffed.

"You're quite sure that you never gave her treatment of any kind?"

"No, never. She didn't need treatment, a young girl like that. I should think she was well under thirty. Most of our patients are fairly old and come here for rheumatism or obesity, and things like that. I have to give them special baths or massage or electric treatment. Miss Blake was very slim and supple. You could see that she didn't need treatment of that kind."

"I see. Then you have no idea why anyone so young as she should have stayed at this hydro for so long?"

"Well, I haven't really; but I did think that she was perhaps some society girl who had got fed up with cocktail parties and had come for a rest. I used to be at a fashionable West End nursing-home, and I know the type, you see. I don't think she ever meant to live here permanently; in fact, I had the impression that she meant to leave here fairly soon, though I can't say that she ever told me so."

"Thank you, Nurse. Have you any suspicion as to who is responsible for Miss Blake's murder?"

Nurse Hawkins pushed an imaginary piece of her strong auburn hair under her becoming headdress, looked down at her lap and smoothed the spotless, shiny surface of her white overall with her fingers. Her face looked serene, but when she looked up Palk saw that her eyes were troubled.

"I don't know anything," she faltered.

Palk nodded sympathetically.

"Any impression you can give me may be of the greatest value," he said, "and you may be sure that I shall only make use of information which materially helps me to solve the murder."

"Well, then, if I had to say somebody, I should say Mrs. Napier," she replied reluctantly. "She is one of my special patients, and I am with her more than the others at the moment. Hers is a peculiar case. She's not normal, of course, but sometimes she's worse than others. She likes making a scene, especially if there are plenty of people near to see her. She pretends that she can't walk if I'm near her, but if she wants to she can walk as well as you or I. It's a kind of hysteria, and the doctor says she's quite harmless; but I think there's no knowing what she might do if she had a sudden fit of wanting to do it. She only pretends to be weak; she's very strong really. I don't think I could hold her if she became violent."

"So you think she's capable of m–"

"I've never known her anything but gentle in her ways," interrupted Nurse Hawkins firmly. "She says dreadful things sometimes, but then, they all do that. I wouldn't like to say any more except that if I had to give a name I'd give hers."

"Thank you. You said that you'd been in a West End nursing-home. Have you been here long?"

"Two years."

"And you like it?"

"It has advantages and disadvantages, like any other place. I hated it when I first came. It seemed all petty scandals and back-biting, with everyone calling everyone else names, like a crowd of kids. I missed the company of the other nurses, too. I'm the only regular nurse here except when the Hydro's full, which isn't often."

"And the advantages?"

"There's not nearly so much work to do here. There's no dusting or taking meals to patients who have to have treatment in bed. The maids do all that, and I must say that they wait on me here as if I were a lady of leisure. All the same, I was going to leave next spring, only..." She looked down again.

Palk waited. All at once she looked up defiantly.

"Oh, I expect you'll hear all about me from other people. They can't stop talking about other people's business here. After all, I don't want to be a nurse all my life."

Palk let this inadequate explanation pass unchallenged.

"You are a properly trained nurse?" he asked, looking at the bronze-and-enamel badge she wore on her breast pocket.

"Oh yes. London-trained in general nursing, with special certificates in massage and radiography."

"Then it would be true to say that you know a good deal about anatomy?"

"Certainly. I couldn't do any massage without that knowledge. My training was a very thorough one. You see, you must know the position of all the bones and nerves and muscles in the body or you might do a great deal of harm by giving the wrong treatment."

"So you understand how it is that a knitting-needle thrust through the back of anyone's head would cause immediate death?"

"Yes, it would pierce the –"

She broke off abruptly as she perceived the significance of his question. A deep flush spread over her face down to the neat Peter Pan collar of her silk blouse which turned back over the top of her overall. Her eyes widened with fear.

"Yes, I – I understand," she whispered.

CHAPTER X

Mrs. Napier entered the library, leaning heavily on the constable's arm, and turning her ankles over more than usual to attract the Inspector's sympathy. She managed to mix her legs up inextricably with those of the chair and table that Palk came over to help in response to the appeal in the constable's eyes. As she stumbled against him he felt the tensed muscles of her lean arms and marvelled at their strength. With some difficulty they managed to lower her square-shouldered figure into the chair, and Palk cursed the luck which had led him to investigate a murder case amongst such a selection of strange characters. He did not expect much assistance from Mrs. Napier.

"You knew Miss Blake?" he asked abruptly – a little too abruptly, he thought.

Mrs. Napier nodded.

"She was kind to me. Not many people are kind here. I have a great burden to bear."

"You know that she is dead," went on Palk.

"Murdered!" she exclaimed excitedly. "I know who did it."

The familiar words irritated Palk, and he said without his habitual caution:

"You think it was Nurse Hawkins?"

Mrs. Napier's eyes stared at him from behind the thick spectacles.

"How did you know? Has someone been spying on me? I've heard whispering at the keyhole. I have enemies all around me."

"No, no, Mrs. Napier, nothing of the sort, I assure you," replied Palk with forced heartiness. "But it is not surprising that you should suspect the nurse. Perhaps you find it a little difficult to get on well with her."

Mrs. Napier began to dust her dress down with her handkerchief, a sure sign of pleasure from her. She leaned forward confidentially, and tears stood in her eyes.

"You understand," she said earnestly. "I was thinking myself alone and misunderstood, but you understand. You will protect me. Perhaps you understand Nurse Hawkins too. No one has a good word for her. She makes my life a misery. She tortures me. I am covered with bruises where she has let me fall. And she is so strong; she can lift me as if I were a little child. The bruises! But not so bad as she would like. I fall soft, thank God! She murdered that poor girl, and one day she will murder me. I am so afraid." Her mouth puckered like the mouth of a child about to cry, but she did not stop talking.

"It's all because we have seen her flirting with the Admiral. It's a disgrace to the Hydro. They do say that he buys all her clothes, and she has got a new fur coat. What does a nurse want with a fur coat? I haven't got one. They say that when a man gives a woman a fur coat he gives her something to put under it. You must put her in prison or she will kill me."

Further questions only brought forth similar accusations, and Palk dismissed her in disgust. Not until she had gone did he realize that he had not asked either her or Nurse Hawkins about the little petrol-lighter.

Admiral Urwin hobbled in heartily on his two sticks, and though his bloodshot blue eyes held their perpetual twinkle, his bluff, red face wore a grave look which sat rather oddly upon it. He made his way to the chair opposite Palk and, subsiding into it without any invitation, slid his sticks underneath with a rapidity which showed constant practice.

"This is a bad business, Inspector," he said.

"It is indeed, Admiral," replied Palk. "I'm afraid I must ask you the usual routine questions."

Admiral Urwin waved an understanding hand.

"Of course. Carry on. I hope I shall be of some help."

"Did you know Miss Blake well?"

"I can't say that I did. Fairly well, would be more accurate. That's about as well as anyone gets to know anyone else here under six months. I know that she was a very charming girl who seemed to have no hobbies except reading and playing the piano; that she was fond of pretty clothes and furs and jewels, as every pretty woman ought to be; that she was kind-hearted enough to try and help me with my crossword puzzles although they bored her to tears; but who she was and where she came from I don't know, and I'm sure nobody else in the Hydro knows either, or we should have heard of it before this."

"Would you call yourself an admirer of hers, Admiral?"

The Admiral shook with suppressed laughter.

"That's Simcox's idea, I'll be bound," he said. "The doddering old idiot got quite upset if she spoke to anyone else but him. I used to join them for the fun of the thing, and he looked as if he could murder me, I can tell you. No, I wouldn't say that I admired her exactly. I liked to see her pretty face, poor girl, but that figure? – no, thank you! I like a woman to show that she is a woman. I like her to stick out a bit here, and go in a bit there…" His gestures left his meaning in no doubt. "Nurse Hawkins, now, is more my type; she's a fine figure of a woman if you like. Knows a good joke when she hears one, too. Nurses always know what's what, eh?"

His eyes twinkled lasciviously, and Palk felt that with the slightest encouragement he would begin to tell his favourite Stock Exchange joke.

"Have you any idea why Miss Blake came to the Hydro?" he asked hastily.

"No. Never even thought about it."

Palk changed the subject.

"Do you knit, Admiral?"

The Admiral swore an oath which must have come out of the stokehold of his ship, and even the constable winced at the sound.

"Me? I'm a man, sir, and a member of the Senior Service. Admirals don't knit! I may do an occasional crossword puzzle to pass the time because I can't get about as much as I used to, but knitting is an old woman's pastime, and, by God, there are enough old women in this place without me turning into one!"

"So you have no knitting-needles in your possession?"

"I have not, sir."

"Then," said Palk, leaning forward a little, "can you tell me how this one" – placing it on the table in front of him – "got into your bedroom?"

But if he had hoped to startle the Admiral he was disappointed, for he only shrugged his shoulders as if it were the most casual thing in the world and said:

"Someone must have dropped it there, I suppose. That damned fool Simcox, I expect. He's always losing his knitting-needles. You'll probably find the fellow to it in his room while you're poking round."

Palk placed the small shagreen-and-gold lighter on the table.

"Can you tell me whom this belongs to, then?" he asked. "No one else seems to know."

The Admiral grunted.

"Yes, it belongs to Sir Humphrey."

"You're quite sure of that?"

"Of course I'm sure. Only a man with a title could afford to walk around with a useless thing like that in his pocket. Besides, I offered to mend it for him not long ago – I've got a knack of making those things work – and I had it in my room for a week fiddling with it. I had to trim down a thicker wick for it because my own lighter takes a larger size. You can see it if you look. I only returned it to him just before dinner on the night of the concert, but I don't suppose it works now." Palk rasped the wheel and produced a tiny shower of sparks but no flame. "I thought not. Those things are no better than toys. Some woman gave it to him, I'll be bound."

"Have you any idea who murdered Miss Blake?" asked Palk finally.

"Not unless Colonel Simcox did it, mad with love," returned the Admiral with a leering wink, as he groped for his sticks.

CHAPTER XI

It was Dr. Williams who spoiled the continuity of the interviews. He asked to see Palk, and pointed out to him that the Hydro was a machine whose mechanism must be maintained if it was to be kept working.

Murder or no murder, there was work to be done: food to be prepared, vegetables to be picked from the gardens, tables to be laid for meals, rooms to be cleaned, beds to be made. Palk had already interviewed the staff, could they not be released for their daily duties, and could he not also see his way to release the doctor himself, who, as commander-in-chief of that staff, had to see that those duties were carried out efficiently?

Palk treated the doctor with friendly candour, but he did not make the mistake of forgetting that he was as much under suspicion as any of the residents in the Hydro.

"Nasty business, sir," he said, as he indicated the chair facing him.

"Very nasty indeed, Inspector Palk. A most unpleasant situation for the Hydro altogether. It's bad enough when such a thing occurs in a private house, but it almost ruins a hotel. I can't think what the directors will say."

"Of course, there's no doubt in your mind that it is murder?"

"None whatever. In the olden days men used to commit suicide by running on their swords, but I don't see how Miss Blake could have run her head backwards on a steel knitting-needle, and she certainly couldn't have driven it into her own head with her hand by such force."

"How exactly did it cause death?" asked Palk.

Dr. Williams looked surprised at the question.

"Surely the police doctor –" he began.

Palk spread his fingers deprecatingly.

"He was rather technical. I should be glad if you wouldn't mind explaining it more simply."

The doctor automatically leaned back in his chair and placed the tips of his fingers together in the familiar attitude of the consulting-room.

"It pierced the medulla, undoubtedly," he said. "That is the life-giving cord which runs from the brain down the spine through the vertebrae."

"I gathered that," said Palk; "but I can't understand how you could pierce through solid bone with a mere knitting-needle."

"You couldn't," replied the doctor; "and if the blow had been struck at any other spot at the back of the head it would not have proved so instantly fatal. You see, it's like this. The skull is not cast in a solid mould, as many people seem to believe, it is divided into an upper and lower part, which are delicately hinged together. When the head is in an upright position with the body, the two halves of the skull are fitted closely together, but if the head is moved forward, say with the chin resting on the chest, a small space is created between them at the back. If you draw an imaginary line from the top of the head to the back of the neck, exactly in the middle, and intersect it by another imaginary line from ear to ear" – neither of them so much as smiled at the well-worn pun – "you will find the particular spot at the point of intersection which becomes vulnerable when the head is in the forward position. The medulla runs immediately behind that one spot, and becomes exposed, so that if a knitting-needle is stabbed into that little space it will pierce the medulla, cutting off life instantaneously."

"I see. You might call it the 'heel of Achilles' of the human body," said Palk reflectively. "Would you say it was an easy thing to stab anyone in that particular spot?"

"Not at all easy, I should say, but quite possible if you had time to study the back of your victim's head beforehand and a chance of finding her with her head in the necessary position. It would have been far more difficult in the days when women wore their hair in buns at the back, stuffed with hairpins."

"So you think that the crime must have been premeditated?"

"Oh, decidedly. The odds against anyone stabbing a needle through that precise spot by accident are so enormous as to render it practically an impossibility. Given such a weapon as a knitting-needle, most people would, I think, attempt to stab it through the heart of their victim, if they were told to commit a murder."

"And would that be equally effective?"

"Not nearly. The chances of failure are far greater. There are all the ribs to feint past, which make a far more impassable barrier than the writers of detective stories seem to think. Also, death would not be instantaneous, and might be a very long time coming. This is a far cleaner way of killing anyone, in more ways than one."

"Thank you, Doctor," said Palk. "All this argues some very specialized knowledge. There can't be many people in the Hydro who know about it, with the exception of yourself and the nurse."

"I'm afraid you'll be disappointed if you work on those lines, Inspector," replied Dr. Williams. "Anyone inside the Hydro might have known as much about it as I do."

"But surely –" objected Palk.

"I don't mean that all the residents have had the specialized training you mention, but certainly anyone who can read could have found out all about it from one of my medical books."

"But if you could remember to whom you had lent the books we could soon narrow down the inquiry."

"It's not so simple as that, Inspector. To my knowledge I have never lent anyone in the Hydro one of my books, but there are plenty of them scattered round the building. You know how it is. You start off with a certain number of books and gradually accumulate bigger and better ones till they overflow from one room into the next. If you yourself want to verify the information I have just given to you, you have only to consult the blue book with the gilt lettering on the bottom shelf of the wall-bookcase behind you."

"I see," reflected Palk. "Do you think, then, that the murder was actually committed by someone in the Hydro?"

"Yes," replied the doctor, "I'm afraid I do."

"Well, then, you won't mind giving me some idea of the kind of people you have here. Does your establishment differ in any marked detail from the usual type of hydropathic hotel?"

The doctor hitched up one perfectly creased trouser leg before crossing one leg over the other.

"Well," he began, "Presteignton Hydro is not the most fashionable type, such as the Imperial Hydro at Tormouth. We are an old-established place and usually get our visitors by recommendation rather than by advertisement. During the summer months we have a number of casual visitors who generally move on to a more modern hotel when they find that we have no licensed bar, but at this time of the year we have some twenty visitors, most of whom are permanent, and most of whom take treatment."

"Are they people of any particular type or class?"

"Well, I hadn't thought about it particularly before, but I suppose they do come from the same class. We get men like Admiral Urwin and Colonel Simcox, who have retired from the Services, and women who are often either the widows or daughters of officers too."

"Then they all have money?"

"Well, as far as I know, none of them works for his living, so I imagine they all have private incomes."

"Have all the people in the Hydro now been here for some considerable time?"

"For years, most of them. Except Sir Humphrey Chervil and Miss Blake."

The Inspector looked interested.

"Did they come here together, then?"

"Oh no, quite separately. They didn't even know each other until quite recently, I believe. Miss Blake came in June and Sir Humphrey about a month or six weeks later. I can find the exact dates for you by looking up their accounts if you like."

"Don't bother, thanks," replied Palk. "I can see them for myself in the visitors' register."

The doctor looked uncomfortable.

"You may not be able to find them," he said. "We're not very strict about keeping it up to date."

Palk banged his hand on the table.

"That's always the way," he said irritably. "You people can't keep even the simplest law properly, and we poor policemen get all the blame."

"Well, you know how it is, Inspector, you can't be bothering people* all the time, and I don't know why it is, but so many visitors hate signing the book when they first arrive."

Palk snorted.

"You've soon caught the habit," remarked the doctor.

"What habit?" snapped the Inspector.

The doctor laughed.

"Snorting," he said. "They all do it here when anything irritates them. I have the greatest trouble in the world to stop myself getting infected."

"Then there is a queer atmosphere about this place," said Palk.

"Oh, I don't know," replied Dr. Williams. "I do think so sometimes, but it's really no more than you get anywhere where the company is a little old, a little warped, a little lonely, and never quite in good health."

"Are they all suffering from some complaint, then?"

"All of them in some minor degree, except –" He stopped abruptly.

"Except...?" prompted Palk.

"Sir Humphrey Chervil and Miss Blake," finished the doctor slowly.

Palk looked pleased at this second association of the two names.

"Didn't it strike you as strange, Doctor, that those two should be at Presteignton Hydro at this time of the year? Surely October is too late for the stragglers of the summer season to be here still."

The doctor thought for a moment before replying.

"No, I can't say that I thought it strange," he said. "You see, they came at the beginning of the summer and just stayed on. I rather wondered that Miss Blake did stay – I think that we all did – for we have no young company, and I don't think she got on well with the others."

Palk asked him to explain.

"Well, she got on too well with the men and too badly with the women, and they were all so much older than she was that there was bound to be a certain amount of jealousy."

"Did anyone appear to dislike her more than the others?"

"N – no."

Palk did not pursue this line of questioning.

"I understand that there is an old lady upstairs who keeps permanently to her room. Is there any chance that she is not really bedridden?"

The doctor laughed again.

"You won't find the murderer there," he said. "She's eighty to my knowledge, and half blind; she's quite incapable of using a knitting-needle for knitting, let alone for murdering anyone. She's genuine all right, and so is Ada Rogers, her attendant. You'd better see them, together. I'll show you their room if you like."

Palk sprang to his feet.

"Do you mean to tell me that one of the staff is on duty in that room and has not yet been interviewed? Why wasn't I told about her? She might be destroying evidence while we are all down here."

Dr. Williams lost his temper.

"Oh, don't be foolish, Inspector!" he said. "Whoever your murderer is, it's not a bedridden old lady or her attendant. Miss Brendon hasn't the strength, and if Rogers wanted to murder anyone she'd murder her mistress. She stands to gain five hundred pounds by her death."

"How do you know that?" asked Palk sharply.

"I can't help hearing things," answered the doctor wearily. "If you knew this place a little better you'd realize that everyone in it knows everything about everyone else, and what they don't know they invent. They mean no harm, but they've nothing else to do all day. I don't mind telling you that I don't envy you your job of sifting the evidence."

Palk intimated that the interview was at an end.

"Thank you, Doctor. Have you any idea who did it?"

"Not an idea in the world."

Palk gave him a crooked smile.

"You may be interested to know that so far you're the only one in the Hydro who hasn't," he said.

CHAPTER XII

Inspector Palk looked up with interest as Sir Humphrey Chervil came into the library. He was a good-looking man of medium height, probably thirty-nine years old. His straight black hair was severely plastered upon his head with brilliantine, so that it shone like the head of a painted wooden doll. He was clean-shaven, but down his cheeks there was a dark suspicion of side-whiskers, as if left deliberately to accentuate the resemblance to some old family portrait. His nose was long and straight; Lady Warme called it aristocratic.

Altogether he had an intelligent and interesting face, but at the moment he looked badly shaken. His dark-brown, almost black eyes were heavy with trouble; his sallow-skinned face looked haggard with anxiety and apprehension; he walked as if his knees trembled, and his hands were not quite steady. Palk noticed that he glanced almost fearfully at the two constables on duty before sitting down. Then he almost tumbled into the chair that Palk indicated and started as his gaze fell upon the little shagreen-and-gold automatic lighter.

"Your name?"

"Sir Humphrey Ch – Chervil."

Palk pointed to the lighter which Admiral Urwin had identified.

"Is that yours?"

"Why – yes."

"You know that Miss Blake was found murdered on the settee in the drawing-room?"

"Yes."

"That lighter was found down the side of the settee. Can you explain how it got there?"

The evident suspicion in Palk's tone seemed to penetrate to Sir Humphrey's consciousness. He pulled himself together and looked the Inspector full in the face.

"I expect it slipped down when I was sitting there with Miss Blake after the concert," he said.

"You admit sitting there with her, then?"

"Of course I do!" exclaimed Sir Humphrey. "What object could I have for hiding it? In any case, the whole Hydro saw us and I don't suppose it's a thing they'd keep quiet about."

"Wasn't it rather strange that you should ignore the rest of the gathering so completely after the concert by staying in the drawing-room when everyone else had gone out for refreshments?"

"I don't think so. They're not a very inviting crowd, are they? It was quite natural that I should prefer to remain there alone with Miss Blake."

"Had you ever met Miss Blake before you came here?"

"No, I hadn't. What makes you think that?"

"You arrived here within a month of each other. You are both the same kind of people..."

Sir Humphrey looked truculent.

"What do you mean by that?"

"You are both younger than the others, and neither of you was here for treatment," Palk explained. "It seems likely that you had been friends before and that you had quarrelled perhaps. Then you followed her here and tried to make it up."

"And when she scorned my advances I murdered her!" Sir Humphrey smiled at last. "If you must know, I stayed on in this god-forsaken hole because she was here. I was very much attracted to her, but I didn't get much of a chance to see her alone because she always had one of the old men hanging around, and for all I knew she might have preferred them. I have taken her for a drive or a walk occasionally, but last night was actually the longest time I had spent with her alone in the hotel."

"Were you in love with Miss Blake?"

"No," replied Sir Humphrey frankly. "But I was deeply interested in her."

"Forgive my asking, but did Miss Blake appear to reciprocate your – interest?" persisted Palk.

"I have every reason to believe that she did." Sir Humphrey suddenly covered his face with his hands and shuddered. "Oh, it's horrible, horrible! Can't you do something, Inspector? It's such a terrible thing not to know anything about it. She was only twenty-six, too young to be brutally murdered."

Palk looked at him reflectively.

"We are doing all we can, sir. You can help me very much by answering my questions. Now, what time was it when you and Miss Blake left the drawing-room?"

Sir Humphrey passed a hand over, his smooth black hair. "It must have been about one o'clock when I went upstairs. Miss Blake went straight out of the drawing-room and I went through the writing-room which adjoins it."

"Wasn't that rather strange?"

"I don't think so. We didn't want to be seen going upstairs together."

A few hours before, Palk might have questioned this statement, but after his experience of the conversations of the Hydro visitors his sympathies were with Sir Humphrey on this point.

"Did you actually see Miss Blake go through the door?"

"N-no."

"So that she might quite easily have remained downstairs after you yourself had gone upstairs?"

"Yes, I suppose so, but I don't think she did."

"Did anyone see you leave the writing-room?"

"No. At least, I saw nobody."

This form of reply always annoyed Palk. I only wish I had your eyes, he said to himself. To be able to see Nobody! Why, it's as much as I can do to see real people by this light!

"You didn't see any of the staff on your way to your bedroom?" he continued.

"No."

"You're quite sure? There was a maid on duty in the corridor, waiting to turn out the lights."

"Well, she wasn't in the corridor. I'm perfectly sure that I didn't see her."

"You went straight up to your bedroom from the writing-room?"

"Yes, yes. I didn't hurry, though. I wanted to let Miss Blake reach her room first."

"What did you do when you reached your room?"

"I went to bed and to sleep in the usual way."

"When did you first hear of Miss Blake's death?"

"At eight o'clock this morning. The maid brought my shaving-water up and told me that the doctor wanted us all down at once to breakfast because Miss Blake had been murdered."

Palk pursed his lips. He had given special instructions that the murder was not to be mentioned to the residents until he had seen them. It was evidently quite impossible to stop people talking in the Hydro. It seemed as if they must talk or die!

"Sir Humphrey," he asked, "do you know who killed Miss Blake?"

Sir Humphrey clenched his fists till the knuckles were drained white.

"I wish to God that I did!" he exclaimed fervently.

CHAPTER XIII

In Winnie Marston, Palk found the first genuine liking for the dead girl by any one of her own sex, and his voice softened when he questioned her, as a tribute to her admiration. He discovered that although Winnie Marston was her mother's "Yes-girl" for the sake of peace, she had opinions of her own to express and did express them very forcibly when the family were out of hearing.

"Murder is always wicked, of course," she said, "but somehow it seems more than wicked to kill Miss Blake. She was so lovely. It's like destroying a beautiful painting or work of art."

Palk pointed out that the women he had already interviewed would not have agreed with her description of Miss Blake.

"They didn't understand," replied Winnie. "You see, they never look under the surface to find out what people are really like. They just take them all the time at their face value. They assume that anyone who belongs to a different age and a different life from theirs must be inferior to them. They don't bother about people's hearts, except in the medical sense, and they'd never met anyone quite like Miss Blake before. But Miss Blake was a damned good sort, whatever they say. She was really sweet to all those old dames. They snubbed her to her face and talked behind her back, but she never got annoyed. They thought that her way of speaking to them was rude, but it wasn't really. It was just her natural way, rather casual and outspoken, you know, but nothing personal about it. I think she had a beautiful face and a lovely nature, and they were all perfect beasts to her – except the men, of course. They all adored her."

"You think, then, that some woman in the Hydro might have killed her?" asked Palk.

"Oh, I shouldn't like to say that," Winnie hastened to reply. "Being beastly to someone and murdering her are two different things, aren't they? But I've certainly seen two people look at her as if they hated the sight of her, within the last two days."

Palk looked mildly interested.

"Oh. Who were they?"

"Nurse Hawkins and Lady Warme." And she went on to give an accurate description of the scene in the lounge on the afternoon before the murder, culminating in Lady Warme's indignant exit before tea, "looking as if she could murder Miss Blake."

Palk did not place too much significance on this, realizing by now that such scenes were of common occurrence in this strange hotel. He knew, however, that clues might be found in the most unlikely sequence of circumstances, and persisted, therefore, with his questions.

"Which of the two do you consider would have been more likely to murder Miss Blake?"

Winnie looked startled.

"Oh, neither of them, Inspector Palk. I can't imagine any woman being so vicious."

"You said that Nurse Hawkins looked as if she could have strangled Miss Blake –"

"Yes, I know." Winnie sounded confused. "We often do say things like that though, don't we, without meaning them to be taken literally. One of my sister's favourite expressions is: 'Honestly, I could have killed her!' but it doesn't mean a thing. I'm quite sure she wouldn't hurt a fly. It's just a form of exaggeration, and we all do exaggerate things in this place. I don't really believe that Nurse Hawkins would have touched Miss Blake, not even to smack her face, but she was just annoyed to hear that Admiral Urwin had been talking to her. It sounds rather funny to think of the nurse and the Admiral being in love – somehow love is more for –" she faltered and looked down at her hands, nervously plucking at the skirt of her frock, "– for younger people, but I believe that they're really very fond of each other and they'd be well suited. I mean that Nurse Hawkins would look after him well and all that. But if the Admiral had preferred Miss Blake, I'm sure that Nurse Hawkins wouldn't dream of killing her. She'd just wait for another man to turn up. Nurses are rather callous, I think. I suppose it's all that training, operations and all that."

She paused.

"And Lady Warme?" asked Palk softly.

"Lady Warme? Oh, she's not a bad sort really. She's very touchy about a lot of things, like all the others here, and she likes to have her own way about everything. She's a most frightful snob, but the others make her like that. They say that her husband was knighted after the Great War because he gave a lot of money to hospitals and things. They hate titles without pedigrees, although they'd rather have titles than good plain yeoman names. Because Lady Warme's husband – that's what they always call him – made his money in cornflour, they refer to her behind her back as 'Lady Blancmange Mould'! But Miss Blake never said things like that behind her back. The only time I ever heard her say anything rude to anyone was when she read that book aloud the other day, and, really, Mrs. Dawson was quite right – they did ask for it. They were so rude to her first, and after all, she only did what they asked her to. I've never seen Lady Warme in such a flaming temper, and she might easily have slapped Miss Blake's face or boxed her ears, but I'm sure she would never wait and plan to murder her, especially after Miss Blake had been so decent and helped her with the concert that night."

But, reflected Palk after he had dismissed her, Winnie Marston would never believe evil about anyone, and the fact still remained that someone in the Hydro had murdered Miss Blake, someone who had found it child's play to camouflage his or her movements among the maze of the comings and goings of so many erratic people. And somewhere amongst this ever-increasing mass of irrelevant details there must lie at least one clue to the identity of that person, if only he could have the patience and skill to discover it.

CHAPTER XIV

Lady Warme sailed in looking, as the Inspector thought, very much like an Elizabethan galleon, for she gave the impression of having sails trimmed and decks cleared for action. She was an imposing woman nearly six feet tall, and heavily built, with large, capable hands and feet. Her dark hair was beautifully dressed, and if she wore a wig, as some people thought, no one in the Hydro had ever succeeded in discovering it. She either had good taste in clothes or the good sense to leave the choosing of them to an excellent dress-designer, for her black-and-white morning dress was well-cut and becoming, and she was exquisitely corseted. Yet, when she spoke, this illusion of femininity was somewhat marred by the masculine tones of a deep, resonant voice.

She evidently believed that attack is the best form of defence, for before she reached the table at which the Inspector was seated, she had spoken.

"You sent for me? No, I won't sit down."

Almost before the Inspector's brain had strummed a warning of "inferiority complex," he had jumped to his feet and was pushing the chair towards her with the manner of an attentive shop-walker.

"I could only request you to come, Lady Warme – my duty to question everyone – purely voluntary, of course. You won't mind if I ask you for your help in this very serious matter?" he murmured, his voice falling into a perfect imitation of the staccato way of speaking so popular in the Hydro. He felt thankful that Sergeant Jago was not there to hear him.

Lady Warme sat upright on the extreme edge of the chair.

"It's all very upsetting for a woman of my position, Inspector, to be mixed up with the police, and when it comes to my having to sit in a room for hours in the company of chambermaids, it becomes most embarrassing. I don't think I've ever spent a more unpleasant morning since I came to live here."

"I'm sorry," returned the Inspector, "but you will be quite free to go back to your own room after this interview. If I'd known, of course –"

His vague words evidently possessed some meaning for Lady Warme, for she did not wait to hear the ending of his sentence, which was fortunate for the Inspector.

"I always thought that the police had a system for questioning people," she said, "and nothing annoys me more than to be kept waiting. But, after all, Sir Humphrey has been in the same position, I suppose. I reckon that I'm a public-spirited woman, Inspector, and if I can tell you anything, you have only to ask. But I must warn you that you will be wasting time because I know nothing whatever about Miss Blake's death, and I'm sure that none of my friends here knows anything either. It must have been someone from outside. There are always a lot of tramps and gipsies about the place, but although I've complained to Dr. Williams about them, he never seems to do anything. Indeed, I've actually seen him give orders to have some food sent out to one awful man. No doubt this is the result."

"You don't think that anyone in the Hydro murdered Miss Blake, then?" Palk asked, in some surprise.

"Certainly not. They are all my friends. I'm quite sure that none of them would do such a terrible thing."

"But you understand that there is no doubt about her having been murdered? It couldn't have been an accident."

"Certainly, I understand. I am a woman of average intelligence, although from your questions I must assume that you don't think so. I tell you that you are simply wasting your time looking for the murderer inside this hotel, and you will only succeed in causing a considerable amount of annoyance to a number of innocent people."

"If your theory is correct," said Palk patiently, "the murderer must have entered the drawing-room after the concert was over. Perhaps you will be good enough to tell me what happened that evening. You organized the concert, I believe?"

"Yes, I always organize concerts here. I suppose I have a certain reputation among the residents as a lover of music, and most English people are so unmusical. Now, in Italy –"

"Yes, of course," agreed Palk, a little too heartily. "They sing so prettily – er – that is to say, Italian tenors, of course." He kicked himself mentally. "But to return to the concert. Miss Blake was the accompanist, wasn't she?"

"Yes, she took the organist's place at a moment's notice, and it was very good of her to volunteer, for, of course, you couldn't have a concert without an accompanist, could you? I mean, Miss Astill's voice, for instance. It's good for a few bars, but after that it needs a little gentle drowning out, and I must say Miss Blake did it extraordinarily well. I was rather surprised, because you don't really expect a low-born adventuress to know how to play the piano, do you?"

Palk could have told her of several low-born adventuresses whose social accomplishments attained higher levels than the mere playing of a piano, but he refrained.

"How do you know she was an adventuress?" he asked instead.

Lady Warme regarded him with a pitying stare.

"By the look of her, of course. Besides, she never said who she was. There are several good families of her name in this country, but she never admitted being related to any of them. There was Admiral Blake and Blake the poet, not that I rate poets very high in the social scale, but still they are *known*, and it does give one something to go on... Miss Blake never spoke of her home or her people, or any friends, and even when she left her handbag in the drawing-room once – well, no one ever got to know anything about her."

"Wasn't it rather strange that she should volunteer to play for you after that quarrel you'd had in the lounge?" asked Palk.

"Quarrel? In the lounge? Oh, you mean that ridiculous affair over the book. I suppose someone has given you all the details already – I must say I don't like all this prying behind people's backs. I should never have called it a quarrel myself, though I admit I was very much annoyed with Miss Blake at the time. Really, I shouldn't like to repeat some of the words she used – it was all in very bad form indeed, but as I said before, you could hardly expect anything better from a low-born adventuress, and when she was so nice afterwards about my concert, I couldn't very well remain annoyed, could I?"

Palk found it difficult to reconcile Lady Warme's present attitude with Winnie Marston's words, "She looked as if she could have murdered her"; but as it was obvious that he could get no further information from her, he indicated as politely as possible that the interview was at an end.

When Lady Warme had reached the door, she turned:

"If you want to find out the real truth," she said, "ask the doctor's secretary. She always knows everything. That's what she's paid for."

CHAPTER XV

In Palk's estimation the doctor's secretary, Miss Lewis, was the most attractive woman he had yet seen in the Hydro. She was small and slim, neatly costumed and shod. Her fair hair was parted in the middle and plaited into old-fashioned earphones. From the frill on her white blouse to the bows on her high-heeled suede shoes she looked the perfect stage secretary, and it seemed almost too good to be true that she could also be an intelligent stenographer. Palk expected her name to be Rosalind, and, surprised to find that it was, in fact, Gwynneth, guessed correctly the nationality which Christian and surname implied. Of all the people he had interviewed, she seemed to express the least emotion, sitting quietly on the chair in front of him and inclining an attentive secretarial ear. The only question Palk wanted to put to her was: "Are you doing anything tonight?" and he with difficulty restrained himself from dismissing her at once from his mind as a possible suspect. As it was, he began with an apology and again was thankful that Sergeant Jago was busy elsewhere, searching all the possible hiding-places in the hotel.

"You understand, Miss Lewis, that I have to interview everyone who has access to the public rooms in the Hydro. I hope you won't mind if I ask you a few questions."

As Miss Lewis's present attitude already indicated her readiness to collaborate in anything the Inspector wished to say, she did not think it necessary to reply to his remarks, but her hands made a quick little movement as if they were about to flick open her shorthand book. Finding them empty, she sat restfully, waiting.

"You knew Miss Blake?"

"Very slightly. She wasn't one of Dr. Williams' patients, and those are the people I come into contact with chiefly. At the most I might have had five minutes' conversation with Miss Blake at a time."

"I see. So you can't very well tell me whether you liked her or not?"

Miss Lewis's green eyes met his frankly.

"I liked what I did see of her. She was always very pleasant and smiling, and seemed to like to pass the time of day with everyone from her chambermaid upwards, but apart from that, she was merely a name in the account-book to me."

"She didn't have any medical treatment during her stay here?"

"No, never. I should have known because I make all appointments for the doctor. I can let you have the books, if you would like to verify them."

"Thank you. I don't doubt your word, but the books might prove of interest. I thought that, perhaps, you might have met Miss Blake in the lounge or dining-room. You're both young, and if she was inclined to stop and talk, as you say —"

"Oh yes, I'm sure she would have spoken to me, but you see, apart from arranging the flowers, I am so rarely in the public rooms in the daytime, and certainly never in the evenings as a general rule. The staff here are not encouraged to make use of these rooms – we have our own dining-room and sitting-room, and are expected to keep to those. There was a terrible outcry one day when Nurse Hawkins sat knitting in the drawing-room. I was kept busy all the next morning receiving complaints about it. Dr. Williams attends to all complaints personally, so that I have to make a note of them in a special book when they are reported. It wouldn't be popular with the housekeeper, either, if she heard of my going too often into the public rooms. It's her job to see that the maids do their work properly, and she would almost certainly think that I was trying to interfere in her department. This isn't a very charitable establishment."

"So I've noticed," replied Palk. "But you were at the concert last night, I believe."

"Oh yes, the staff is always invited to anything in the nature of an entertainment, but we always sit on hard benches at the back of the room, just to remind ourselves that we are only the staff, and we have our coffee and cakes in our own dining-room, although I actually helped to pour out coffee last night. I can't think why I was asked, but I was."

"Don't you find all those little things rather unpleasant?"

Miss Lewis smiled.

"No," she said, "I'm used to them, and they don't really worry me. I'd rather work for Dr. Williams than for anyone else in the world, and these petty little rules and regulations are mere incidentals. My work is the real thing to me, and it's congenial and well paid. I'm sure there are similar disadvantages in all jobs."

"What, exactly, are your duties?"

Miss Lewis tapped a reflective heel on the floor.

"Letters first of all, then Dr. Williams comes into my office at ten to the minute every morning, and discusses such things as special menus for patients who are on a diet, and fixes times for the various treatments in the Baths. This is most important, because we have only one set of treatment rooms, and it's very necessary to avoid any possible clashing between men and women patients."

Palk visualized the horror-stricken look which Miss Astill would bear if suddenly confronted by a semi-naked Colonel or Admiral, and smiled.

"Most necessary," he agreed, with suitable gravity.

"Well, then, diet sheets and treatment time-tables have to be typed in duplicate, and Nurse Hawkins comes to see what arrangements have been made for her day's work. For instance, Lady Warme has a chronically stiff shoulder, which needs frequent but not regular massage, and Admiral Urwin is always trying some new treatment, especially if it means extra attention from the nurse." She bit her lip. "I shouldn't have said that," she apologized, "but in this place it's so difficult not to repeat scandal. One hears so little of anything else, and only Dr. Williams seems to be above that kind of thing."

"I find it rather catching myself," sympathized Palk. "And then?"

"Oh, well, then I take the menus to the kitchen, and usually have to listen while the chef explains exactly why he cannot cook what Dr. Williams has ordered. It doesn't mean a thing, really. He's just one of those foreigners who wake up every morning wondering why he was fool enough to leave his native land, and always starts the day in a bad temper. I've never known him unable to carry out the doctor's orders."

"A foreigner," repeated Palk slowly.

A smile started in Miss Lewis's eyes and wreathed itself round her mouth.

"Yes, he's French, as a matter of fact. But I don't think you can pin the murder on him, because he doesn't sleep in the Hydro. He goes home after dinner every night."

The Inspector moved uneasily in his chair.

"I didn't realize that my thoughts were so transparent," he remarked ruefully.

"Don't worry about that," smiled Miss Lewis. "You see, I'm used to watching people to find out what they are thinking. I have a regular procession of residents coming into my office nearly every day and demanding to see Dr. Williams without giving any reasons. I just have to fish around until I find out what they want, or else Dr. Williams would never get his work done."

"But there are so few people in the Hydro," returned Palk. "Surely there can't be so many complaints."

Miss Lewis laughed, and Palk caught himself thinking that a woman's laugh can be a very pleasant sound, and so frequently is not. This laugh was neither too high-pitched, like Miss Astill's, nor too deep, like Lady Warme's – if Lady Warme ever did laugh, which he doubted. It was not a giggle like Millie Marston's, nor a bellow like Mrs. Napier's; it was, in fact, everything that a laugh should be, and it expressed genuine merriment, which was reflected in the twinkle in Gwynneth Lewis's eyes.

"Not many? You've no idea what most of the residents here are like. They go around the place hoping to find something wrong, and inventing something when they fail to find it. Dr. Williams has had to give up one day entirely to hearing complaints, but even that doesn't prevent some of the regular ones coming on all the other days in the week. They remind me of Wendy's children in *Peter Pan*."

Palk nodded. He knew his Carroll and Barrie, and with little effort brought the reference to mind.

"Slightly is coughing on the table... The twins began with mammee apples... Nibs is speaking with his mouth full... I complain of Curly... I complain of Nibs... I complain of the twins," something like that, if he remembered aright.

"One or two complaints are of long standing," went on the secretary. "Colonel Simcox likes the rooms heated to a temperature of seventy-five degrees, or higher, while Admiral Urwin likes open windows and a temperature of fifty or fifty-five degrees. They're always complaining of each other, as you may imagine. Then Mrs. Napier wants us to buy a new bath-chair because she doesn't like sharing one with Miss Brendon, and so on. So you may understand that I spend a large part of my time sitting in the office and persuading them all that Dr. Williams is engaged."

The Inspector seemed suddenly to realize that the conversation had wandered a long way from the subject of Miss Blake's murder. Perhaps it was because Miss Lewis's way of talking was so expressive; she moved her hands about and raised her eyebrows when she spoke, and every feature seemed to share in her smile.

"You probably know the people here better than most of the staff," he said, "I suppose you didn't notice anything out of the ordinary during or after the concert?"

"No. They all looked quite – er – normal to me. I've been to concerts here before, and this was exactly the same, even to the names of the songs: their repertoire is rather limited. The only thing I did notice was that everyone had his eyes focused on Miss Blake as if she were the chief attraction, or the reverse, but that was nothing new, really. She was so striking that as soon as she entered a room everyone stopped talking and gazed at her. All the men admired her and all the women envied her. I envied her myself."

"And after the concert?"

"We all went into the lounge for coffee, as I told you, and I helped to pour out. Everyone talked about the concert and then everyone talked scandal about Miss Blake and Sir Humphrey Chervil."

"And that was nothing new either, I imagine."

"No," agreed Miss Lewis. "They had both been the subject of a good deal of talk, chiefly because they were both so different from the other residents, but they hadn't really taken much notice of each other until the last week or so, so there hadn't really been any scandal about the two of them together. But on Sunday they went for a walk in the woods, and two young people of opposite sexes can't do that and then sit up alone until after midnight in this place without someone making mud of their names."

"How did you know that they were sitting alone together till after midnight?" persisted the Inspector.

"Weren't they?" she asked ingenuously, and for the first time Palk, with a sickening feeling in his heart, felt suspicious of her.

CHAPTER XVI

Palk interviewed the other three Marstons without adding a jot of information to that which he had already collected. Everyone, except Sir Humphrey Chervil, Dr. Williams and his secretary, had confided in him the name of the murderer, but in each case the accusation was based solely on personal spite without a vestige of evidence to support it.

"If I believed half that I've been told this morning I should think I'd strayed into a regular murderers' kitchen," he told Sergeant Jago.

He was poring over his notes, once again at a dead end, when a constable came in and placed a small red notebook in front of him.

"From Room 16," he said.

Palk read through the pencilled contents, then paused at one page and whistled softly. He looked down his list of the rooms and their owners, murmured a name, and the constable on duty at the door went automatically, and returned with Mrs. Dawson.

She was a heavily built woman of the old-fashioned head-mistress type, with fair hair drawn back from her forehead, and yellow horn-rimmed spectacles resting on her wellshaped nose. She wore a severely tailored blouse and skirt, thick grey stockings and low-heeled shoes, and was one of those breezy-mannered women whom Palk instinctively disliked.

"This is a terrible thing, Inspector," she said. "It has shocked me deeply."

She certainly looked very much upset, thought Palk, and so she should if it was really her notebook he had just been reading.

"You knew Miss Blake well?" he asked.

"No, I can't say that I did. She wasn't my type exactly."

Palk agreed. It would have been difficult to have found two women more unlike each other.

"You disliked her, then?"

"Oh no. I found her most interesting."

Palk leaned forward earnestly.

"Mrs. Dawson, was this murder a surprise to you?"

"More than a surprise. A very great shock, Inspector."

"You had no reason to suspect that it would be committed?"

Mrs. Dawson looked at him fearfully. She moistened her lips with the tip of her tongue.

"I – I – I certainly didn't expect it."

"Then may I ask you to be so kind as to explain this."

He thrust the notebook in front of her, and Mrs. Dawson's composure broke as she saw it.

"You found it, then," she said. "I have been afraid that you would, but now I'm glad. Now I can tell you all about it."

"I must warn you –" began Palk, with a glance at the constable, who still sat at his shorthand in the corner, but she interrupted him.

"I know all about that, but it's been haunting me. You must see that it has."

Palk did not see very clearly, and said so.

"This is a very serious matter, Mrs. Dawson," he said. "A lady is found murdered in this Hydro, probably by someone in residence, and a notebook is found in your room, giving notes about the victim, the place of the murder, and the manner of it." He read aloud from the notebook, "'First murder. Miss B. Settee in drawing-room. Knitting-needle.' Don't you see that unless you can make some satisfactory explanation I shall have to take you into custody on suspicion of being, if not a murderer, at least accessory after the fact?"

Mrs. Dawson's pale-blue eyes stared at him in horror.

"Oh, but you can't think that I had anything to do with it! I don't know anything about it. Don't you see how terrible it is for those notes to have come true? If I'd really been the murderer I should never have kept them."

"Come, come, Mrs. Dawson," said Palk. "Murderers have been known to make mistakes sometimes. You will have to explain more clearly than that if you expect me to believe you. What was the point of writing such a thing? It must have been put down before the murder."

"Of course it was, weeks before. That's why it's so horrible. Can't you understand? They were notes for my new book."

"Oh, you write books, do you?" asked Palk, who possessed the greatest contempt for women writers.

"Yes, thrillers. I haven't had any published yet, but my agents will tell you it's true. Webster and Hadley, Fleet Street; they've got two books of mine, but they've not found a publisher for them yet. This would have been my third, and I did want to make it a success."

Palk, whose estimation of Mrs. Dawson had gone up contrarily as he realized that her books were still unprinted, began to think that there might be some truth in what she said, although it certainly seemed to be stretching coincidence very far.

"So they were the notes for a new thriller," he repeated. "Let's assume, for the moment, that I believe you. Would you mind telling me why you chose Miss Blake as the victim? I suppose you don't deny that 'Miss B.' represented Miss Blake?"

"No. It was meant to be Miss Blake. I told you that I found her interesting. Besides, she was by far the prettiest woman in the place, and seemed the obvious choice for the victim. Can't you see what a perfect setting this Hydro is for a murder, Inspector, with everyone wanting to murder someone else at times? I've seen Mr. Marston look as if he could murder Lady Warme when she played a wrong stroke at croquet, and Colonel Simcox look as if he could murder Admiral Urwin when he joined his *tête-à-tête* with Miss Blake, and Mrs. Napier look as if she could murder the nurse when she saw her talking to the Admiral."

Palk had a suspicion that she was trying to lead him away from his questions.

"I must remind you," he said, "that in view of those notes you are under very strong suspicion. I am going to give you every chance to answer the questions I put to you, but I must caution you that –"

"That everything I say will be taken down and used in evidence against me," supplied Mrs. Dawson. "I know, I've written it down often enough myself. I'm not a fool, and, of course, I see that I'm under suspicion. It's bound to look queer for me to plan a murder that comes true, even to the knitting-needle, but I don't know anything about the real murder."

"Why did you choose a knitting-needle as a weapon?"

"Because it was the only original one I could think of. Daggers and bullets have been overdone, and the women here always carry knitting about in their needlework bags; anyone could get hold of one. I hadn't definitely decided on it, you know. You'll see a question mark after the words 'knitting-needle', if you look. There were so many details to think out in connection with it. For one thing, the murderer would have to have a handle for the needle before it could be made into a serviceable weapon."

"So you'd thought about that, had you?" asked Palk.

"Of course I'd thought about it. A writer of thrillers has to think about these things, Inspector." Mrs. Dawson was fast recovering her natural manner.

"Perhaps you also understand how the knitting-needle caused Miss Blake's death?"

"It pierced the medulla through the gap between the two halves of the skull when she bent her head forward, didn't it? It's no use, Inspector, I've told you that I intended to write it up in a story; naturally, I read up all the necessary details."

"I suppose you bought a book for that purpose, then. Can you let me see it?"

"There was no need to buy a book, Inspector. The doctor's medical books are scattered all over the Hydro, and all who run may read."

"Did you mention this method of murder to anyone in the Hydro?"

"Probably. I'm not what you'd call a silent worker. I like to discuss ideas with other people."

There was no doubt about her telling the truth there, thought Palk.

"So that it is quite possible that you discussed the theory in some detail to several people here?"

"Yes, I'm almost sure to have done, but I don't actually remember doing it."

"I see. And where had you thought of hiding the handle after the murderer had done his job?" Palk asked sarcastically.

Mrs. Dawson took his question quite seriously.

"I'm afraid I hadn't worked it out far enough for that," she said. "But I should have made it fairly obvious, I think, like the dagger in *The Cat and the Canary*. If you make your clues too involved you defeat your own ends, because people soon get tired of following them. You don't write, Inspector, so you probably won't understand what I mean."

Palk thought of the long, elaborate records he would be expected to write for headquarters, and smiled to himself.

"Will you tell me what your object was in writing 'First murder' in your notes?" he asked.

"Well, there were to have been several murders in the book. Two or three, at least. The reading public nowadays is never satisfied with only one murder. They like plenty of thrills for their money."

She had now quite recovered from her nervousness and answered quite frankly, with a kind of professional interest.

"There's no accounting for tastes," replied Palk. "One is too much for me, but, then, I don't read thrillers. Do you write for a hobby, Mrs. Dawson?"

Mrs. Dawson was not offended.

"Oh no, I don't like writing sufficiently well for that; it's very hard work. But I'm a widow, and have a small son."

Well, she's not my type, thought Palk, but some man must have thought her attractive.

"I've enough income from my husband's shares to keep us both comfortably now, because Bobby is only seven, but I've been fairly hard hit by the conversion loans, and when Bobby is older I shall need more than I have for his education. There seems to be such a demand for thrillers, and the only thing I have any flair for is writing, so I've been trying it for the last three years without any luck. I didn't wish any harm to Miss Blake, but if she had to be murdered sometime in her life, I can't help feeling glad that it was when I was here. It will be such marvellous publicity."

Inspector Palk snorted. That's just typical of a woman, he thought, in the superiority of his bachelorhood. Vultures, all of 'em!

"This is a police inquiry," he said scornfully, "not a publicity agent's."

He asked a few more questions, then dismissed her, more than a little convinced of her genuineness, despite his own personal feelings. As she reached the door he halted her.

"By the way," he said, "whom had you chosen as the murderer?"

Mrs. Dawson smiled.

"Miss Astill," she said sweetly, "because she seemed the most unlikely of the lot!"

CHAPTER XVII

Miss Astill came into the library wearing a fussy dress which gave the impression of her entering the room amid streamers. The first thing that the Inspector noticed was that she was carrying a deep tapestry needlework bag in her hand, and in sudden suspicion, which he hoped was not engendered by Mrs. Dawson's last words, he said:

"I suppose that bag has been searched, Miss Astill."

Miss Astill looked startled.

"Yes, yes, it has certainly. By a police officer. He said he was looking for knitting-needles, but I don't knit. I never could, even as a child, though I can't think why. I told him to try Colonel Simcox; he's very clever at knitting."

Palk hesitated a second, then said:

"Would you object very much if I asked you to allow me to have another look at it?"

She handed it to him without a word, and sat almost at attention while he emptied everything out on to the table. A white satin cloth partly embroidered in red silk and gold thread first came to light, wrapped in an old cream silk handkerchief; then a packet of crewel needles; tiny scissors in the shape of a stork, the two blades forming the beak; a small bag of round, white peppermints of extra strength; a book of Bible readings. He satisfied himself that there was no knitting-needle hidden in any part of the bag, and began to put the contents carefully back again.

"It's a new altar cloth I'm making for the dear Vicar," Miss Astill explained anxiously. "I'm not very clever with my needle, but it's such a labour of love to me."

Palk handed the bag over to her and she settled it comfortably on her knee.

"So upsetting, all this legal procedure," she twittered, eying the two constables.

"I'm sorry, but it has to be done if we are to catch the person who murdered Miss Blake," replied Palk. "You don't mind answering a few questions, I hope."

"Yes, yes, of course. Anything I can do to help... But all this is a very hard experience for me, Inspector. I have been so delicately reared; my dear parents kept me away from the hard knocks of life, and now to be plunged into a – a murder – I don't know what my poor mother would have thought."

The words, though apparently stupid coming from a woman well past middle age, evoked a certain amount of sympathy from Palk. Miss Astill looked so definitely a product of an older age, so unfitted, as she had said, to be involved in a crime of violence. She belonged to the placid Edwardian days, when, as a girl in her twenties, she had no doubt waited on an irascible father and an invalid mother, slowly watching her chances of marriage fade into certain spinster-hood. She exuded a faint odour of moth-balls, and looked as if she ought to have worn a dress of red plush trimmed with antimacassars.

Palk treated her as tenderly as he would have treated his own mother.

"You have heard about the... death of Miss Blake?"

Miss Astill raised her hands, palms outward.

"Yes, yes. The poor girl –"

"You knew her well?"

The hands were lowered, and moved restlessly in her lap.

"Not well, no. We did not see each other much. I am sensitive. I always was sensitive as a child. I felt she despised me. She was young and beautiful and healthy, all the things which I am not. Oh, indeed, I know!" as Palk made a slight gesture of protest. "She drank cocktails in her bedroom, and wore immodest clothes, and smoked cigarettes. I belong to a different age, when girls were taught to cover their bodies decently and to speak softly, and behave like ladies."

"You thought her immodest and indecent?"

Miss Astill sat very erect, as if she still felt the straps of the backboard she had worn as a child. A sudden blaze of anger came into her faded eyes like a white flame.

"I did. Exposing her naked body to the gaze of all the men on the premises!"

"But surely, not naked," protested Palk.

She glared malevolently at him.

"What else could you call it? She used to wear those disgusting things called shorts, and no stockings in the summer. You could see her legs right up to her thighs and beyond, if you cared to look. And her evening dresses! No back and very little front! What else could you call it but naked? She was immodest and immoral!"

She had some difficulty in controlling herself, but suddenly the anger died away from her eyes, leaving them dull and brown.

"It's very wrong of me to say such things about her," she said. "She's dead now, and won't wear any more of those clothes."

Palk waited for a second, then, as if a new thought had struck him, asked: "Did Miss Blake wear much jewelry?"

"Yes, indeed, she did. No one could help noticing it. She had some lovely jewels, and I know something about them. They were real stones, I'm sure, and not synthetic rubbish. Her diamonds must have been worth hundreds of pounds. She used to wear them with tweeds as no real lady would have done, but they were really valuable."

The Inspector wrote a hurried note and sent it to Sergeant Jago by a constable.

"Then you think she might have been murdered for her jewelry by some burglar?"

"By a burglar? Oh no, surely not. Someone in the Hydro murdered her."

"How do you know that?" Palk barked the question at her, and she gave a start.

"But you – you think so yourself, or why would you forbid us all to go out of the Hydro?"

"You have no suspicions of anyone yourself?"

Miss Astill's eyes gleamed eagerly.

"I'm not of a suspicious nature, Inspector," she said, in tones which seemed to presage ill to someone, "but when I see people under suspicious circumstances I can't help having suspicions, can I? When I saw Miss Blake upstairs in the corridor after the concert –"

"What?" The Inspector's exclamation was like the crack of a whip. "You saw her upstairs after the concert? At what time?"

"It must have been after one o'clock in the morning, because I know I didn't feel well. I'd taken a cup of coffee, and it always upsets me, but I thought that just one cup during the evening wouldn't have any bad effect. It just shows you that you can never relax your dieting for a second when you have such a delicate digestion –"

Palk interrupted her. If you once let people talk about their digestions here, he thought, there's no stopping them.

"When did you see Miss Blake?"

Miss Astill looked aggrieved.

"I'm telling you, Inspector. I didn't feel well after the concert, and I was going along the corridor upstairs –"

"Where were you going to?" asked Palk bluntly.

Miss Astill hung a modest head, and Palk began to think that there was much to be said for the modern girl despite her shorts, at least where police questionnaires were concerned.

"Well, go on," he said.

"I heard someone coming along the corridor, so, of course, I went back to my room and waited for them to go past."

"But you saw who it was, first?" Palk knew that there was no need to ask such a question in the scandal-loving Hydro.

"Certainly I saw them. I'm not blind. If people will walk about the corridors at that time in the morning they must expect to be seen."

Palk thought the argument faulty, but did not say so. "You say that you saw them. Who were they?"

"Miss Blake and Sir Humphrey Chervil, of course."

Palk whistled.

"You're quite sure of that?"

"I'm the daughter of an Army officer, and am not accustomed to having my word doubted," said Miss Astill stiffly. "Besides, you can find out from Sir Humphrey himself." Palk secretly thought that this might not be so easy as she seemed to think.

"I'm sorry," he said. "I don't doubt your word. Did you happen to hear anything they were saying?"

"No, they were too far away."

"So you did not see either of them again?"

"No, and I didn't hear them, either!"

But Palk was tired of chasing clues.

"What, exactly, do you mean by that remark, Miss Astill? If you have any further evidence, I must ask you to give it to me at once."

Miss Astill leaned forward eagerly.

"Well, Sir Humphrey's room is along the corridor to the left of my room, so that he has to pass my door to reach it. Of course, I left my door open a little so that I should know when he had gone past... But," she paused impressively, "I never did hear him come past. I waited for ten minutes, then risked looking out. The corridor was empty and Miss Blake's door was shut."

"Perhaps he passed so quietly that you couldn't hear the sound of his footsteps," suggested Palk.

"But I should have seen him. I had switched off the light in my room and was standing looking through the gap in the door. The corridor lights were still on. He couldn't possibly have passed without my seeing him."

Palk had a sudden vivid picture of the little spinster standing in her bedroom, clutching a scarlet flannel dressing-gown, with a purple collar, around her scanty figure. She was probably wearing metal hair-curlers under a decorous boudoir cap, he thought, glancing at the waves in her hair, which were narrow and crimped, where Miss Blake's had been so smooth and wide.

"Where do you think Sir Humphrey went, then?" he asked.

"Into Miss Blake's bedroom, of course," replied Miss Astill, in triumph. "I heard voices from her room when I passed afterwards. I don't know what else you could expect from a girl who wore such clothes."

CHAPTER XVIII

Sergeant Jago entered, looking very pleased with himself.

"Found it, Sergeant?" asked Palk.

"Not the handle yet, sir, but we've got the jewels." He placed a large pigskin jewel-case on the table. "You didn't send me a list to check them by, but I should think they're all here. There do seem to be a powerful lot of them."

"I suppose there's no doubt about their being Miss Blake's."

"Hardly, sir. Her name's inside. We found them in room twenty-seven. They weren't hidden much; just the usual place, on top of the wardrobe."

Inspector Palk ran his finger down the list of rooms, then leaned back in his chair, and threw his pencil down with a satisfied air.

"I think that settles it, Jago," he said. "Just stay at that door. I may need you. Bring Sir Humphrey Chervil," he said to the constable.

Sir Humphrey looked still apprehensive, but more collected than at his first interview. Some of his composure vanished, however, when he saw the jewel-case.

Palk nodded to him pleasantly.

"I want to ask you a few questions about that, Sir Humphrey," he said, while Sergeant Jago felt ashamed of his superior's lack of finesse. To his way of thinking, the jewel-case should have been concealed at the beginning of the interview, only to be whipped out at the crucial moment when the witness had perjured himself. But Jago read detective novels in his spare time, and Palk did not.

The Inspector had his own methods, and did not care whether they were orthodox or not. He preferred to place all his facts before a suspect, leaving him to explain them away. If anyone was disposed to tell lies, he argued, those lies were more likely to stand out against the nucleus of truth around which they must thus, inevitably, be woven. But he could never get the sergeant to see this, which is probably why he remained a sergeant for a very long time, while Palk's promotion was more speedy.

After cautioning Sir Humphrey, Palk went on:

"I have reason to believe that the jewels in this case be-long to Miss Blake. They have just been found on the top of your wardrobe. Can you explain how they got there?"

"No." Sir Humphrey's neat black moustache served to accentuate the pallor of the tensed skin round his mouth.

"You have been cautioned about the seriousness of your replies. Do you still persist in the assertion that you had not met Miss Blake before you came to this Hydro?"

"Yes."

"Before you met her here, she was a complete stranger to you?"

"Yes."

"Very well. I believe that you told me that you last saw Miss Blake in the drawing-room, that she was going upstairs from there, but that you did not actually see her go through the door."

"Yes."

The monosyllables were strange. Palk, suddenly had the feeling that this man was not unused to official police questionings.

"Yet you were observed by a witness to be walking along the upstairs corridor to Miss Blake's room after one o'clock. Is that true, Sir Humphrey?"

A ghastly pallor spread over Sir Humphrey's face. He put up his hand to steady the trembling of his mouth.

"Yes," he said again.

"You went upstairs with Miss Blake, and you entered her bedroom? Why?"

"She wanted to give me her jewels."

The reply was so ingenuous that Palk was taken aback for a moment.

"What for?" he asked at length.

"To – to take care of them for her. She was nervous about having so many valuables in her room."

Palk smiled.

"I see," he said. "And you really expect me to believe that although she had never met you before she came here, and although you had never been alone together for long until last night, Miss Blake handed over jewels worth a few thousand pounds so that you could put them on top of your wardrobe, instead of handing them to the doctor to put into his safe?"

"Yes, you see, I... yes."

He put up his hands to shield his face.

"Let me remind you of a few things you have forgotten," said Palk. "A lady is murdered. Your cigarette-lighter is found down the side of the couch on which she was lying. You are the last known person to have seen her alive. Her jewelry, of very great value, is found concealed in your room. You have tried to clear yourself by lying. If you want to tell me the truth, I'll listen. Have you anything to say?"

"I didn't murder her," Sir Humphrey said dully.

The Inspector waited.

"Well?" he asked, after a long pause.

Sir Humphrey shook his head. He looked a stricken man, and Palk had no compunction in placing him under arrest.

"A clear case," he said to the sergeant, feeling permissibly well pleased with himself. "I may not be like the brilliant detective who, I am sure, strides through Mrs. Dawson's books, but this old tortoise gets there just the same."

It was not until the following morning that he remembered that he had not interviewed Miss Brendon and her attendant, Ada Rogers.

CHAPTER XIX

The shadow which had been thrown over Presteignton Hydro by Miss Blake's murder was lifted by Sir Humphrey Chervil's arrest. The next day the residents awakened to a morning of brilliant sunshine and the knowledge that they were free once more to enjoy it as they would, out of doors. The thought was particularly pleasant after the gruelling hours of police questioning which they had been forced to spend in closer proximity with the staff and their fellow-guests than they liked.

Chambermaids drew up the heavy green Venetian blinds with a clatter for which they were, for once, not reprimanded. Early-morning tea was sipped without the grudging thought that it was an extra and not worth sixpence. The women all wore their brightest clothes. No one was late for breakfast.

Any qualms which Dr. Williams might have had about the residents packing up and moving to another hotel on account of the murder were soon dissipated, for no one showed any tendency to move. Possibly it might have been different if any of the older residents had been involved in the murder, but Miss Blake and Sir Humphrey had been like visitants from some other world whose actions left them entirely unaffected. It might have been different, too, if the case had dragged on for several weeks instead of being so quickly and satisfactorily solved by Inspector Palk, but, as it was, the murder merely became an engrossing new scandal which would serve as a topic of conversation for many months to come, and they all pursued the insignificances of their daily life as if they had never been disturbed by anything so upsetting.

The more sensational morning papers gave the first jolt to their complacency, but the residents were comforted by the fact that the reporters, in their eternal desire for new expressions, had only succeeded in making the headlines unintelligible. "Murder-Baronet's Beautiful Bride", they said, with more alliteration than truth, and "'Unique Murder Weapon in Hotel Crime." A syndicate consisting of the Chief-Constable of Devonshire, Inspector Palk, Sergeant Jago, Dr. Williams, Miss Lewis, and the housekeeper, had succeeded in keeping the reporters from contact with the residents and staff of the Hydro, so that the only photographs appearing in the Press were those of the official view of Presteignton Hydro, and a blurred photograph of Inspector Palk *(right)* talking to Sergeant Jago *(left)*. There was also a photograph of "Miss Molly O'Shea, pretty Irish girl, who discovered the body," which effectively destroyed the hitherto unbroken friendship between her and Amy Ford.

Thus it was not until the following Sunday, when the first dusty grey charabanc jaunted up the hill and halted on the terrace, that the residents at Presteignton Hydro suffered any discomfort from Miss Blake's murder. The charabanc relieved itself of its passengers and bumped round to the old coaching-yard to make room for two of its fellows. They had come to Presteignton on an advertised "Grand Surprise Trip," but no one was more surprised than the doctor when he beheld the hundred excited, shouting, gesticulating people who stood on the terrace in their stiff Sunday clothes, criticizing the view and everything else in sight.

He took one look at the strangers and gave hurried instructions to Miss Lewis.

"I'll lunch in my own rooms," he said. "I can see no one at all today. You understand?"

"Yes, Doctor," replied Miss Lewis, understanding full well that every resident would demand to make a personal complaint to the doctor and would insist that charabancs must, in future, be abolished from the Hydro.

Such an unexpected crowd of visitors had never been known in the Hydro in the experience of any resident, but the Hydro was a public hotel and, as such, could not refuse to accommodate visitors seeking refreshment. The staff set to work rearranging the dining-room, crowding the residents' tables into one corner of the room, and bringing in long trestle-tables from the staff dining-room for the extra people. The kitchen staff, hastily reinforced from the garden, was working at full speed already, washing extra dinner services which were covered with layers of dust from long disuse, cleaning vegetables, opening tins of soup and fruit, while the chef and the housekeeper shouted and coaxed and sweated, and somehow contrived to have a four-course luncheon ready on time.

"Is this the way to dinner, Ma?" one of the party asked Lady Warme, who replied with a frosty, "Luncheon will be served in there, if that is what you mean. Really," she said, turning to Mrs. Marston, "they can't expect us to eat in the same room as these low people. I shall go up to my bedroom and ring for a luncheon tray. I advise you to do the same. This is intolerable."

She went, but after half an hour she returned to the dining-room, tired of ringing a bell which no one attempted to answer. All the chambermaids had been pressed into service as waitresses, and no one was in attendance in the corridors. She found things considerably calmer. Only occasionally could a remark be heard.

"Now eat your meat, Albert, or you won't have no pudding."

"Gosh, ain't it tough?"

"Here, miss, me and this lady's been waiting hours for that fruit."

"Plums or apples. Is that what I came out of the Army for?"

"Don't 'ave any rice, Gert, it's sticky."

"Did you hear that? Sixpence for a cup of coffee. No, you can't have any. We'll get a few oranges instead."

Most of which were, after all, the usual remarks heard during Hydro luncheons, if expressed somewhat differently.

Lady Warme walked slowly towards her table.

"Not so bad now that they're having food," she remarked to Mrs. Dawson, as if she was speaking about a new consignment of animals for a zoo.

"No, but you should have heard those American girls ordering sidecars – cocktails, you know."

"Sidecars? I thought they were Irish." Lady Warme's knowledge of things Irish was limited. "Where's my table?"

A waitress passed by with a loaded tray.

"I'm sorry, Lady Warme, but we thought you were out, so we used your table. Could you sit with Miss Astill? We're very busy."

She passed on. Lady Warme subsided at the table indicated, her face red with anger.

"Really, this is beyond an insult," she exclaimed loudly. "I shall complain to the doctor. Cluttering the hotel up with common people who drive about in charabancs! Huddling the regular guests into a corner like this! Do you know that someone actually asked me to show him where the murder was committed? As if it's not bad enough to be pitchforked into a murder without people coming to gloat over it. It's disgraceful. I shall give notice at the end of the week without fail."

But she did not do so, for before the week ended Inspector Palk and his attendant band of constables were again in the Hydro, and the questioning had begun again.

CHAPTER XX

Mr. Marston stood on the terrace throwing gravel at his wife's bedroom window to attract her attention. She kept him waiting until she judged that he was in danger of throwing a full-sized stone, then threw up the window and leaned out.

"Hallo, dear," she said. "It's going to be a lovely day."

"It won't be day much longer if you don't hurry up. What the devil are you and the girls doing? Have you seen about a luncheon basket yet? Does anyone know we've arranged to go out?"

"Just a minute, dear." Mrs. Marston withdrew into the bedroom. "Your father's in one of his usual morning tempers," she remarked to her two daughters. "Spoiling things as usual."

"I don't think he slept well last night, Mother," said Winnie.

Mrs. Marston snorted.

"Rubbish, child! That's an old tale of his. I used to be worried to death every time he complained of a sleepless night until I realized that it was just a habit of his to say so. Angling for sympathy, that's all it is. I've no patience with a man who can't make the best of things. Your father's never so ill as he pretends to be."

"He's getting jolly mad now," said Millie, who was looking through the window. "He's stamping about like a wild bull. You'd better say something to him or he'll go and insult the first person he sets eyes on, and everyone is annoyed enough already about his language. They'll be complaining about him to the doctor again, and we shall be asked to leave this place just as we had to leave all the others. There soon won't be a hydro in the country that we can stay at."

Mrs. Marston stabbed a brooch into her blouse.

"Well, why are you both standing there doing nothing? My life's a perfect misery what with you and your father. Millie, go and ask them to pack a luncheon basket for four and the chauffeur. You'd better tell Matthews that we want the car brought round to the front at once, Winnie."

Millie giggled.

"If you want Matthews as quickly as all that, you'd better fetch him yourself," she said.

Mrs. Marston swung herself round.

"What do you mean by that?" she asked.

Millie drew back. She was afraid of her mother and had already regretted her words.

"Nothing – only – well, if you want to know, it's all over the Hydro that Winnie and Matthews –"

Mrs. Marston advanced on her unfortunate daughter and boxed her smartly on the ear.

"Don't ever let me hear you say anything like that again," she said. "Isn't this place full enough of scandal without your repeating lies about your own sister? I'm ashamed of you, Millie. You know that Winnie can't help being seen about with Matthews. He's teaching her to drive the car."

The two girls hurried out of the room and Mrs. Marston composed her face at the mirror and once again leaned out of the window, apparently quite oblivious to the fact that she had kept her husband waiting so long.

"It's all right," she called down. "The girls are seeing about lunch, and the car will be round at once. You'll just have time to take your exercise while we are getting ready." She waved her hand and closed the window.

"Oh, blast!" roared Mr. Marston, stepping backwards into Miss Astill, who was reading her morning prayers as she slowly paced along the terrace.

"Really, Mr. Marston," she began indignantly, as the black leather book turned turtle on the path, scattering little printed texts from its gilded leaves.

"Sorry." He stooped down to collect them and thrust them ungently into her hand, then leaned for a second on his walking-stick, his breathing heavy with annoyance.

Miss Astill sorted out her texts, selected one, and pressed it into his hand.

"If only you could believe..." she murmured, and turned from him with a coy smile.

Mr. Marston stared after her, speechless with rage, then looked down at the little card with its serrated edges and its printed forget-me-nots and roses wreathed round the text.

"Oh, blast!" he roared more loudly than before, and, tearing the card into minute pieces, scattered them on the gravel and stumped off to Bachelors' Walk, where he usually took his morning exercise.

Bachelors' Walk was a level strip of gravel eighty yards long. At one end stood a wooden garden seat painted green, and at the other a stone urn painted red. From the seat to the urn and back again was thus a hundred and sixty yards, and to cover this distance eleven times meant that you had walked a mile under the most advantageous conditions, since there were no hills to negotiate. A scale plan of the path was pinned up on the notice-board in the hall, with a kind of ready-reckoner for the quarter, the half, and three-quarter mile.

Mr. Marston selected eleven small smooth pebbles from the gravel, and placed them in his outer left-hand jacket pocket. Then he stood squarely in front of the seat, and set off at a brisk pace. He turned sharply when the urn was reached, and when he arrived back at the seat, he placed one of the pebbles on the green wood and repeated the whole process again.

Urn. Seat. Urn. Seat.

He knew nearly every stone on the path, for he always paced it with downcast eyes, and no one but himself knew the tricks it played on him.

Seat. Urn. Seat. Urn.

Sometimes he took an imaginary run to bowl one of the fast spinners which had done so much to put his name in the lists of cricket. His mind went back twenty years. In imagination he saw himself picked for the Test Match, saw the smooth pitch, the waiting field, the Australian wickets falling to his bowling. The Ashes...

Urn. Seat. Urn. Seat.

He stopped for a moment, leaning against the seat and breathing heavily.

Here he was, an old man at forty-eight, he thought bitterly. His life for the last fourteen years had been spent in voyages in the winter and in hydros for the rest of the year. All forms of sport were denied to him; he had to spend his recreation hours playing croquet or clock-golf, and then people wondered that he couldn't keep his temper. He, who had been so essentially masculine, was now deprived of everything which makes a masculine atmosphere. He must not drink, he must not smoke; his life was as full of "don'ts" as that of Robert Louis Stevenson had been. He hadn't even a son in whose exploits he could live again the hazards of his own youth, but only two daughters, Winnie and Millie. The Marston sisters. It sounded just like one of those hateful crooning turns on the wireless, which Millie loved so much.

He resumed his walk.

Seat. Urn.

How he hated all this necessity for taking care of himself. He could never get away from his wife's constant questions: "Have you taken your exercise, Charles?"

"Have you had your medicine yet, Charles?" or "You know I'm only telling you for your own good, Charles." She never let him out of her sight for two minutes, and raised hell if he so much as looked at another woman.

Urn. Seat.

There they were now, standing on the terrace round the car. He hated driving. He hated closed cars. It was damned unhealthy to sit in a glass-sided box for an hour or more with four other people, but he couldn't stand the windows open. Ever since that bout of rheumatic fever he had caught cold so easily.

He sighed. He was an old man now, an old man.

He reached the seat again and put down another pebble, then counted the number in the little row he had made along the seat.

Eight. Oh, well, call it eleven. No one would know.

He swept the pebbles on to the path and went to join his wife.

"There you are, dear," she greeted him brightly. "I'm afraid you didn't finish your mile this morning. Never mind, you can take a little walk after lunch."

He glared at her.

"Where are we going?" he snapped.

"Through Newton St. Mary and straight on to Excester. The girls want to do some shopping. We can come back along the coast road."

"You never ask me where I want to go. You decide everything and expect me to follow like a dog on a lead," grumbled her husband.

Mrs. Marston smiled because the chauffeur, Matthews, was within hearing, and replied with forced cheerfulness:

"My dear Charles, if we waited for you to decide we should never arrive anywhere."

She settled herself in the far corner at the back of the car, and Winnie and Millie followed her. Mr. Marston lowered himself carefully into the front seat beside the chauffeur.

Mrs. Napier approached, taking a walking lesson from Nurse Hawkins. She smiled at them icily.

No one ever gives me any consideration, she thought. They go off on a pleasant trip and never offer me a seat. That chauffeur always draws the car right up in my path on purpose, just to make me walk round it. They all know I can't walk properly. There ought to be a rule against such cruelty. I shall complain to the doctor.

She stumbled in self-pity.

"Now, Mrs. Napier," reprimanded Nurse Hawkins, "you have not got your mind on what you're doing. You must think about it all the time. Now keep pace with me: left, right, left, right."

"Poor soul," remarked Mrs. Marston. "I am so sorry for her. I wish we could take her for a drive, but there's no room."

"I suppose you'd like me to give up my seat to her and stay at home. Is that what you're hinting?" demanded her husband.

"Certainly not, Charles. You know that I meant nothing of the kind. But she looks so lonely, and that husband of hers comes to see her so rarely. Of course, I know that he lives over two hundred miles away, but still... I hope that if I ever get like that you will have more consideration for me.

Mr. Marston made no reply, but his expression seemed to indicate that if such a calamity should ever befall her, he would cheerfully murder her.

Matthews pressed the self-starter and the car hummed into life.

"Have you filled up with petrol, Matthews?"

"Yes, madam."

"Is the luncheon basket in?"

"Yes, miss."

"I suppose you know the way?"

"Yes, sir."

The big saloon car moved off. Its five occupants were silent.

Mrs. Marston was thinking how disheartening it was to try and arrange an outing which would please them all. Charles always contrived to be more than usually irritable on such days. He tried to make out that it was because she nagged him about taking medicine and exercise. But if she didn't take the trouble to remind him he simply made no attempt to take either, and she had to sit up with him all night if he had one of his attacks. Of course, it was dreadful for Charles to be tied down by ill-health after he had been used to such an active life, but he ought to have become sufficiently used to it by now to endure it more cheerfully, instead of that, he spent his time fretting about the games he could no longer play, forgetting that in any case he was now too old to be included in any cricket team. He exaggerated his own prowess in the game too. "A spin bowler and a forcing bat," was his usual description of himself to any stranger, so that most people went away with the idea that he was a combination of Verity and Hammond, and felt regret that England had never had the chance to play him in the Tests. But, of course, Charles had not even played in county cricket, and who cared for the game in a little village like Marston Magna? Why, he hadn't even been chosen for the first team there, so what chance had he ever had of being selected to play for England?

She was growing tired of his temper. The real reason for it this morning was that she had asked him whether he had remembered to wear his thermogene. Perhaps it had been rather tactless of her, in front of other people, but still, standing about in the draughty front porch was enough to give him a severe chill, and he should have had the sense to know it. If it were not for the girls, she might...

Millie was thinking what a nice day it was, and how much she would have enjoyed a picnic with a handsome, attentive young man like Ronald Colman, and what a pity it was that all the men in the Hydro were so old and uninteresting. She wished she was like that exotic-looking Miss Blake who had somehow contrived to look like the Dietrich in *Desire* at nine o'clock in the morning. She wished she had the technique of other women. Technique was important in love-making, she thought.

She was thinking, too, of her ear, which still tingled from her mother's blow. Hard blows didn't stop you thinking about things, so why pretend they did? She couldn't help wondering if there really could be anything in the Hydro rumour about Winnie and Matthews. It was no good asking Winnie, anyway; she kept her affairs too much to herself. Well, perhaps she would marry him, and perhaps he would turn out to be a duke's son who had been forced to earn his own living before he could succeed to an old and honoured title. It would be just like that film she had seen last week...

Winnie was thinking that there was something very attractive about Matthews when you considered him as a man and not as a chauffeur, as she had always done up to now. She wondered who had started the scandal about her, for she believed that Millie was telling the truth when she said she had heard of it, and she thought how unkind everyone was in this place. She had not taken much notice of Matthews before, although she had been having driving lessons from him for some time. She suddenly realized that his brown uniform matched his eyes, which she could see reflected in the windscreen, and that he had a rather tender mouth and firm chin. Yes, there certainly was something attractive about him – he had a nice smile, too, though it wasn't much in evidence when Father was there.

She glanced down at her well-worn tweed suit and comfortable brogues, and wished she had worn her new green two-piece and the green suede shoes. She wondered what Matthews was thinking about...

Matthews changed down to second gear grudgingly.

She ought to have taken that hill easily on top, he thought. Surely she couldn't need decarbonizing again. He'd said it would be no good to fill her up with Commercial Spirit. It never did pay with a car in the long run; but the boss was a stingy old devil. Well, arguing never did a chauffeur good, whether he was right or wrong. There she was, knocking again. Damn all Devonshire hills, anyway!

He changed down to bottom gear.

What a row! Now he'd hear a bit of language from the boss, and what would Miss Winnie think?

He glanced surreptitiously sideways. But Mr. Marston was fast asleep.

CHAPTER XXI

A few days later, Miss Astill, swathed in a shapeless knitted garment, was sitting at a rickety table in her cheerless back room writing letters, when a loud double knock on the door disturbed her. A chambermaid entered at her reply.

"What is it?" she asked irritably, for it annoyed her to know that if she could have afforded a front bedroom the maids would have taken pains to convey a more apologetic note to the panel of the door.

"Miss Brendon's compliments, miss, and will you take tea with her this afternoon at four o'clock?"

"Say that I shall be delighted, and don't bang the door."
Almost as soon as she had finished her letters it was time to

dress for tea. She put on a blue serge frock, fixed a large lace collar to it with barely concealed safety-pins, and hung a row of cheap imitation pearls round her neck. She chose a hat of dusty velours, and fixed it with a knobbed pin to the little sausage of hair on top of her head. Then she took up a pair of white cotton gloves and her needlework bag, and set out for "Spinsters' Corridor."

As she left her room the chambermaid watched her, and running along to her companion on the same corridor, whispered, "Miss Astill has gone to call on Miss Brendon." And the whisper, too, twisted along the corridors and down the stairs, increasing in intensity until it reached the ground floor and blew out at the front door, roaring at the people outside on the terrace: "MISS ASTILL HAS GONE TO CALL ON MISS BRENDON!"

Miss Brendon, as Inspector Palk had so recently discovered, was an old lady whose age was given as anything between seventy-four and eighty-two, and was therefore known to the other residents as "the oldest inhabitant." Her skin was of the texture and hue of the leather effigies which used to be carried in procession round the streets of old Chester, but, for the rest, she reminded you of a particularly unattractive bird. Her nose was beaky, and her hands clawlike, and her dark violet-lensed glasses, seen beneath a fuzzy crop of white hair, gave her the appearance of a peering white owl.

She was attended by a stocky little woman with straight grey hair, who always seemed to have walked recently out of a laundry, with her striped dress stiffly starched, and her face and hands smelling of yellow soap. This was Rogers, who had first entered the Brendon household as a girl of sixteen, and had insisted on remaining with Miss Brendon when she took up her residence in the Hydro.

Both of them had been at the Hydro for fifteen years, though, as a matter of principle, Miss Brendon gave notice every Lady Day.

Miss Brendon nodded with pleasure when Rogers announced her visitor.

"Glad to see you, Eppie," she said. (Miss Astill's Christian name was Ephemia.) "Come and let me have a look at you."

Miss Astill crossed the room and bent down over the couch under the window, which Miss Brendon occupied during the day. She allowed the old lady to pass her gnarled hands over her dress, which was her way of looking at her.

"That's a nice collar you're wearing, Eppie. Irish crochet, I can see. Ah, they don't make it so good as that nowadays."

"Oh, Miss Brendon," said Miss Astill, in the high-pitched, girlish tones she always adopted as being suitable in one so much younger than her hostess, "you make such beautiful lace yourself!"

"Indeed and she does, miss, and so I often tell her," agreed Rogers, nodding towards a faded red velvet tatting-cushion on a side table. "But it's hard to get her to do any nowadays. The only time she'll touch it is when she knows you're coming. Peevish, she gets."

"Rogers has a new way of doing my hair," said Miss Brendon, abruptly changing the subject. "Show her, Rogers."

Rogers took an inch-wide black velvet ribbon, and depressed Miss Brendon's untidy halo of hair with it, while her mistress listened for approval.

"Perhaps it does make you look younger," said Miss Astill cautiously, and was quite unprepared to see the ribbon torn off and flung on the floor.

"Take it away, take it away!" screamed Miss Brendon. "I won't have it. At my time of life I must look older, not younger. Who cares whether I'm seventy or eighty? But if I were a centenarian I should have a telegram from the King! It's only foolishness for us to try and look younger than we are at our age, Eppie."

Miss Astill's reply was luckily checked by the arrival of a maid in neat black house-dress and pleated cap and apron, balancing a large metal tray on her shoulder.

Miss Astill removed her gloves.

It was not pleasant, she thought, to take tea in an overheated room where an old lady lay during the day and night with all the windows closed except when the doctor was expected. She trusted that her visit would be a profitable one.

When she had accepted her first cup of tea, and had bitten off a corner of buttered toast, she inquired after her hostess's health in the earnest manner which befitted the most important of all Hydro subjects of conversation.

Miss Brendon smiled with pleasure. Eppie was so correct and ladylike, she thought. Now she could discuss all her most interesting symptoms during tea.

"As you see, my dear," she said, munching a piece of soft toast, "I am well enough to receive you, but my tubes are still very raw. I didn't sleep a wink all night."

Rogers stooped and removed a crumb from the carpet.

"She slept like a log, miss," she whispered, then straightened herself and said aloud, "I heard you snoring, Miss Brendon."

Her mistress smiled patiently.

"Ah, that's what you think, Rogers; but I never snore. It's the wheezing in my tubes that you hear. I wonder that it doesn't keep the whole Hydro awake."

"It sounds rather bad," said Miss Astill, inducing a note of sympathy into her voice.

"Oh, I'm used to it, my dear, I'm used to it. But the worst is that I can't get any action."

"You mean...?"

"Yes, dear. I don't believe in all these new-fangled medicines the doctor recommends. Senna pods were good enough for my mother, they ought to be good enough for me. I've had no action for six days!"

But this was too much for Rogers.

"Oh no, miss," she said emphatically, "you forget. Your memory isn't as good as it used to be, miss. Two days, miss, it is, and time yet."

Miss Brendon turned her short-sighted eyes towards Rogers.

"How often must I tell you not to interrupt the conversation?" she said; then, apologizing to Miss Astill, "Rogers is such a trial. I ought to have given her notice years ago, poor thing, but I haven't the heart."

This had no noticeable effect on Rogers, and Miss Astill welcomed the break in the conversation, for she had not come to hear all about Miss Brendon's ailments.

'These family retainers are so much better than hired servants," she said. "You are very lucky to have someone like Rogers, I assure you. Just look at the trouble Mrs. Napier has with that awful Nurse Hawkins. She grossly neglects her."

"Flirting with the Admiral still, is she?" asked Miss Brendon with relish.

"Yes. It really makes you wonder whether –"

"Oh no, I shouldn't think there's anything like that in it, Eppie. It's marriage she's after. I don't think she'd be put off with anything else. Now, that Blake girl was different, she deserved to come to a bad end."

"I try never to speak ill of the dead," said Miss Astill piously, "but when I think of her running about naked, and taking the name of the Lord in vain, I have no regrets. None."

"She was a bad lot, from all accounts," agreed Miss Brendon. "But what about the eldest Marston girl and the chauffeur? There's another one for you, and I wouldn't say that she wasn't a good bit worse than the others."

Miss Astill stiffened.

"What do you mean?" she asked.

Miss Brendon cackled with laughter.

"I could tell you, couldn't I, Rogers?"

"Indeed and you could, miss, if it so happened that you had a mind for it," agreed Rogers.

"Yes, I saw them sitting in the car right underneath this window. She was pretending to drive, but I saw him put his arms right round her and kiss her. You mark my words, there'll be a scandal about them before long."

"Yes," said Rogers, "such an exhibition I never before saw in my life. Whatever would they get up to in the dark if that's the way they carry on in broad daylight?"

Miss Astill recovered from her first surprise that Miss Brendon could have seen the pair as she had described them: it was always a little confusing to remember that she saw things through Rogers' keen eyes.

"The brazen little hussy!" she exclaimed, when the full significance of the incident had become clear in her mind.

"Of course, I wouldn't dream of saying anything about it to anyone but you, Eppie, but I know how discreet you are."

Miss Astill set her lips very firmly together, then suddenly she smiled.

"Well, really you have amazed me," she admitted. "But now that you have mentioned it, I did have a feeling about it myself. Nothing I could have put into words, you know, just a feeling. But what a disgusting thing! A common chauffeur! How shameless!"

The conversation passed from Hydro scandal to old times, and Miss Astill, realizing that she had exhausted Miss Brendon's stock of scandal for the day, rose to go.

"Is that really the time?" she exclaimed, drawing on her gloves in readiness for the journey up to her own room. "Well, good-bye. Thank you so much for a delightful afternoon."

She moved across to the door, and as she passed the walnut table which the velvet tatting-cushion occupied in full glory, she bent down over it, touching the noisy bobbins.

"You must really use this more than you do, dear Miss Brendon," she said.

CHAPTER XXII

The following morning Winnie Marston came down from her bedroom on the first floor by the main staircase, and, turning right, walked along the corridor until she reached the double glass-panelled doors marked, "Treatment-Rooms," and entered the ladies' section on the left.

Nurse Hawkins was standing at a table in the centre of the largest of the three rooms, heating a poultice over an electric ring. She smiled cheerfully, and Winnie found herself wondering who had originally designed the softly draped headdress which is so becoming to most women.

"Good morning, Miss Marston. Douche and massage, isn't it?" she said brightly. "Will you come and take off your clothes, please?"

She led the way to one of the cubicles opposite the door and drew back the dark-brown curtains with a sharp jingle of brass rings.

"Have you brought a bathing-cap? That's right. Call when you're ready."

Winnie quickly undressed and fitted the rubber cap on her head. At her call, the nurse handed her a hot towel through the curtains, and Winnie, wrapping it round her body, stepped out on to the cold tiled floor, holding a folded piece of linen in her hand.

"Is this anything to do with me?" she asked.

"Oh yes," replied Nurse Hawkins. "You tie it round your waist with the tapes."

Winnie shook it out of its folds, and gazed at the plain, machine-hemmed material, with its long strips of tape at either end.

"What on earth for?" she asked. "Won't it get wet when I have the douche?"

"Yes," replied the nurse, "but it's just to keep you covered. Our patients don't like to be naked altogether."

"Well, do you mind if I don't wear it? I can't bear the thought of having a clammy piece of linen clinging round my middle. I'm afraid I'm not ashamed of my body."

Nurse Hawkins thought that Winnie had no need to feel ashamed, as she glanced at the firm young limbs which she sluiced up and down in the spraying water. She increased the heat gradually, until the finger of the indicator crept towards a hundred degrees and Winnie's body became rosy, then decreased it again, and after a final tepid flourish, turned off the water, and wrapped a fresh hot towel round her patient.

When she was dry, Nurse Hawkins again changed the towels, and led Winnie into a smaller adjoining room in which were several couches ready made up with pillows, sheets, and grey hospital blankets. The clothes on the nearest couch were neatly turned down, and Winnie got between them and found her feet against a welcome hot-water bottle.

"It's the right leg, isn't it?" asked the nurse. She shook up a pillow and slipped it under Winnie's leg, tipped some talcum powder into her hand, and began to massage it with preliminary tentative strokes. "How did you manage to hurt it?"

"I was playing tennis with my sister, and the grass was slippery after the rain. I fell and twisted my leg under me and strained it in some way. The doctor says I might easily have broken it." Her eyes glanced round the room. "It feels so strange to be in here," she went on. "My sister and I always look on the treatment rooms as a place for old people only. I never thought I should come in for treatment myself one day."

"Oh, we'll soon put you right," smiled the nurse. "It's surprising how comforting massage can be when there's something wrong."

It was not long before their conversation turned to the subject which of late had superseded all others in the Hydro.

"It was dreadful about Miss Blake, wasn't it?" remarked Nurse Hawkins.

Winnie shuddered.

"Yes, awful. I liked her and I liked Sir Humphrey too. It's hard to believe that he could have murdered her so callously. I wonder what really happened."

"Oh, there's no doubt that he was guilty. I expect he was in love with her and got her into the usual trouble. Some girls are such fools, though I must say that she looked pretty smart, but you can never tell. Girls do the silliest things when they're in love. They do say that he was always in and out of her bedroom, and though I don't hold with all this scandal-mongering, there's no smoke without fire, you know."

"I suppose he had a wife alive and couldn't marry her," reflected Winnie. "It was a dreadful shame. She was so pretty."

"Yes, she was," replied the nurse. "But to my way of thinking, she spoilt herself with all that make-up."

"Oh, I don't know. After all, it's the fashion. I'd do the same if I had the chance; but Mother and Dad are so old-fashioned. Why, Millie and I had a terrible struggle to get them to allow us to have our hair shingled even! Just because some silly ass once said that a woman's glory was her hair."

"Well," said Nurse Hawkins, increasing the firmness of her rhythmical strokes on Winnie's leg, "a little powder and lipstick in reason help us all, but these London girls are getting a bit too flighty, and overdoing it altogether. I was in a big West End nursing-home before I came here, and I could tell you a few things about them that you've never heard before. They'd come in with beauty-boxes as large as week-end cases, full of skin tonics and creams and eyelash pencils and false eyelashes. You should have seen them make up their faces before they went in for an operation... Laugh! I used to die of laughing nearly. If only they could have seen their faces when they were under the anaesthetic they'd never have done it, I can tell you. The ether makes all the colours run together, and you never saw such sights as they look. The surgeons used to get hopping mad about it, and we'd have to clean up the faces before they'd begin to operate. You'd think that they'd be glad of a chance to give their faces a rest while they were in a nursing-home, wouldn't you? But not they! It's 'Nurse, where's my beauty-box?' almost as soon as they come round after the operation's over." She looked at her watch and gave a final stroke to the leg. "There," she said, pulling down the bedclothes, "you must rest now for a good half-hour."

Winnie looked dismayed.

"Oh, but, Nurse, I'm not ill! I must get up now. I – I've a most important engagement to keep. I can't stay, really."

"It's no use having massage unless you rest afterwards," said Nurse Hawkins professionally. "The doctor is most particular about that. Could I give anyone a message for you?"

Winnie blushed.

"No. Oh no, thanks. I expect it will be all right."

"Very well. I've got another patient to attend to now. You can get up in half an hour, but you'll probably find that you feel sleepy in a minute. I'll give you a call if you're not up when I come back." With a nod and a smile as bright as her clean white overall, she rustled starchily away.

She busied herself for several minutes at the long table in the centre of the largest room of the baths, placing a tin of antiphlogistine (known to members of the nursing profession more familiarly as "Auntie Flo") in a saucepan of water and substituting it for a pan of sterilizing instruments over the electric burner standing on a square mat of asbestos. She had barely taken her hand from the saucepan handle before Mrs. Dawson walked into the room. Nurse Hawkins greeted her with a smile.

"Just on time, Mrs. Dawson," she said, for the majority of her patients in the Hydro were so lax that she had learned to appreciate punctuality.

"I always try to work to a time-table," answered Mrs. Dawson. "You have to if you're a writer, you know. If I didn't sit down for my regular two hours a day with a pen in my hand and manuscript paper in front of me, I should never have finished one book, let alone three. But I nearly forgot my appointment altogether this morning, and I must say that I don't see why you had to change it so suddenly from yesterday. I'm sure the doctor knows nothing about it. He knows that this is a very inconvenient time for me because I usually write in the mornings. I never could concentrate after luncheon."

Nurse Hawkins chose to be uncommunicative.

"It was more convenient," she said, and ushered her patient through the door marked "Electric-Room."

This room was small and severe, with no windows or skylight, so that, whatever the time of day, it was yellow with electric light. Around the walls was a dado of electric plugs in front of which stood a variety of machines – silent robots ready to spring into life with the turning of a switch. At the moment only one plug was in use, connected by a thick black flex with an enormous kettle of shining aluminium, which puffed out great clouds of steam. Nurse Hawkins switched it off, and added some of the boiling water to a small waist-high bath which already contained cold water, testing it with a muscular elbow, while Mrs. Dawson seated herself in a chair beside it and took off her silk shirt blouse.

"You needn't bother to fetch me a magazine," remarked Mrs. Dawson. "I've brought a book."

Nurse Hawkins finished her preparations with quick but careful fingers, moved to one of the smaller machines, turned one switch and then another. A low humming began to fill the room and increased in intensity as she watched the control dial.

"Are you quite comfortable?" she mouthed, for her voice could not now be heard in the little room above the sound of the machine. Mrs. Dawson replied with a cheerful nod, and the nurse left the door of the electric-room ajar and went to test the temperature of the heating poultice. Apparently satisfied with this, she rapped her overall pocket to make sure that the tin of talcum powder was still there, switched off the electric heater, took the metal canister of antiphlogistine out of the hot water with a pair of metal forceps, wrapped it in a towel, tucked a roll of lint under her arm, gave one swift glance round the room, and walked out of the baths.

Winnie lay obediently still, her leg pleasantly stimulated by the massage, and her body glowing from the warmth of the douche.

It was true, she was thinking, that her engagement was an important one: how important, the nurse could never guess, but it was not a bit of good making a fuss about it. Tomorrow would do as well. The Hydro was such a place for gossip that she couldn't be too careful.

She bent her head forward on the pillow and tucked up her knees, snuggling like a kitten in the warmth of the couch.

She smiled to herself as she visualized Matthews' firm chin, and the brown eyes which seemed the same colour as his chauffeur's uniform. How strange that she would never have thought of Matthews as a lover if those old cats in the Hydro hadn't started to make up all that dreadful scandal about them, just because she went out with him alone when she was learning to drive the car. She would never have thought of him as a man otherwise, but only as a useful and necessary robot. She would never have learned to thrill to the touch of his hands, would never have made such shameless eyes at him, nor allowed – well, encouraged him, then – to kiss her. She was just twenty, and had never been kissed by any man before. She and Millie had never had the chances that other girls had in these modern days. Mother was so old-fashioned that she behaved like a duenna of pre-Communist Spain, and never allowed them to go to dances or parties unchaperoned. Mother would have sixty fits if she knew that she had fallen in love with Matthews, but then, Mother was no judge of men. Look at Father! Look at the way she had thrust herself and Millie at Sir Humphrey Chervil, and he had turned out to be a murderer.

Her eyes grew dreamy.

She and Bert would have to live in a town planned house and eat high tea at six o'clock. Bert would cut the pocket-handkerchief lawn on Sunday mornings in his shirt-sleeves and no collar. She wouldn't mind. She hated late dinner, anyway, and she had often seen Bert in his shirt-sleeves and dungarees, without a collar, when he had been cleaning the car. She thought that he looked nice like that, lovable and reliable somehow. Oh, she would be happy with Bert, and there was no need to have an aspidistra in the window after all –

A slight sound attracted her attention and she opened a sleepy eye.

"Hello!" she said. "What are you doing here?"

CHAPTER XXIII

Nurse Hawkins entered through the door of the ladies' baths and put a large box of thermogene on the table. She glanced through the open door of the room in which Winnie Marston had been resting and, noticing that she was still there, called out brightly, "You can get up now, Miss Marston!" then went into the electric-treatment room, where Mrs. Dawson was still sitting facing the thermostat machine, book on knees.

She looked up and smiled as the nurse touched her on the shoulder, but did not attempt to speak, for the noise of the machine was so great that only a high shout could possibly have penetrated through it. Nurse Hawkins glanced briefly at her wrist-watch, turned an indicator on the machine slowly, then switched off the current and removed the plug from the wall.

"There," she said, "I hope you were all right while I was away. Did it prickle much?"

"I didn't notice it," replied Mrs. Dawson, "and if I had, I could have turned it down a little. I've watched you doing it enough times. But I was far too much interested in my book."

"I think I'll give you the massage in this room, Mrs. Dawson. It's warmer than in the big one."

The nurse went out into the large main room for a light table and pillow. She noticed that the curtain of Winnie Marston's cubicle was swaying slightly as she passed, and guessed that she was dressing.

"Same time on Thursday, Miss Marston," she called out, and without waiting for a reply, went back to Mrs. Dawson.

For the next half-hour Nurse Hawkins was silent, not so much because she was engrossed in her thoughts as because Mrs. Dawson liked to hear the sound of her own voice, and started a monologue which covered a variety of subjects and theories mostly concerned with new and fantastic methods of murdering people, for the writing of thrillers was a kind of fever with her and she looked upon other people's lives and emotions as so much "copy."

"They say it's an ill wind that blows nobody good," she said, "and there's no doubt that Miss Blake's murder will be a great help to me. It's good publicity; couldn't be better. The last letter from my agents was distinctly encouraging, and I shouldn't be surprised to hear that they've been able to place one of my books at last. After all, if one has to be mixed up in a case of this kind, one might as well get some good out of it. The trouble is that if I really based a book on Miss Blake's murder and put all the Hydro people in it, nobody would believe that such a collection of oddities could ever exist. And in any case, one murder isn't enough for the reading public nowadays; it would be better to have at least two... Oh, have you finished already? Surprising how the time goes when one is busy talking, isn't it? I talk far too much, of course. It's one of my failings, I know. I hope to goodness that this wrist of mine will soon be well. It's a great handicap to a novelist, but I must be thankful for small mercies, I suppose. It's lucky that I can write with my left hand."

By the time that she had finished this last sentence, she had once more buttoned herself into her blouse, and with a little nod of farewell, she walked briskly away.

Nurse Hawkins began cleaning up the electric-room, for it was part of her job to leave all the treatment-rooms in perfect order before going to her lunch. Mrs. Dawson had slopped some water on the floor, and the nurse wiped it up with a clean towel.

She resented such menial tasks, and thought it strange that in a hotel as over-staffed as this, she should not be provided with an assistant to keep the rooms and apparatus clean. To be sure, one of the maids washed the floors and polished the brasswork of the shower douche, which looked like part of a ship's engine-room with its round pipes and clock-faced indicators, but she had to clean up after her patients, who always seemed to take a fiendish delight in leaving everything as untidy as possible. And was she a trained nurse or was she not? she asked herself resentfully. Why should she have to put things in order for that lazy lout Ted Cox, the men's bath-attendant? A nice soft job he had. Why, he wasn't even a proper masseur! If any patient, man or woman, needed massage in this place she had to do it. If anyone developed a sudden temperature or was taken ill in the middle of the night, she was sent for. If some old half-wit like Mrs. Napier decided not to walk, she had to go and help her. And as if that was not enough, she was expected to mop up floors and clean saucepans.

If she'd complained to Dr. Williams once, she had complained fifty times, but what was the use? He only looked at you with his most charming smile and said, "If you're overworked, Nurse, what about me?" and of course you couldn't do anything then except smile back at him. He was a hard taskmaster, but he never spared himself. No wonder Miss Lewis was crazy about him. She'd been a bit potty on him herself when she'd come first. But you might as well fall in love with a crepe bandage for all the notice he ever took of women. He was entirely wrapped up in his work and his little daughter. Besides, the doctor wasn't her sort. She liked a man to have a bit more go in him – to slap you on your backside and tell you you were a fine buxom wench. Thank God, she was no lady!

Well, if things turned out as she expected, perhaps she wouldn't have to mop floors in this place much longer.

She bunched pillow, towels, and lint under her left arm, picked up the kettle, and put them in the proper places in the middle room. Then she hesitated.

"Shall I light a fag?" she asked herself. "I could do with one after listening to that human gramophone record for half an hour. Ten past one. Just time to finish one before luncheon, and take a turn outside to blow the smoke out of my hair. Yes. Oh, blast it! I've forgotten the rest-room! Water carafe to fill up, I expect; glass to wash; hot-water bottle to empty. There won't be time, unless Miss Winnie thought of making the bed after she got up. She's a good sort and might have thought of it. I'd better go and find out the worst..."

As she walked through the open door into the rest-room she saw Winnie's fair head still lying on the pillow, and halted in surprise.

"Why, Miss Marston!" she exclaimed. "I thought you had gone some time ago!"

As Winnie did not move, she walked briskly towards the bed and put her hand on her shoulder.

"You've been fast asleep," she said, shaking her gently.

She bent forward suddenly as she perceived the unnatural stillness of Winnie's face, and pulled down the bedclothes with professional concern to feel her heart. But as she drew aside the towel in which Winnie was wrapped, she started hack, for the light from the window glinted on something like a steel arrow which projected from the back of the bowed head.

CHAPTER XXIV

When Inspector Palk entered the ladies' treatment-rooms, the first person he saw was Nurse Hawkins standing beside the old-fashioned wall telephone, with the earpiece in her hand. He went up to her.

"What are you doing with that?" he demanded.

Dr. Williams answered for her.

"Merely a precautionary measure," he said. "Nurse Hawkins volunteered to remain here alone while I telephoned for you. But as it seems certain that there is a homicidal maniac at large somewhere in the Hydro, I didn't like to leave her alone without the means of calling for help if she were attacked. This 'phone is plugged in to my consulting-room, which we have just left."

Palk made a sign to Sergeant Jago, and kept the others waiting until he judged that he had had time to reach the consulting-room, then he took out the plug, which caused the telephone to whistle at the other end, and spoke down the mouthpiece.

"Sergeant Jago speaking," was the reply.

"Right. Lock the door behind you and bring the key."

He hung up, and spoke apologetically to the doctor.

"Sorry, sir, but it's my habit to clear up as I go along. It's not Sir Humphrey this time, you know, because I've got him safe in a police cell. Now will you show me, Nurse, how you found Miss Marston?"

Nurse Hawkins led the way through the door to the left of the telephone, and motioned towards the bed. Her face was pale but expressionless.

Palk's inspection did not take long.

"She was lying in this position when you found her?"

"Yes."

"Were the bedclothes tossed about as if there had been any struggle?"

"No, they were neatly folded round her and tucked in at the sides just as I had left them. The towel was drawn tightly round the body. I pulled it away so that I could feel her heart."

Palk looked carefully round and under the bed, then worked his way round the room. He indicated a metal tray on the table beside the bed, containing a water-flask and a used glass.

"Did Miss Marston drink some water?" he asked.

"I didn't see her do so, but it's most likely that she did. Nearly all the patients do while they're resting. I always refill the carafe and put out a clean glass before each patient comes in."

"Better take charge of them, Sergeant," said Palk. "You might get something from them, though I doubt it."

He walked to the nearest cupboard and, opening it, saw piles of clean linen and towels. Then he walked over to the glass-fronted cupboard facing the couch, in which could be seen rows of bottles, most of them marked "Poison," rolls of lint, and boxes of bandages. He tried the doors and found them locked.

"Where is the key to this cupboard kept?" he asked.

Nurse Hawkins produced it from her pocket, and Palk unlocked the cupboard and peered inside.

"I have a duplicate key," said the doctor, taking it off a split ring. The Inspector took it without comment, locked the doors with it, and handed both keys to the sergeant. He moved across to the other couches, inspected their coverings, moved sheets and pillows, and left them untidy. He then proceeded to a closed door at the end of the room and, on opening it, found himself in a box-like lavatory with tiled walls and floor. He sniffed the air, and beckoned Sergeant Jago inside.

"Smell anything?" he asked.

The sergeant sniffed tentatively.

"Moth balls," he said. Then, "That, I expect," indicating a small square cage fixed to the wall, containing a decreasing piece of bright pink, frosted antiseptic.

"Yes, perhaps," agreed Palk, returning to the massage room and indicating to the police doctor and photographer that they could proceed with their routine tasks. He turned into the electric-room, which was equipped with a couch, two chairs, and several elaborate-looking machines, whose intricacies would have delighted the heart of a Heath Robinson. The doctor explained their purposes as if Palk had been any ordinary visitor.

"And where does that door lead to?" the Inspector asked at length, pointing to a door immediately opposite the one through which they had entered.

"Into the men's treatment-rooms," the doctor replied. "They are almost exact replicas of the two rooms we have already seen in the ladies' section, but the electric-room is common to both. Electrical apparatus is exceedingly expensive, and we are not sufficiently busy to feel justified in duplicating this room. The men have their electric treatment in the afternoons so that the times do not overlap, so there won't be anyone in there now."

He threw the door open, and there, in full view, stood a dark curly-haired man of about thirty, his coat off and shirtsleeves rolled to the elbows.

"Who is this, then?" asked Palk.

"Ted Cox, the men's bath-attendant and masseur," replied the doctor, unperturbed. "He naturally has access to the rooms at any time of the day."

Palk stepped up to the table at which Cox was standing.

"What are you doing?" he asked.

Cox answered as if he were speaking to any casual visitor.

"Sterilizing instruments, sir."

"This is Inspector Palk, Cox," said Dr. Williams. "He wants to ask you a few questions."

Cox looked startled but said nothing.

"Where were you when Miss Marston was murdered?" asked Palk.

"Miss Blake, you mean, don't you, sir?"

"No. Miss Marston was murdered this morning in the massage-room within a few yards of where you are standing."

A glass dish crashed to the floor.

"My God!" exclaimed Cox, his hands trembling.

The Inspector looked at him curiously.

"I haven't seen you before," he remarked. "Where were you when I interviewed the rest of the staff about Miss Blake's murder?"

Cox moved his eyes restlessly from left to right. He looked pale.

"I – I wasn't in the Hydro, sir."

"Why not?"

"I don't live in, sir. I have my own house down in the village. I leave here at six o'clock and come every morning at eight. I wasn't allowed in the building on the morning after the murder, sir."

"Where were you between six o'clock in the evening and six o'clock on the morning of the murder?"

"I – I don't remember, sir. I don't think I was anywhere except home."

Palk turned to the doctor.

"Surely it's rather strange not to have this man on the premises," he said. "Suppose one of the men patients were taken ill at night?"

"It's quite a usual arrangement," replied the doctor. "If anyone were taken ill, Nurse Hawkins would attend to him. Cox is only an attendant, not a trained nurse or masseur."

"So he couldn't give an injection to any patient?"

"Oh no! Nurse Hawkins or I would do that," replied the doctor in some bewilderment.

"Then why are you sterilizing that hypodermic?" snapped Palk to the unhappy Cox.

The man moved restlessly on his feet.

"I just thought I'd do it, sir."

"Is any injection to be given this morning?"

"Not that I know of, sir. I saw it there and I thought it looked dirty and thought I'd clean it."

Palk made a swift movement with his hand.

"And I suppose you thought you'd clean this as well," he said, holding up a plain steel knitting-needle which he had snatched out of the metal container holding numerous other instruments.

Cox looked terror-stricken.

"I never saw it before, sir. You can't think that I had anything to do with killing Miss Marston!"

"How do you know that Miss Marston was killed with a knitting-needle?" came the quick question, and Cox relapsed into a scared silence.

Palk looked round the room and saw that it was, as the doctor had said, almost a mirror-image of the ladies' room. "How long have you been in this room?" he asked Cox. "About an hour, sir, I think. Perhaps more."

"What have you been doing all that time? Not sterilizing instruments, I imagine."

"No, sir. I've been dusting and tidying the rooms. They're in my charge, sir. I do them every morning."

Palk strolled into the smaller massage-room and sniffed.

"Someone's been smoking in here," he remarked. "You?"

Cox looked furtively at the doctor.

"No, sir. No one is allowed to smoke in the treatment-rooms."

"Has anyone else been in here this morning?"

"No, sir... that is, no."

"So I suppose that the smoke drifted in through a closed skylight. Come, you'd better tell me the truth. I shall find out eventually."

Cox became more and more ill at ease.

"Well, sir, my pal Bert Matthews did drop in for a few words, sir. But only for a minute or two, sir. He didn't even shut the door behind him, but just stood in the doorway."

"Did he smoke?"

"He did have a fag in his hand, sir."

"Who is he? What does he do?"

"Bert Matthews, sir. He's Mr. Marston's chauffeur."

"He had no business to be in this part of the building at all," put in the doctor.

"Which way did he go out?" asked Palk.

"By the door leading to the main corridor, sir, the same way that he came in. He just came to the door and then went away again."

"Did he close the door after him?"

"Yes, sir."

"So that you didn't see where he went after he left you?"

"No, sir."

"And what did he come here to say so specially?"

Cox moistened his lips.

"I – I'd rather you asked him that yourself," he said miserably.

"You're not doing him any good by refusing to answer."

"Well, then, he wanted to know if Miss Marston was in there," he said, jerking his thumb towards the ladies' treatment-rooms.

CHAPTER XXV

Palk returned to the ladies' treatment-rooms and began the serious business of questioning Nurse Hawkins.

"What time did Miss Marston come in for treatment?" he asked.

"Treatment was fixed for ten past eleven and she was almost on time."

"By that clock?" glancing at the round, wooden-rimmed clock which hung on the wall.

"Yes."

"Tell me all that happened from the moment that she came in."

Nurse Hawkins gave him a clear account of all that had occurred from the moment of Winnie's entry into the rooms to the moment when she had made her gruesome discovery.

"How long did the douche last?"

"About twelve minutes. It is just to bring the blood to the surface of the skin to assist the massage."

"Then she dried herself. That would take a good five minutes, I suppose," went on Palk.

"Oh no! Not more than two, I should think."

The doctor smiled.

"Women never dry themselves properly," he said. "They use one large towel instead of two small ones, and have no idea of giving themselves a brisk rub down. I don't suppose she troubled to dry herself properly."

"Say three minutes at the outside, then. That brings us to eleven twenty-five. How long did the massage take?"

"Twenty minutes."

"Eleven forty-five. Why didn't she get up and go then?"

"She did want to," replied the nurse, "but I wouldn't let her. She said she had an important engagement, but all patients have to rest after treatment." She glanced at Dr. Williams.

"Yes, most essential," he agreed, rather unnecessarily, Palk thought. "The limb needs rest after the treatment. Massage is really more strenuous than most people seem to think. The body needs to get back again to a normal temperature. Rest is most essential. The fact that patients feel naturally sleepy afterwards is sufficient indication of this."

"Miss Marston was your first patient this morning, Nurse?" Palk continued.

"Yes, Inspector."

"So that there was no one else in these rooms at eleven-forty?"

"Yes. I had another patient down for that time for electric treatment. She was waiting for me in the next room when I'd finished with Miss Marston."

"Who was it?"

"Mrs. Dawson."

"That confounded woman again!" the Inspector said to himself, as he moved into the electric-room and asked what kind of treatment Mrs. Dawson had been having.

The doctor explained.

"Mrs. Dawson is suffering from strain to her right arm," he began. (Palk's brain supplied: "Writer's cramp. Why doesn't he say so?") "She would be sitting in this chair facing the thermostat machine, with this bath" – indicating a deep, narrow bath fixed to elbow-height by an adjustable iron stand – "on her right, her forearm lying beneath hot water."

"The chair and bath haven't been moved since she was here," added the nurse.

"You put on the usual pad, of course, Nurse," the doctor inquired.

"Yes, Doctor."

She picked up a thick, folded bandage of white lint and handed it to the Inspector. He took it into his hands and noticed that it was soaked through with water.

"That pad is placed on the arm, with this," the doctor held up a square metal disc, attached by a black rubber tubing to the machine, "on top. They are bandaged to the arm, and the machine is turned on."

The nurse turned a switch at Palk's request, and the room was filled with loud humming, like the sound of an electric vacuum-cleaner.

"So Mrs. Dawson would be virtually attached to the machine?"

"That is so," replied the doctor.

"Could she move?"

"Oh, yes, but I don't suppose that she did. Nurse Hawkins will tell you that we find our patients usually get a complex about this machine. They feel tied down by it and will hardly even turn their heads during treatment. It's rather like a hen who think she's tied to a string if you draw a chalk-mark from her beak to a stick in the ground."

"How long did Mrs. Dawson's treatment last?" Palk asked the nurse.

"An hour altogether. Half an hour for electric treatment and half an hour for massage. I stayed in here for the massage instead of going into the other room, because I thought it would be warmer."

"So that Mrs. Dawson would be ready to go at a quarter to twelve."

"No, later than that, Inspector. It takes nearly a quarter of an hour to prepare the electric treatment, fetching hot water and fixing the bandage on the arm. I did not finish the massage till one o'clock."

"Did you remain in here while Mrs. Dawson was having the electric treatment?"

"No. I went upstairs at twelve to give Lady Warme her massage in her bedroom."

"So that for half an hour you and Lady Warme have an alibi?"

Nurse Hawkins flushed, but did not reply.

"Is it usual to leave a patient alone when she is having treatment?"

"It depends. I should not think of leaving a stranger at any time for the first few treatments, but Mrs. Dawson was familiar with the procedure, and could have turned off the current if anything unusual occurred."

"Oh, could she?" exclaimed Palk. He calculated a little. "Then you were here till about twelve, when you had prepared Mrs. Dawson for treatment. At twelve-thirty you came back and remained in the electric-room until one o'clock. You say that you called out to Miss Marston at twelve-thirty, so that she must have been alive then."

Nurse Hawkins looked upset.

"How do I know that? That's the awful part of it. If I'd looked... But I just called out that it was time for her to get up, and didn't wait for a reply. Then I went to fetch a table for the massage, and saw the curtain of her cubicle move, so I imagined that she was dressing. I called out to her again, but, you see, I never expected an answer, so I don't know whether she was still alive."

"She was most probably killed, then, while you were upstairs with Lady Warme," said Palk. He walked into the larger room in which Miss Marston had had the douche. "Which cubicle did Miss Marston use?" he asked.

Nurse Hawkins walked to the fourth one from the left.

"This one," she said, jerking back the curtains, and there, sitting on the upholstered bench among her own clothes and Winnie's, attired in a linen apron and a bathing-cap of red rubber, sat Mrs. Napier, scowling in hatred at the nurse, and gibbering between her clicking, ill-fitting teeth.

CHAPTER XXVI

Miss Blake had been merely a corpse to Inspector Palk, but he had spoken with Winnie Marston and had seen her walking about the Hydro, so that this second murder affected him personally far more than the first. Miss Blake, as far as he could ascertain, had no friends or relations, but Winnie Marston had parents and a younger sister: he did not relish the forthcoming interviews with them.

Mr. Marston came in first; a man of athletic build with blue eyes, reddish hair, a cruel mouth, and a reputation for bad temper unrivalled even in the Hydro.

"Well, couldn't you have stopped it?" he barked at Palk. "You knew that there was a killer about, didn't you? The whole lot of us will be murdered before you find him. Why don't you do something?"

Palk pointed out that the previous murder had been committed by Sir Humphrey Chervil, who was already in prison.

"Nonsense!" Mr. Marston stamped up and down the room, drawing in noisy, asthmatic breaths. "He never murdered anyone. He's the wrong type. He might be a twister, but he's no murderer. If he'd got a girl into trouble he'd have run away. You want to use a bit of psychology, Inspector. I could have told you at the time that he wasn't guilty. Now perhaps you'll believe that I'm right." He sat down suddenly and bowed his head to his hands. "Oh God! Why did he have to choose my Winnie?"

Palk, making every allowance for Mr. Marston's grief, remembered, nevertheless, that Winnie Marston had been alone for one fatal half-hour, during which anyone could have had access to the ladies' baths unseen, and that Mr. Marston was as much under suspicion as anyone else in the Hydro.

"He?" he repeated. "Do you suspect Matthews then?"

Mr. Marston looked up in amazement.

"Who? Me? Suspect Matthews? Of murdering my daughter? My chauffeur? Good God, no! Why should I?"

"It appears to be an understood thing in the Hydro that they were in love with each other," replied Palk.

He was unprepared for the effect of his words. Mr. Marston leaped to his feet, his face suffused with anger, and pumped his arms up and down in the air amid a stream of profanities which he might have learned from Admiral Urwin.

"It's a lie! A damned lie!" he yelled. "Do you think I shouldn't have known about it? Do you think I should have kept him in my employment if there'd been a word of truth in such a scandalous insinuation? My daughter has been murdered... murdered, I say... and you sit there listening to gossip! Why don't you do something?" He stood still, breathing audibly, then placing his hands on the table, he leaned across towards Palk. "Will you find the man who did this terrible thing?" he asked quietly. "I'll give a hundred, five hundred, a thousand pounds if you'll only find him."

His lowered voice was impressive, but the effort to keep it in check was too great for him. The sight of Palk sitting immobile aroused him to further fury, and he thumped his fist on the table.

"Will you do something," he yelled again, "instead of sitting there like a smug ape? Get up and do something!"

Palk got up, a good head taller than Mr. Marston, and thumped the table in return.

"Sit down!" he ordered, in the same tones he had used to quell the hysterics of the chambermaid, Amy, and Mr. Marston, surprisingly, sat down. "I haven't time to listen to your histrionics, Marston," the Inspector went on. "If you want me to find your daughter's murderer you'll answer my questions soberly..."

"Soberly!" roared Mr. Marston. "Do you mean to suggest?"

"I haven't time to waste in idle suggestions," cut in Palk. "I know that you're upset, and I've tried to make every allowance for that, but you're hindering me considerably by this objectionable manner, and you will please curb your temper and answer my questions as concisely as possible. Your daughter's murderer is still at large somewhere in, or near, this building, and the longer you keep me here the better chance he has of going free."

"Keep you here! Me? Why, I'm trying to —"

Palk ignored him.

"You say that you did not suspect any kind of love-affair between your daughter Winnie and your chauffeur?"

Mr. Marston made as if to rise from his chair, caught Palk's eye, and subsided, replying in surly tones:

"No. There was nothing, I tell you, nothing. They had been out together several times. I don't deny that. He was giving her driving-lessons. Everyone in the Hydro knew it."

"You're quite sure that there was nothing in it? A young girl alone in a car with a young man... surely there was some temptation there?"

Mr. Marston controlled himself with difficulty.

"There was no temptation. He was not a young man in her eyes; he was only a chauffeur, and no more to her than the steering-gear of the car. She was my daughter, a Marston of Marston Magna; she would no more dream of allowing a chauffeur to take liberties with her than – than I should dream of taking liberties with a chambermaid!"

"You don't consider that Miss Marston's life was so restricted here that she might have been driven to seeking the company of someone young and good-looking whom she would not otherwise have noticed?"

"Certainly not. What was wrong with her life here? She had her mother and sister and me, and a reasonable allowance, and no worries of any kind. What more could a young girl of twenty want?"

"You think that she was quite happy, then?"

"Of course she was. She'd have been very foolish if she had been anything else."

"How do you account for the fact that Matthews went to the treatment-rooms and asked the bath-attendant if Miss Marston was in there this morning?"

"I don't try to account for it, Inspector," retorted Mr. Marston. "That's your job. Why don't you ask Matthews? He was there; I wasn't. He certainly didn't mean to stay there long, I can tell you that, because he knew that I'd ordered the car for twelve-thirty, and when I give orders, Inspector, I see that they're obeyed."

"Mr. Marston," asked Palk finally, "can you give me any idea who murdered your daughter, and why?"

"No!" replied Mr. Marston flatly. "That's your job. For God's sake get on with it!"

Millie Marston's reaction was different.

"I want to ask you some questions about your sister," Palk began, and to his consternation Millie burst into tears.

"It's awful to think of her lying there alone like that!" she sobbed.

"I'm so sorry," said Palk sympathetically. "It must have been a great shock to you. I suppose you were great friends."

"No, we weren't," replied Millie, when she could control her voice. "We never got on well together, and it wasn't my fault, either. I always wanted to be friends and share her secrets, but she was so reserved; she treated me as if I was a baby, and she was only two years older than I."

"I don't suppose you could have any idea who killed her then," said Palk.

Millie brushed away the last of her tears.

"Oh yes, I could!" she exclaimed. "It was Matthews. I know a good bit more about Winnie's affairs than she thought I did. If she wouldn't tell me, you can't blame me for trying to find out, can you? After all, you do want to know when it's your own sister. She and Matthews were as thick as thieves, I can tell you that much. Winnie was crazy about him."

"But if she never told you anything, how could you know?"

Millie sniffed.

"I could tell," she replied with a superior air. "I used to rag her about Matthews. If there'd been nothing in it, she'd only have laughed, but she didn't. She used to fly into a temper as bad as Father's, and say that she'd kill me if I ever breathed a word about it."

"You did tell someone though, didn't you? Someone must have started the rumours about them in the Hydro."

"Well I didn't," said Millie truculently. "The only thing I ever said was that everyone in the Hydro was talking about Winnie and Matthews. I told Mother, and she boxed my ears for me."

Palk could well understand it; he was possessed with a desire to do the same himself.

"So you think that Matthews murdered her. Why?"

"Who else would want to?" retorted Millie. "She never had anything to do with anybody else. Do you know what I think? I think that they were planning to run away together this very morning! Winnie was excited about something, anyway, and goodness knows, there's nothing to get excited about in this foul hole. It's worse than being at school. I don't think that she wanted to go for her treatment this morning at all, and she cried with temper when she twisted her leg at tennis, but she had to go. She daren't cry off in case Mother or Dad suspected anything."

"But why should Matthews murder her? If he didn't want to go away with her, as you seem to think, surely he could have gone away without telling her?"

Millie grinned.

"You didn't know Winnie," she said. "She was one of the clinging sort, and if she wanted a thing badly enough she'd get it whatever anyone else said. If he'd tried to go away from her she'd have screamed blue murder!" She stopped, scared by her own words, then went on suddenly, "If she'd only told me, I'd have helped her. It's because she was so secretive that I was mad with her. I'd have helped her to run away with him, even though he was only a common chauffeur. Dad's always talking about the honour of the Marston family, but it's not much use to anyone in a dead-alive hole like this. We never have a chance of any fun. Besides, Matthews might turn out to be a duke's son who has to earn his living for a year before he can succeed to the title. I saw a film last week in Newton St. Mary with Cary Gable in it like that..."

Mrs. Marston was the calmest of the family. Small, plump, and pretty, she gave the impression of being naturally a vivacious and talkative woman, but now she sat quietly in her chair, and Palk felt her grief hanging like a semi-transparent curtain between them.

Yes, she would tell the Inspector everything she knew, though it seemed rather late, didn't it? She didn't much care about having anyone hanged; revenge couldn't give Winnie back to her, could it? Still, for the sake of other people... Millie might be the next, mightn't she?

Yes, she had heard rumours about Winnie and Matthews. When? Oh, quite recently. Within the last week, she thought. It was Millie who had first drawn her attention to them. It happened in this way. They had arranged to go for a drive. Charles had been in one of his frequent tempers and was stamping about outside, throwing gravel at her bedroom window because they were late, and really it was his own fault, for until the very last minute he had said he wouldn't go with them at all. She had sent Winnie to the garage to tell Matthews to hurry, and Millie had said that if she wanted him to come quickly she ought not to have sent Winnie. Asked for an explanation, Millie had said that it was all over the Hydro that Winnie and Matthews were "mad about each other." No, she didn't believe it. She had boxed Millie's ears and forbidden her to speak of it again. But no doubt the people in the Hydro had gossiped about Winnie and Matthews; they talked nothing but scandal about anyone. Of course there was no truth in it whatever. Winnie was a good girl and well brought up, not flighty like that poor Miss Blake who was always ogling the men, even if they were other women's husbands. Well, really, she had seemed to set her cap at Charles, and he was so susceptible to a pretty face, even if it belonged to a chambermaid...

No, she couldn't imagine why anyone should want to kill a sweet-tempered girl like Winnie. It must have been some terrible mistake, unless it was part of a plot to make them move away from the Hydro. She knew that most of the other residents disliked them. It was Charles' fault, of course; he had such a terrible temper, and it was hard for outsiders to realize that he didn't mean half he said.

Everyone had been so kind to them today, but it was dreadful to feel that any hand which had been stretched out in sympathy might have been the one which took Winnie's life from her. Mrs. Napier had been specially kind, but then she had actually been in the baths when Winnie was... had died... hadn't she? And she wasn't quite... was she? And she had never really liked Winnie, so it did look as if... didn't it?

They sat in silence for a few moments, then Palk said softly:

"Mrs. Marston, I don't want to intrude upon your grief, but can you think of any reason why anyone in this Hydro or outside it should want to kill your daughter?"

For a moment Mrs. Marston's calm was replaced by grief and her next few words were broken with sobs.

"Such a lovable girl she was, Inspector, such a sweet nature. She never made an enemy in the world. Millie is different: she's a little too outspoken for most people, though I'm sure she will grow out of it. But Winnie wouldn't say a word to hurt a living soul. How anyone could...it must have been a lunatic escaped from some asylum... to kill her so callously. She must have looked so defenceless lying there like that. Winnie always looked so pretty when she was asleep. She always slept curled round like a kitten, with her head bent forward on the pillow."

Palk helped her from her chair and escorted her to the door, but as she was going out he stopped her with another question.

"Did your husband believe that there was any truth in the rumours about Miss Winnie being in love with your chauffeur?"

"Oh no!" she replied quickly. "If he'd believed that, he'd have murdered her!"

Then, aghast at her words, she turned and fled.

CHAPTER XXVII

Try as he would, the Inspector could not rid his mind of the moment when he had swept back the curtain of the cubicle and revealed the incongruous figure of Mrs. Napier seated amongst Winnie Marston's clothes. Both Dr. Williams and Miss Lewis had confirmed Nurse Hawkins' statement that Mrs. Napier had had no appointment in the baths for that morning, and the more he thought about it the more he was inclined to believe that Mrs. Napier had stolen into the massage-room, stabbed Winnie, and, finding her retreat cut off by the nurse, had slipped into the cubicle and awaited discovery. But if she had been cool enough to achieve this, why had she failed to seize the opportunity to escape at the moment when Nurse Hawkins had discovered Winnie's murder? He decided to ask her, with no real hope of receiving an intelligible, let alone an intelligent, answer.

Mrs. Napier's entrance into the room did not help to allay the Inspector's suspicions. She came in alone, walking with much greater ease than before, and while Sergeant Jago was still moving forward to assist her, she reached the chair and seated herself in it unaided, with surprisingly few bumpings and twistings.

It might of course be, thought Palk, that she was always of intention at her worst when the nurse was present, but all the same it looked decidedly strange. Was it possible that she was not so harmless as the doctor believed? That was his opinion as a medical man, of course, but even the best of doctors made a wrong diagnosis sometimes, and Nurse Hawkins, who saw a great deal more of Mrs. Napier than anyone else did, had believed her to be capable of murder. She had not been absolutely normal when she first came for treatment, and possibly the murder of Miss Blake had provided a shock sufficient to turn her brain and had produced a homicidal tendency in her. If this were so, the murder of Winnie Marston was purely imitative. This solution certainly provided a perfect reason for the choice of Winnie as a victim, for both she and Miss Blake were young, good-looking, unmarried girls. In his profession accuracy was a habit, and he had learned to be careful in his usage of the old-fashioned word "virgin" in these enlightened days.

The more he thought of this theory the more feasible it seemed. Mrs. Napier's whole manner pointed to the fact that she was pleased about something. In her last interview she had been sullen and vindictive, now she was smiling and had a contented look as if some urgent desire had been fulfilled. Well, he must not allow his thoughts to run away with him.

Theories were all very fine, but until you proved them they were not facts, and the Chief Constable was a stickler for facts. It wasn't even wise to say "I think this" to him, but was always more advisable to preface remarks with "I believe" or "I consider." Palk did so now to keep in practice.

"I believe I interviewed you before about the murder of Miss Blake."

Mrs. Napier nodded.

"Yes. She was murdered. Sir Humphrey, they tell me. It was very sad."

Palk hesitated. If he could only ask the right questions in the right way he might get the truth from her at once, he thought. Mrs. Napier appeared to be quite content to wait until he had made up his mind.

"What were you doing in the baths this morning?" he asked eventually.

Mrs. Napier smiled brightly.

"My treatment. I always have treatment in the baths, for my legs, you know. They're very weak. Sometimes I can't walk at all. I ought to use a bath-chair really, but there is only one."

"Yes, I know, Mrs. Napier. But you were waiting there this morning at a quarter past one. Dr. Williams tells me that he never makes an appointment after half past twelve."

Mrs. Napier looked in no way disconcerted.

"That nurse kept me waiting. She always does. Other people can be attended to on time but not me. Oh no! She keeps me waiting deliberately, but I'll be even with her yet, you'll see. She's a wicked woman."

"If you were waiting for a long time you must have been in that cubicle when Winnie Marston —"

"She was murdered. I was there. Yes, murdered just like that other girl." Mrs. Napier beamed at him, and her eyes behind their thick-lensed spectacles positively gloated.

Palk drew a deep breath.

"Mrs. Napier," he said impressively, "how do you know that she was murdered in the same way as Miss Blake?"

"I was there. I heard it all."

Sergeant Jago gasped. This was an unexpected development.

"You mean that you were really there all the morning hidden in the cubicle? You heard the murderer enter the baths and kill Miss Marston? You know who did it?"

"Yes, yes, I know," she said excitedly. "I saw her. I was there. I was very frightened. She might have murdered me too." She drew a handkerchief from the pocket of her woollen cardigan and began to dust her skirt down with it.

"Who was it? Whom did you see?" Her excitement was catching.

Mrs. Napier looked up in surprise.

"Who? Why, Nurse Hawkins, of course. Who else was it likely to be? If she stays here we shall all be murdered, and I shall be the next one. She hates us all, but she hates me the most. It's because we see her flirting with the Admiral when she ought to be at work. The way she neglects me is a disgrace. She lets me fall down. I can show you the bruises. She's a wicked woman, I tell you. You must lock her up, and then I shall be safe."

Palk interrupted the familiar words with a snort of disgust and dismissed her. As if she suddenly remembered that she had entered the room with less trouble than usual, she endeavoured to make her exit as difficult as possible so that Sergeant Jago at length re-entered the room mopping his brow with a yellow handkerchief surprisingly decorated with pink elephants, and was for once too breathless to make any suitable comment.

So much for my handling of the situation, Palk thought irritably. She's either entirely innocent or else too clever by half.

But in either case it was obvious that he would get no further information from Mrs. Napier, and as a matter of routine he sent for Nurse Hawkins again. She affirmed again the fact that Mrs. Napier's appointment was for the following day, and this was confirmed by Miss Lewis's appointment book.

Palk then sent for Mrs. Dawson and greeted her with: "Well, Mrs. Dawson, did you foresee the second murder?" and she hesitated in her walk towards the chair to which Palk had waved his visitors in the previous case.

"Are you still suspicious of me, Inspector?" she asked in a forced, roguish manner which accorded ill with her flat-heeled appearance, and did not effectively cover her real feelings. "No, I never got so far as visualizing the second murder, thank goodness, or I might find myself under arrest. As it is, I could have done the murder, I suppose."

"You admit that?" asked Palk.

Mrs. Dawson looked straight at him.

"I'm not a fool, Inspector, as I believe I've told you before. I realize that I was unpleasantly near to Winnie Marston when she was murdered, and that it's to my benefit to tell the truth and do all I can to help you to solve the mystery."

Trying to make a good impression on me, was Palk's first thought, and, Talks like a detective novel, was his second.

"I understand that you were having treatment for your wrist. How long have you been having it?"

"For three weeks. I began it before the time of Miss Blake's murder, and I go twice a week."

"Is today one of your regular days?"

"No. Nurse Hawkins asked me to come today instead of yesterday."

"Did she give you any reason for the change?"

"She said that Dr. Williams had altered her time-table for this week, and so she couldn't fit me in yesterday."

"Did anyone know that your time had been changed?" Mrs. Dawson smiled.

"Oh, everyone knew, I should think. You see, I was annoyed about it, because I like to work to a time-table. If you're a writer, you have to."

Inspector Palk restrained a snort.

"You arrived for treatment this morning, then, at what time?"

"Just after twenty to twelve. I was a few minutes early and had to wait. I heard Nurse Hawkins talking to Miss Marston in the massage-room when I came in, then I went into the electric-room and began to read my book."

"How do you know that it was Miss Marston whom the nurse was talking to? Did you recognize her voice?"

"I heard..." Mrs. Dawson hesitated. "Well, I don't know really. I just assumed that it must be she afterwards."

"Then you actually heard another voice besides Nurse Hawkins'?"

"No, I can't say that I did. I just heard the nurse's voice and assumed that she was talking to another patient. Oh, you mean that Nurse Hawkins might have killed Winnie before I went into the baths, and was only pretending to talk to her for my benefit?"

Palk did not encourage her to pursue this line of thought. "Was Nurse Hawkins late in coming to you?" he asked. "No, she was on time by my watch. She fetched some hot water for the arm-bath. You see, for my treatment the arm is immersed—"

"That's all right," interrupted Palk. "I understand what the treatment consists of. Your arm is actually attached to the machine which sends an electric current through the water on to the metal plate clamped to the pad on your arm, so that you are unable to move. Isn't that correct?"

"I... I could move if I wanted to, I'm sure, but I've never tried."

"You understand the working of the machine?"

"Yes, partly. I know, that is, how to turn it on and off."

"So that you could have turned it off this morning and taken the pad off your arm, and gone into the other room if you'd wanted to?"

Mrs. Dawson's face paled.

"It would be difficult to replace the bandage with my left-hand," she said, "but I think I could. Only I didn't."

"You realize that a girl was being murdered in a room alongside the one in which you were sitting? You're sure you heard no sound?"

"No. The machine makes such a noise that you'd have to shout to make yourself heard even if you were in the same room. I couldn't possibly have heard anyone call from the next room."

"There are two doors to the electric-room; one leading to the ladies' baths, and one leading to the men's. I suggest that you saw someone come through the one door and go out through the other."

There was no doubt about Mrs. Dawson's fear now.

"No, no. I saw nobody," she said.

"But if anyone had passed through that room you must have seen him."

"I don't think so," she replied nervously. "The machine would drown any sound, and I was sitting reading my book, with my back turned towards the doors. Oh, Inspector, you don't really think that the murderer did pass behind me, do you?"

"1 think it quite possible," he replied. He leaned forward and said, "Mrs. Dawson, who do you think killed Winnie Marston?"

"Oh, the chauffeur, of course," she replied. "Everyone knows that they were carrying on an affair together, and I suppose he'd got her into trouble."

"So you would make Matthews responsible for the second crime?" he asked sarcastically.

"Oh no," replied Mrs. Dawson. "If I were writing it as a thriller I should make the same murderer responsible for the two murders. Both were young, pretty girls; both were murdered with knitting-needles; surely the similarity is striking."

"How do you know that Winnie Marston was murdered with a knitting-needle?" Palk asked pointedly.

Mrs. Dawson looked very much taken aback.

"I... I... wasn't she?" she stammered.

Palk ignored her question and returned to her previous remark.

"If your detective had arrested Sir Humphrey Chervil," he inquired, "whom would you have made responsible for the second murder?"

Mrs. Dawson smiled brightly.

"My detective would never have been such a fool!" she replied.

CHAPTER XXVIII

Bert Matthews, his brown eyes serious, his firm chin showing even greater firmness than that which Winnie Marston had admired, came into the library. His chocolate-coloured uniform was beautifully brushed and pressed; his leggings shone with polish, and his hair with cheap-scented brilliantine. He held his brown peaked cap in his horny, well-scrubbed right hand, on the little finger of which he wore a tight-fitting gold ring. He was altogether a dapper figure, and if the rumours about him and Winnie were true, it was not difficult to understand why he had appeared attractive to her in a place where young, good-looking men were rare. If he had been applying for a post as chauffeur Palk felt that he would have engaged him on the spot, and in that first instant he did not believe him guilty of murder. It was not Palk's business, however, to judge people by first impressions, and he turned to the task of questioning Matthews.

"Your name is Bert Matthews?"

"Yes, sir."

"You are employed as chauffeur to Mr. Marston?"

"Yes, sir."

"You knew his daughter, Miss Winnie Marston?"

"Yes, sir."

"You have lately been giving her driving-lessons?"

"Yes, sir."

"Did you at any time become intimate with her?"

"Intimate, sir?"

"Yes. Did you make love to her? Kiss her?"

"No, sir."

"Did she make any advances to you?"

"No, sir."

Palk realized that the man was playing with him. These answers were rehearsed; they were not natural. Only by surprise could he hope to gain any proper information from him.

"Miss Winnie Marston was murdered this morning in the ladies' massage-room," he said suddenly, looking sharply at the chauffeur.

Matthews' start of surprise was overdone.

"Murdered?" he cried.

"You knew," snapped Palk. "Who told you?"

Matthews twisted his cap round in his hands.

"Ted Cox, sir."

The Inspector swore audibly. He should have guarded against this possibility, he thought, but there were so many doors in the Hydro that it was almost impossible not to overlook one, and Ted Cox must have slipped through that one to waylay Matthews on his return from the car.

"You went to the treatment-rooms this morning and asked for Miss Marston," stated Palk.

Matthews nodded.

"What did you go for?"

"I went to speak to Ted Cox, sir. I had a few minutes on my hands."

"If you've seen Ted Cox since, you'll know that he told us that you went specially to ask if Miss Marston was having treatment. Wasn't that a very unusual thing to do?"

"Well, yes, I suppose it was," said Matthews sullenly, "but I only wanted to leave a message for her. It was about her driving-lesson at ten to twelve."

Palk checked him, then, thinking better of it, said:

"Go on. At ten to twelve, you said. When was that arranged?"

"Yesterday evening, sir. Miss Winnie came into the garage when I was cleaning the car."

"What message did you want to give her, then?"

"I wanted to let her know –" The chauffeur's voice faltered, then he made an effort and continued, "I couldn't give her a lesson after all. The boss sent round word this morning for me to have the car ready for him at twelve-thirty, and I had to let her know."

"Can't you see that it looks very strange for you to have gone to the ladies' baths yourself?" persisted Palk.

"What else could I do?" returned Matthews. "I couldn't send a note, could I? And I had to let her know somehow, didn't I?"

"How did you know that she would be there?"

"Because she told me. She said: 'I've got to have some massage in the morning, but we... we can go afterwards. Be ready about ten to twelve.'"

Palk tapped the table with his pencil. The story was a straightforward one and was most probably true, yet he had an unaccountable feeling that Matthews was lying.

"How long have you been teaching Miss Marston to drive?" he asked.

"Six weeks, sir."

"And couldn't she drive yet?"

"She drove well enough, sir, for a woman, that is, but the boss wouldn't let her go out alone yet," replied Matthews, and again Palk felt that though he might be telling the truth, he was not telling the whole of the truth.

"Matthews, did you murder Miss Blake?" he asked.

"May I be struck down dead if I did, sir," he cried passionately.

There was a long pause. At the end of it Matthews still remained standing.

Palk dismissed Matthews and sent for Sergeant Jago.

"Any clues?" he asked.

"Nary a one, sir. Not even a scrap of blank paper. Doesn't it strike you as peculiar, sir, that two different girls should be murdered in the same way by two different men? Do you think that baronet fellow is really guilty of Miss Blake's murder?"

"You've been talking to Mrs. Dawson," returned Palk. "Of course he's guilty. From what I can gather he wasn't so well-off as he pretended to be, and the few thousands he'd have been able to raise on her jewels would have set him up for quite a time. This other murder is an imitative one. You know yourself that any crime, however small, brings a crowd of imitations."

But Palk almost seemed to be talking to convince himself, and the sergeant, encouraged by his superior's perplexity, went on:

"As you say, sir, but I think Mrs. Napier did both of them myself. She walked in while the nurse was upstairs with Lady Warme, in the second crime, then undressed herself and sat in the cubicle after she had stabbed Miss Marston. She knew we'd find her there, and that we shouldn't suspect anyone who stayed near like that. We all know that she's a bit peculiar, and people like that are very cunning."

"It's a possibility," replied Palk. "That's the trouble. As long as we don't know where everyone was during that half-hour, everyone is suspect, and everything's a possibility. I don't mind admitting that I'm not satisfied with that nurse."

Jago looked surprised.

"But she's about the only one who has an alibi," he objected. "She was upstairs with Lady Warme during that half-hour."

"I know," replied Palk; "that's partly why I'm not satisfied. Alibis can be faked too easily, and have you noticed the way she keeps looking at the doctor all the time when I'm questioning her, as if she wants him to give her a hint about what to say? Half the time this morning I didn't know which one of them I was supposed to be talking to. There's always the possibility that there were two people in league together."

"What about the chauffeur?" asked Jago. "He knew Miss Marston was in the baths. He may have gone in to her without being seen. He could have got a knitting-needle from Cox. You may depend that if there was one amongst the instruments there was another too."

"If there was, we can't prove it," returned Palk. "Time enough to talk about Matthews when we get the P.M. result and find out whether she was as good a girl as her mother thinks she was. Matthews is playing at being a tar-baby at present, and 'ain't sayin' nuthin'. If we can pin a motive on him we might be able to alter all that, but the trouble is that, so far as I can see, no one had any motive whatever for murdering Winnie Marston."

The result of the medical examination on Winnie Marston did not give Palk the help he had hoped for. Winnie was pronounced *virgo intacta*, the motive remained obscured, and the Inspector had to content himself with a temporary verdict of "murder by imitation by some person or persons unknown, but probably residing in Presteignton Hydro." He set one of his men to shadow Matthews, and issued an order in his arbitrary way, forbidding anyone to leave the Hydro; but, failing to gain any further information about anyone's movements at the time of the murder, he realized that his inquiry was virtually at a standstill.

CHAPTER XXIX

As a result of Palk's order, everyone in the Hydro began to suffer from a specialized form of claustrophobia; a fear of being shut up with their fellow creatures. They realized fully that the Inspector had no authority to enforce such an order, and that they were free to leave the Hydro if they wished, but fearing lest any such departure would be taken as an indication of complicity in the murder, no one would be the first to leave. And so they remained on, each suspecting the others, and spending their time in solitary confinement behind the locked doors of their bedrooms. But after a few days of this they herded together again even more than usual, having found isolation unbearable. For one could not talk to oneself, and habit had made it necessary for the Hydro residents to hear the sound of their own voices.

It was therefore with a feeling of great pleasure that they welcomed a new arrival into their midst.

At any other time Mr. Winkley would have passed unnoticed among the visitors to the Hydro, so unassuming and insignificant was his appearance, and so gentle and unobtrusive his manner. His skin was pink, his hair and moustache fair, the latter stained brown at the straight-clipped edge with nicotine, and matched by the skin between the first and second fingers of his left hand. His eyes were of a mild blue, and he blinked frequently as if he ought to have worn glasses. One felt that he should have been short and stout, and it was rather surprising to discover that he was well above the average height, and that his carriage was upright and soldierly.

Lady Warme put him down as a retired grocer ("and she ought to know if anyone does, having been in that trade herself, my dear!"), and this seemed borne out by the fact that he wore red leather slippers with his dinner-suit. But after she had spoken with him by accident one evening, Lady Warme was not quite so sure, for there was no getting away from the fact that he spoke like a gentleman, "and really if he brushed his hair back instead of wearing it in that ridiculous bang over his forehead he would look quite distinguished!"

Miss Astill was convinced that he was a detective from Scotland Yard, and though everyone else laughed at the idea of Mr. Winkley's being anything so decisive as a detective, she maintained her belief and obstinately refused to have anything to do with him. This seemed all the more noticeable since Mr. Winkley appeared to be a great man for the ladies, and needed no invitation to join any one of them when he happened to be passing through the lounge and saw her sitting alone. For the matter of that, he was equally anxious to chat with the men, and was altogether a very friendly and comforting person to have about the Hydro at this trying time. Even the doctor, who was notoriously unfriendly, and in the opinion of all the residents overdid the standoffishness of his position, made no secret of the fact that he liked Mr. Winkley's company, and invited him more than once to his private rooms for a quiet smoke. But Mr. Winkley did not often accept the doctor's invitation, and this more than anything, perhaps, made him sure of a high position in the good opinion of the residents, who abominated any sign of favouritism, especially as he played a really useful though uninspired hand at whist, and could be relied on to lose at billiards.

It was soon noticeable that Mr. Winkley was fond of detective fiction, and was rarely seen about without the latest thriller under his arm. But though the residents had experienced more thrills at first hand than Mr. Winkley, to judge by his appearance, was ever destined to know, no one so much as mentioned the recent murders in the Hydro. Miss Astill explained to Miss Brendon that she personally kept silent "out of a sense of loyalty to the dear doctor," but the others did not claim any such noble motive. They held their peace, partly because they had had their fill of cross-questioning from Palk, partly because they remembered that Winnie Marston's murderer was still at large, and perhaps partly because they were badly in need of new faces around them, and feared lest a man of so gentle a nature as Mr. Winkley might be scared away by the knowledge that a drama as shocking as any he had ever read had been enacted in the Hydro.

So they talked of the weather and their ailments and family affairs and certain special days which stood out in the memory of the Hydro, such as the visit of Charles Laughton at luncheon one day, looking "not a bit like that dreadful Captain Bligh, and how the man can bear to take such a part I can't imagine; though really I suppose it's very naughty of me to say so, for after all, he was a Bligh, wasn't he, and I suppose he was related to the Blighs, or wasn't he, do you think?"

So the warm, sunny October drew to its close and ushered in November with such cold winds and persistent rain, that the tension which had been bearable when all could get out into the grounds to take their daily exercise, increased, and their nerves were frayed with the strain of keeping silent on the one subject about which their tongues longed to wag. Worst of all, perhaps, they were driven out of the room which, since the murder of Miss Blake, had become their general sitting-room, for the sun-lounge was the most depressing of all the public rooms in bad weather. Its three sides of clear glass showed vistas of mist-obscured tors and rain-swept coast. In the foreground the croquet and tennis lawns and paths, which appeared to be level in dry weather, showed themselves to be a mass of depressions, in which the rain gathered in little pools. The rain gurgled monotonously in the gutters and ran continuously down the windows; nevertheless, for several days the Hydro residents sat shivering in the cold draughts of the glassy room, until ever-widening damp patches appeared ominously on the ceiling and the one solid wall, and drove them reluctantly into the drawing-room, which few of them had entered since Miss Blake's death.

They sat there in chairs drawn almost too close for bodily comfort, and plied themselves a little too earnestly to their several occupations; Admiral Urwin with the less difficult crossword puzzle from last Sunday's *Observer*; Miss Astill with the altar cloth she was embroidering for the Vicar; Lady Warme with a bedjacket she was crocheting in pink wool; Mrs. Dawson with her little notebook; the Colonel with a newspaper marked "Not to be removed from the Library."

It was noticeable that nobody was knitting, and that they all avoided the deep, comfortable settee which now stood crosswise at the left-hand side of the hearth. It was only natural that Mr. Winkley should walk towards it; and, looking around in his short-sighted way, should sit there after a smiling, "Does no one else want to sit here? Sure?"

Lady Warme shuddered, and drew her black velvet bridge-coat more closely round her, and casting long fearful glances towards the curtained window behind, murmured, "It's very draughty in here tonight, isn't it?" and began crocheting at a feverish rate.

The conversation languished until the only sounds in the room were the crackle of the fire and the Admiral's laboured breathing. After half an hour's silence, Mr. Winkley let his book slide from his fingers on to the settee, lit a cigarette, and leaning forward to toss the match into the hearth, said aloud:

"I wonder what would be the best way to commit a murder?"

The sudden question jerked the automatons into life. Lady Warme screamed, the Admiral dropped his pencil with an oath, Colonel Simcox jumped to his feet with a muffled, "My God!", Mrs. Dawson pulled up her skirts as if a mouse had just run over her foot, Miss Astill pricked her finger and looked down at it with startled eyes, while Mrs. Napier, who had been sitting unnoticed in a corner muttered, "Blood... blood!"

Explanations inevitably followed, and they all began to talk at once, so that it was some time before Mr. Winkley could be made to understand what they were telling him.

"I... I'm sorry," he stammered at length. "I assure you I had no idea. Crime interests me; I was merely speculating aloud. I really hadn't any idea... you must forgive me. I quite understand that you don't want to talk about it."

But now that the subject had been brought into the conversation, they all wanted to relieve their repressed fears by talking about them.

Mr. Winkley's blue eyes opened wider and wider, and his murmured exclamations of interested surprise stimulated the residents, who so often had to relate their scandal to unwilling ears. They each told him in their different ways the story of the two crimes, and even Miss Astill was prevailed upon to alter her first hastily formed opinion of him, and contribute her own experience, agreeing that no real detective could ever take such a morbid interest in murder.

"Well, well," Mr. Winkley said when they had all paused for breath, "it is most astounding... such an amazing experience. I have always been interested in crime, and to think that I missed two murders by only a few days. I almost wish I had been here. I shall probably never have another chance. It does seem a pity, doesn't it?" and his eyes blinked rapidly round the circle of faces.

CHAPTER XXX

Reputations were quickly made in the Hydro. Because Lady Warme had once been to the Scala as an insignificant unit in a mighty audience, she had become, in the eyes of the residents, a musician; because Mrs. Dawson dabbled in writing, therefore she was pointed out on every possible occasion to casual visitors as "the well-known lady novelist, my dear!" It is not, therefore, surprising that by the following morning, everyone, from the doctor down to the boy who cleaned the shoes, knew that crime was Mr. Winkley's hobby. Before long they had suggested that he should try and solve the murder of Winnie Marston.

Mr. Winkley seemed willing enough to oblige them, and apparently never grew tired of hearing the same things over and over again, for he would often come to one or other of the residents, and, peering into the little pocket-book which he now carried about with him in place of the neglected thrillers, he would begin, in words which soon became familiar to them all, "Oh, by the way, you know what you told me about..." and they would tell him their stories all over again with great relish.

They all seemed like so many Ancient Mariners, cursed to tell their tales to ease their minds, and somehow it did seem to take away part of the horror from the recent tragedies to talk about them to this good-natured, simple-minded man.

"Of course, the Inspector may be right in thinking that Sir Humphrey Chervil and the chauffeur are the two murderers," he said diffidently, "but in all the books I've read on crime, the inspector is always wrong, and it is the private investigator who finds the missing clue."

His "fame" spread over the Hydro. Miss Brendon, defying the severe Hydro conventions, invited him to tea in her bedroom, and even the Marstons received him in the private room which they had used since Winnie's death, and presumably told him their stories too. Guests and staff alike grew accustomed to stumbling over him in dark corners, when he would rise to his feet, pocket magnifying-glass in one hand and miniature torch in the other, and blinking in embarrassment, would murmur something in-distinct about "examining the wainscot..." They would smile and, relating the incident over the tea-cups, would say, "Old Dr. Thorndyke-Holmes is at it again! Time he showed some results, isn't it?"

One evening after dinner, they were sitting uneasily in the drawing-room, when Mr. Winkley came up to them with a stammered suggestion which for a moment made them think that his hobby had turned his brain.

"Don't you think it would be a good idea...? It's quite in the right tradition... I wonder Palk didn't think of doing it himself... I mean, we might learn something from it... But, of course, I can't do it without your help."

He continued in this incoherent strain until Colonel Simcox lost his temper.

"Goddammit, man!" he roared. "What are you blethering about like an old nanny-goat? Can't you speak Queen's English and have done with it?"

Mr. Winkley blinked at him apologetically.

"I thought I'd explained. I was only thinking... reconstruction, you know. It's usual with a crime."

Lady Warme gave a horrified gasp.

"Do you mean...you want us to act... murder?"

"Yes," replied Mr. Winkley, "that was the idea. Oh, not if you have any objection, but it couldn't do anyone any harm, and it might do a little good."

"It's sacrilege, Mr. Winkley," said Miss Astill, sitting up very straight in her chair. "I for one shall refuse to take part in it.

"Nonsense!" contradicted the Colonel, now thoroughly aroused. "You women use such hysterical expressions. I can't imagine how you think of them. It's certainly an unusual request, but sacrilege... Huh!"

"I agree that it can't do any harm," said Admiral Urwin, "but what good will it do, eh? What good will it do?"

Mrs. Dawson sucked at her cigarette. She did not really enjoy smoking, but thought it fitted in with her pose as a successful novelist. "Personally, I'm all for it," she said. "It's been miserable enough sitting here every evening, goodness knows. I'm in favour of anything that will cheer us up a bit."

Lady Warme snorted.

"Well, if you think it will cheer us up to reconstruct a murder which has altered all our lives for the worse, and reacted on us all in a most unpleasant way," she retorted, "you can do it. But you needn't ask me to help you." Nevertheless, she remained in the room, as if morbidly attracted by the idea.

"If you're determined on this tomfoolery," said the Admiral, "I suggest that you have Nurse Hawkins in. She can explain about the position of the wound and all that. She's a very clever little woman, Winkley, and would be a great help."

"By all means," said Mr. Winkley, and pressed the bell.

"I agree that Nurse Hawkins is a clever woman," said Miss Astill, "a little too clever, if the truth were known, perhaps."

"What d'you mean by that, ma'am?" the Admiral shot a glance full of hatred at her from under his shaggy eyebrows.

"I'm firmly convinced that she had a hand in Winnie Marston's murder," she said placidly, "and what's more, I think Inspector Palk agrees with me. After all, she was alone in the baths with the poor girl."

"Why, you –" began the Admiral, but Mrs. Dawson interrupted him.

"You can't start accusing people like that, Miss Astill," she said. "There's no evidence that she had anything at all to do with the murder. If it comes to suspicions, you might as well choose me. I was alone in the treatment-rooms with Winnie, too, and for all that we know you might have been there as well."

"That's all beside the point," remarked Lady Warme. "It's not a question of suspicion. You've no right to have Nurse Hawkins in here. You know perfectly well that none of the staff is allowed to make use of the public rooms. I'm surprised at you, Admiral, for suggesting such a thing. You'll only put wrong ideas into the nurse's head."

"I did that a long time ago," roared Urwin, leaning over and digging delighted fingers into the Colonel's unwilling ribs.

While this was going on, Mr. Winkley had sent a message to Nurse Hawkins by the maid who had answered his ring, but when the door opened, it revealed Miss Lewis, the doctor's secretary, to the Admiral's evident disappointment.

"I heard that you were asking for Nurse Hawkins," she explained, "but she's off duty and lying down with a headache, and I didn't like to disturb her unless it's absolutely necessary. I'm off duty myself," she went on with an apologetic glance at her neat, navy-blue woollen frock, "but if there's anything I can do..."

"Sit down, sit down," bellowed the Admiral, dragging a light chair close to him with the crook of one of his ash-sticks, and patting the seat. "Mr. Winkley's going to play murder."

Miss Lewis gave a perceptible start and put her hand up to her throat.

"Murder!" she exclaimed, looking apprehensively round the room.

Mr. Winkley moved towards her.

"Don't be alarmed," he said soothingly. "I'm only going to try and reconstruct the murder of Miss Blake, and I think you might be able to help me."

Miss Lewis looked relieved.

"But I wasn't here... I didn't see..." she said.

"Just so," replied Mr. Winkley in his reassuring voice, "but I want you all to help me. Of course, it isn't serious, you know. I'm not a professional like the Inspector, but I'm extremely interested in crime...In fact, I almost wish there'd be another murder while I'm here." His hands fluttered. "Oh, please don't get alarmed. I merely thought it would be fun, you know."

"Fun!" snorted the Colonel. "The man's a lunatic!"

"Well, if no one has any objection, we'll begin," went on Mr. Winkley, blinking rapidly in his excitement. "Miss Lewis, perhaps you wouldn't mind taking Miss Blake's place, as you're the youngest woman here." He was apparently unaware of the hostile looks which the other three women cast in his direction, and guided Miss Lewis to the high-backed settee. He stood back, frowning, as she sat nervously on the very edge. "The housemaid said that it was quite a long time before she found the corpse." They shivered at the blatant word. "I can't understand why she didn't see it as soon as she came into the room. It's obvious enough."

"I can tell you that," remarked Miss Astill. "The settee wasn't in that position. It stood in front of the fire, quite close to the hearth."

"Yes, of course, that's it," agreed Mr. Winkley, pushing it into that position with Miss Lewis's help. He walked over to the large bay window and drew back the curtains. "Now if you'll all come over to the corner of the room," he said, "we'll try and think out how the crime was committed."

Admiral Urwin began to slide his sticks out from under his chair, then slid them back with a grunt.

"It's all a lot of tommy-rot," he growled, "and I'm not going to come over. It's too much trouble for me to move, and I don't suppose I shall be murdered for it!"

"Now," said Mr. Winkley eagerly when the others had all joined him, "we can't see Miss Lewis from here at all, so she would not be able to see the murderer, and the murderer would not be able to see her."

"Twice one are two. Here endeth the first lesson," mocked the Colonel, losing his temper again. "What the devil is the fool getting at? What's the good of trying to reconstruct a crime when the criminal is already in gaol? I'll be damned if I'll –"

"I wonder if I've forgotten anything," said Mr. Winkley tremulously, taking no notice of him.

"Shouldn't you put the lights out?" asked Lady Warme, quite forgetting her earlier decision to have nothing to do with the affair.

Mr. Winkley hesitated.

"The lights," he said slowly. "The lights. Oh yes, certainly, the lights."

Mrs. Dawson tapped her temple significantly with her forefinger, and laughed.

Mr. Winkley walked over to the switches and turned out all the lights in the room.

"Mr. Winkley," came Miss Lewis's voice from the settee, "I don't think I can –"

"It's quite all right," said Mr. Winkley. "You're quite safe, and you've no idea how much you're helping me." He returned to the window. "Now I want you to concentrate on the crime," he said in a voice full of importance. "The room is dark, the victim is sitting on the settee; all is ready for the murderer."

A choked, hysterical noise came from one of the women.

"For God's sake, Winkley," came the Colonel's voice from the darkness, "stop all this nonsense!"

"Hush," said Mr. Winkley. "Listen."

The room remained silent.

"What do you think happens next?" asked Mr. Winkley, as indefatigable as a good hound on a clear trail.

"I should think the door opens," suggested Mrs. Dawson facetiously, then stifled a scream as the knob turned.

There was no need now to tell them all to keep quiet. Each one of them could hear the beat of his own heart. The door opened slowly, paused, then as slowly closed. But now there was someone inside it. The little group of people in the window stood as if turned to stone. Then the silence was broken by the clatter of sticks and a shout from the Admiral. Mr. Winkley leaped to the light switch and gazed in astonishment at the scene which was not of his staging.

At the side of the settee nearest the door stood Mrs. Napier, holding something which glittered like a steel arrow in her uplifted hand. Stumbling towards her was Admiral Urwin. Even as he reached her, she moved her hand, and as the steel streaked downwards, the body of Miss Lewis rolled off the settee on to the floor.

Mrs. Napier shook out the large silk handkerchief which had been wrapped round the knitting-needle, and began dusting down the wide skirt of her flowered silk dress. Little beads of moisture glistened on her forehead and upper lip, and her eyes were very bright behind the thick-lensed spectacles.

"She is dead," she said in pleased tones. "I killed her. The others too. They will never be cruel to me again. You can tell Inspector Palk."

CHAPTER XXXI

"I don't like it," said Palk.

He was sitting in the small room which the doctor had placed at his disposal ever since the unsolved murder of Winnie Marston, and which the Inspector used periodically when he visited the Hydro, "like the visiting music master to a girls' school," as he remarked bitterly. He had just interviewed seven of the people who had been present in the drawing-room on the previous evening during Mr. Winkley's reconstruction of the first crime, and had been treated to an exhibition of varied emotions which the pupils of a school of dramatic art could not have bettered. Admiral Urwin had been blustering, Mrs. Dawson over-cheerful, Colonel Simcox indignant, Miss Astill protesting, Miss Lewis hysterical, and Lady Warme had washed her hands of the whole affair with biblical thoroughness. Worst of all, there had been Mrs. Napier, ogling and mouthing, and insisting that she had always said she was the murderer and now perhaps they would all believe her; in spite of the fact that Miss Lewis remained very much alive.

"I don't like it," repeated Palk as Sergeant Jago made an indistinct noise apparently indicative of sympathy. "As if things weren't bad enough before, with Winnie Marston's murderer still free, without this half-baked amateur sleuth running about and upsetting everybody! What in the name of heaven did he want to reconstruct a solved crime for? It makes you think that he wanted to see who would go crazy first. Well, now he knows: Mrs. Napier. I shall have to take up residence in the Hydro if this sort of thing is going to continue. If I leave it for a week this is what happens. I expressly told the doctor that it was against my wishes for him to take in any more guests till these murders were cleared up."

"Aren't you talking a bit as if there'd been another murder, sir?" asked Jago apologetically. "After all, Miss Lewis only fainted. I bet it gave them all a fright when she rolled off the settee like that." A delighted grin began to deepen on his face, but was immediately suppressed at the sight of his superior's scowl. "Do you think Mrs. Napier really intended to kill Miss Lewis, sir?"

"No," replied Palk shortly.

"I've always rather fancied Mrs. Napier as the murderer myself," went on Jago. "She's very cunning, and Nurse Hawkins always suspected her, if you remember."

"She never said so," said Palk. "All that she said was that if she had to name someone as a possible suspect, she'd name Mrs. Napier. That's quite a different thing. No, Mrs. Napier was only imitating the murder last night. I suppose all this talk of reconstruction got on her nerves."

"But she wasn't in the drawing-room when they were talking about it, according to the others."

"I know, but that doesn't mean a thing in a place like this. The maid probably told her when she went to fetch Nurse Hawkins."

"She did have a steel knitting-needle in her hand, sir," persisted Jago.

"And stuck it into the arm of the settee for about an inch," retorted the Inspector.

"Where did she find the needle, though? I thought we had confiscated the lot."

"Well, you didn't. Mrs. Napier said that she'd found it in Miss Brendon's room, but she might as well have said Mrs. Dawson's room or anyone else's, for all the use it is to us. It's not a bit of good trying to get information out of Mrs. Napier. She just says the first thing that comes into her head."

"But, sir, couldn't she –?"

Palk turned on the sergeant savagely.

"No, she couldn't. Haven't you any brains in your head at all, Sergeant? The handle, man, where was the handle? No one could get a grip on a plain steel needle unless it was fitted with a handle. Mrs. Napier was just showing off. I don't believe she'd hurt a fly."

The sergeant rubbed his chin reflectively.

"You don't think there was any chance of her killing the Marston girl, then, sir?" he asked tentatively.

"No, I don't," snapped Palk.

"She was in the baths, sir."

"So was the nurse. So was Mrs. Dawson. So was Ted Cox, and God knows who else besides," replied the Inspector. "If it was anyone, it was Mrs. Dawson: she's cool enough for anything, and there's plenty of suspicion attached to her. Look at all those notes she made about Miss Blake's murder. She was a V.A.D. during the end of the war, too, and knows enough about anatomy to have stabbed her with the needle, but then" – he broke off abruptly – "so do they all, as far as I can make out. Besides, after the first murder, anyone in the place would know how to do it. I still think it was the chauffeur."

"That's enough to show that he's innocent, then," said Sergeant Jago, without thinking.

Palk's heavy fist crashed on to the table in front of him.

"Have you taken leave of your senses?" he demanded.

Sergeant Jago blushed so deeply that the colour was perceptible even beneath his naturally highly coloured cheeks.

"I beg your pardon, sir," he said. "I didn't mean to make any reflection on you. I was only thinking of the usual detective novel. The chief suspect always turns out to be innocent, sir."

Palk snorted.

"Haven't I enough to do, with a crazy fellow like Winkley making ridiculous speculations about the case, without you talking like your favourite Sexton Blake? Bring that amateur sleuth in here; I want to talk to him."

Sergeant Jago, looking deeply offended at this slur on his reading, for he belonged to a well-known subscription library, and prided himself on borrowing "A" books on a "B" ticket, went out to fetch Mr. Winkley.

The sight of his lean shoulders and peering eyes annoyed Palk more than ever, and without preliminaries he asked why he had come to the Hydro.

Mr. Winkley blinked rapidly and began to stammer, as if overawed at the idea of being in the presence of a real detective.

"Well... I... I..." he began. "I had to take a holiday and I wanted to go somewhere new. There was an advertisement in a paper that looked rather attractive, I thought... I believe I've still got it in my pocket."

He pulled out a little notebook, which Palk noticed was full of scribbled notes, and extracted a newspaper cutting which he handed over to the Inspector. It showed a representation of Presteignton Hydro set imposingly on the very edge of a deep precipice, and apparently half blotted out by a blizzard. Underneath was written:

Regain your lost health at Presteignton Private Hydro. Well-equipped treatment-rooms. Resident Doctor. Peaceful surroundings. Private bathing-beach. Tennis. Croquet. Special residential terms.

"Very attractive, if you like that kind of place," remarked the Inspector, "though 'peaceful surroundings' isn't so good for the scene of two murders. At least," he added, looking first at the persistent rain beating dismally against the window, and then at the photograph, "you have no cause to complain that you were not warned against the weather. They've distinctly indicated the rain in the picture." The fancy amused him, and he continued in more pleasant tones, "You seem to have upset the Hydro pretty thoroughly since you arrived. Whatever induced you to try and reconstruct the murder of Miss Blake?"

"I was interested," blinked Mr. Winkley. "You see crime's a little hobby of mine. I'd been talking with the others here about the two murders, and they seemed so much alike that I can't help thinking that they must have been committed by the same hand. I thought I might find some clue that had been overlooked by the police, because the reconstruction of the crime would make them all think about it more clearly, and it might bring to light something which no one had remembered to tell you when you were questioning them."

"You wouldn't be so interested in crime if it was your job," said Palk. "You'd soon get tired of routine work and report-writing. Being a detective doesn't mean going about picking up cigarette-ends all the time and making brilliant guesses. Now perhaps you'll give me an account of your detective-work last night."

Mr. Winkley complied eagerly, and his account agreed in all details with those which Palk had already heard from the others.

"Did you arrange for Mrs. Napier to enter the room after the lights were put out?" asked the Inspector.

"Oh no," replied Mr. Winkley. "It was quite a surprise to me."

"Was it part of your plan, then, for Miss Lewis to roll off the settee?"

"No, no!" protested Mr. Winkley. "It was a genuine faint. I sent for Dr. Williams immediately, and he said it was genuine."

"Yes, I know," replied Palk, "but the doctor might be – er – let us say, an interested party. You say that you remained by the switch after you had put on the lights. Didn't you think that another murder had taken place before your eyes, and think of catching the culprit?"

"No," fluttered Mr. Winkley. "I knew Miss Lewis had only fainted."

"Oh," smiled Palk. "You knew. That was very clever of you. If you hadn't already arranged for Miss Lewis to roll off the settee at a given signal from you, how could you know that she'd only fainted? You saw the steel knitting-needle in Mrs. Napier's hand, didn't you? And you knew that two other people had already been murdered with a steel knitting-needle, didn't you?"

"Oh yes," said Mr. Winkley earnestly, "but Mrs. Napier obviously couldn't have done any damage. She just jabbed the needle into the arm of the settee."

"But there might have been an accident even if Mrs. Napier had not intended to kill Miss Lewis. She might have become flustered by the Admiral's shout. Why didn't you run towards her as everyone else did?"

"Well, you see," said Mr. Winkley, blinking less than usual, "I knew that she could do no damage because she had no grip on the needle. She had only wrapped a silk handkerchief round it, which would be worse than useless. The real murderer had some kind of handle."

Palk's smile faded and he looked suspiciously at Mr. Winkley, who seemed to think that perhaps he had said too much, and added, "Of course, that's only what I think."

"By the way," said Palk after a short pause, 'you say you're on holiday. What is your job, Mr. Winkley?"

Mr. Winkley hesitated before replying.

"I suppose you'd call me a... sort of a free-lance," he admitted.

Palk snorted more loudly than before.

"A free-lance!" he exclaimed looking significantly at Sergeant Jago, who had been standing quietly in the corner throughout the interview. "I ought to have guessed it as soon as I heard about last night's affair. No one else would have had the nerve to try such a thing. You journalists would take a morbid interest in the murder of your own mothers if it brought you in any money. As if it isn't enough to have a woman writer of thrillers in the Hydro without your coming as well! And you thought you'd put me off the truth with that precious newspaper advertisement of yours! I suppose you don't mind admitting that you really came here because of the murders?"

"That's... that's really the case, I'm afraid, Inspector."

"I've a good mind to tell all the people in the Hydro who you are," said Palk. "I suppose you wouldn't like me to do that, eh?"

"No, no," said Mr. Winkley hastily. "Don't do that. It would place me in a very awkward position."

"Well, I won't," replied Palk, "but you needn't think it's for your sweet sake. I shall take steps to see that none of your stuff gets out of this hotel by post, hand, or 'phone, so I shouldn't bother to write any of it, if I were you. And now that you are here you'll have to stay here till you have my permission to leave the place."

Mr. Winkley did not appear to be taken aback in the least.

"I have every intention of staying, Inspector," he replied.

"It's a charming place, and the people are so interesting to talk to."

"That's a matter of taste," replied Palk. "You can go now, but, remember, no leaving the hotel."

Mr. Winkley got up and moved towards the door.

"Oh, by the way," Palk called out in sarcastic tones, "I hope you found some interesting clues last night."

Mr. Winkley turned.

"Yes, thanks," he said quite seriously. "I think I may say that the reconstruction was quite a success. I gained some very valuable information. You ought to try it yourself, Inspector."

"Well, whadda'ya know about that!" exclaimed Sergeant Jago to the closed door. The crime story he had last borrowed from the circulating library was one hundred percent American.

CHAPTER XXXII

On Friday morning, Dr. Williams awoke with the feeling that the day was going to be more unpleasant than usual, and felt puzzled until he realized that this was the day in the month when he received, in person, complaints from anyone in the

Hydro who had a grievance, either real or imaginary. As he walked along to his secretary's office for his customary before-breakfast consultation about the day's work, he found himself anticipating the form which those complaints would take.

He would hear that the library was stuffy, and the drawing-room draughty; that the bedrooms were not fit for dogs to sleep in; that a chambermaid had been insolent; that the housekeeper was inefficient; that it was useless to have a wireless set which was always out of order; that the deckchairs were always sopping wet and why couldn't someone take them out of the rain; that the gardener ought to supply flowers for the bedrooms; that there was a croquet mallet missing and it might be found in someone's bedroom; that the teapots were chipped and no wonder, since Presteignton Hydro must be the only hotel in the British Isles which did not have metal ones; that there had been a slug in the cabbage.

Then would come the complaints from the staff, for the doctor prided himself on being scrupulously fair.

He would hear that the gardener would not dig enough vegetables for the chef; that if the chef more fruit must bottle, 'e more bottles must 'ave; that some b–, h'm, somebody had wheeled a bath-chair over a flower bed; that the bath-attendant had sworn horribly at the electrician; that the electrician had sworn even more horribly at the bath-attendant; that if certain people in the Hydro didn't stop interfering with the wireless, they must put up with the consequences; that the deck-chairs walked outside on their own legs whenever it rained, after they had been carefully put away; that the gardener wouldn't be dictated to by that old Admiral who didn't know a Worcester Pearmain from one of his walking-sticks; that the kitchens, store-rooms, potting-sheds and greenhouses needed enlarging; that there weren't enough flower-pots, fuses, saucepans, tables, trays, dusters, towels, buckets... and so on.

People might be murdered in Presteignton Hydro, but complaints would still go on, and if the doctor secretly thought that no other man of forty-one would be fool enough to take on a job in which he was expected to be doctor, manager, host, arbitrator, and peacemaker, he never said so.

He found his secretary, Miss Lewis, awaiting him in the office which served as an ante-room to his consulting-room. For three years she had served the doctor faithfully and well, a fact which he knew and appreciated; for two years and a half she had loved him, a thing which he did not even suspect.

"Well, Miss Lewis, have you quite recovered from your shock of the other evening?" he asked in his cheerful voice.

"Quite, thank you, Doctor," she replied. "It was very foolish of me to faint like that. You said that Mr. Winkley could be trusted."

"Yes, but I didn't realize what he was going to let you in for, or I might have stopped him. You're looking rather pale. Would you like me to make you up a tonic?"

Gwynneth Lewis thought that he did indeed hold the prescription which would have put colour immediately into her cheeks, if he only knew it, and wondered what he would have thought if she indicated as much to him. A soft little smile played about the corners of her mouth as she replied demurely, "Oh no, thank you. I'm quite all right."

"Very well. Is there anything special down for today?" he asked, turning abruptly to work. "Shelve everything that isn't urgent, won't you. I've got those damned complaints to listen to, and you can just imagine how many more there are likely to be since we've had the police searching everyone's rooms and generally turning the place upside down. I haven't heard the last of those charabanc trips yet."

"I don't think there's anything out of the ordinary," replied Miss Lewis. "Mrs. Napier was making a fuss again yesterday about having to share the bath-chair with Miss Brendon."

"That woman's like a sheep-tick!" exclaimed the doctor. "Once she gets her head into a subject you can't get it out again. We certainly can't afford to buy a new chair for her, and, by the look of Palk, she may be arrested at any minute and won't need a bath-chair for a long, long time. He'll never convince me that she's a murderess, however big a nuisance she may be. I've told him that it's a psychological impossibility, but he doesn't take any notice of me. Thinks I'm trying to divert suspicion from myself probably. After all, I never believed that Chervil is a murderer, though, if I'd been in Palk's place, I should have arrested him, I expect. No, Miss Lewis, there will be no new bath-chair. Mrs. Napier is able to walk perfectly well if she wants to. Besides, I'm not spending any more money on this place for a long time. It's quite possible that there will be no residents left here when these murders have been nicely tidied away. They could all leave today if they wanted to, instead of complaining about everything. I can't imagine why they don't."

"I'll keep Mrs. Napier quiet," Miss Lewis assured him, "but she isn't the only one. They all want to talk to you about Inspector Palk's order for them to stay here, whether they believe in it or not; but I'll do my best to keep them away from you."

"Good," he said, patting her shoulder. "Then you don't want me for anything else now?"

"No, Doctor," replied Miss Lewis, wondering how it was possible for the man to be so dense as to believe her.

"Good," he said again. "I don't know what I should do without you," and Miss Lewis smiled wryly as he went out, knowing that the words meant nothing to him.

The morning routine over, Dr. Williams returned to breakfast in his own rooms. These were cut off from the rest of the Hydro by an inner baize door and an outer wooden one marked "Private" in large gilded letters. They were occupied by himself, a cook, a housemaid, a governess, and the little girl who had cost his wife her life nine years ago. Here the doctor slept, smoked, took breakfast and tea, and spent any leisure time he could snatch from his work.

After breakfast, he entered the sunny day-nursery where Grace was getting ready for lessons. When she saw him she ran and flung her arms around him.

"Daddy, Daddy, come and see the blue-tits on my coconut."

The doctor bent down and kissed her, then ran his fingers up and down the smooth, soft nape of her neck.

"Not now, Grace. I'm in a hurry."

Grace pouted.

"Oh, but, Daddy, it's only nine o'clock. You always stay with me till half past."

She took his hand and tried to drag him towards the window.

"Not this morning, dear; I've a lot to do."

Miss George, the governess, took Grace by the shoulder.

"You mustn't worry your father, Grace."

Grace wriggled away.

"It's complaints day!" she cried. "I know it is. Horrid, horrid old complaints!" Then, as Miss George held her again, "I shall complain to the dear doctor!" she said, tossing her head in a perfect imitation of Miss Astill, and walked across the room, crossing her legs like Mrs. Napier.

The doctor smiled guiltily at Miss George, and Grace ran and bunted her head lovingly against his coat.

"You'll promise to come and have tea with poor Grace," she coaxed.

"Of course, dear. You know that nothing could make me miss my nursery tea." He pinched her chin between his thumb and forefinger. "She's looking a little pale this morning, Miss George," he went on. "Let her off lessons for today. It will do her good to run about with young Bobby Dawson for a bit."

Grace held her breath and stood quite still lest anything she did might put an end to such a splendid idea. Miss George bridled.

"I'm sure it isn't overwork that makes her pale, Doctor," she said. "I'm most careful –"

"I know that," replied the doctor hastily. "I'm not questioning anything you do, and I know that her lessons are important. But we are all a little sun-starved just now, and the children show it more quickly. I think we should take advantage of this lovely sunny day; we shan't get many more like it. I think it would be a good plan to try Grace and Bobby with the sun-ray lamp this winter. I must see about it."

"Very well, Doctor."

"There, you may run off and find Bobby," he said, smiling at Grace's excitement.

"Oh, thank you, Daddy, you are simply wizardly!" Grace danced up and down for a few minutes, then her face fell. "I wish you could come too," she said.

"So I will one day next spring. You and I will go off on our own together in the car, and nobody shall know where we've gone to, not even Miss George. Good-bye."

"Good-bye, Daddy. Horrid old complaints!"

About half an hour later, Grace ran out of the Hydro porch, closely followed by Mrs. Dawson's seven-year-old son Bobby.

"Just look at those children," exclaimed Mrs. Napier. "They ought to be taught to walk properly and not allowed to rush about like young hooligans. Really, I'm surprised at the doctor allowing it. Where's the governess?"

"She doesn't seem to be with them," said Lady Warme. "If she weren't such a fright one might think that the doctor was... well... interested in her." But the doctor had chosen Miss George well, and they did not pursue the subject.

Bobby had succeeded in catching Grace, and they walked along quietly enough in an aimless direction.

"Where's your mother?" asked Grace.

"Trying on a new hat. I think she's going in to make a complaint to your father."

"I wish she wouldn't worry him," sighed Grace. "I hate complaints day. It makes him so tired. Can't you stop her, then there'd be one less anyway?"

"'Fraid not," said Bobby apologetically. "I don't think she really means the complaint though. I think it's just an excuse to see him. I think she'd like to marry him. Wouldn't it be grand if she did? But I suppose you wouldn't like it much."

"Oh, it isn't that," replied Grace politely, "but I don't want anyone except Daddy."

"I shall marry you when I grow up, then," said Bobby solemnly.

"Oh, Bobby, you can't do that. I'm two years older than you."

"Do girls always marry someone older than themselves then?" asked Bobby.

"Of course they do. Daddy was older than Mummy, and Mr. Marston's older than Mrs. Marston, and Admiral Urwin's older than Nurse Hawkins."

"But Nurse Hawkins isn't married to Admiral Urwin," objected Bobby.

"I know she isn't," replied Grace loftily, "but I heard someone say that if she wasn't she ought to be, so I suppose it comes to the same thing. Let's play at being married."

"But you said we couldn't be married because I'm younger than you."

"Never mind, let's pretend."

They ran down the sloping bank from the terrace on to the croquet lawn.

"Look where you're going," called out Millie Marston. "You mustn't run about on the croquet lawn. It's bad for the turf."

Grace, followed by Bobby, swerved down Bachelors' Walk, narrowly avoiding a collision with Mr. Marston, who had just placed the seventh pebble out of his pocket on the seat to denote that he had walked seven-elevenths of a mile.

"You children are not supposed to be seen round the front of the Hydro at all," he wheezed, envying their supple young limbs, and thinking of Winnie's stiffened, dead ones. "This path is for exercise only."

Grace and Bobby found a deserted seat a little farther on, and began their play. After a few minutes Miss Astill approached and sat down on the same seat, although there were three others vacant within easy distance.

"Don't go, my dears," she said, smiling. "Go on with your game. I shan't interrupt. It's so nice to see you playing about on this lovely sunny morning." She watched them silently for a few minutes, then asked, "What are you playing at?"

"Being married," said Grace.

"She's just going to have a baby," explained Bobby.

Miss Astill flushed all over her face and down her neck beyond the narrow velvet ribbon she always wore.

"You disgusting little boy!" she cried. "How dare you say such a thing to me! Go away, both of you, and don't come near me again."

They went, much surprised.

"What's the matter with her?" asked Bobby. "I didn't say anything, did I?"

"Oh, don't take any notice of her," said Grace. "I expect she's cross because she isn't married herself. Let's go to the little round pond and catch tadpoles."

Neither stopped to think whether it was the right time of the year for tadpoles; they could always pretend. But Miss Brendon had chosen to have her bath-chair wheeled down to the pond. The sound of the children's voices aroused her to a gibbering frenzy.

"Go away!" she screamed.

"I've told you children more than once that you're not to come worrying Miss Brendon," said Rogers severely. "She likes to be alone, and so will you when you're as old as she is. There are plenty of places you can play in without bothering us. Be off, now!"

"There are plenty of places for her too," muttered Grace. "Why does she come here? She can't even see the pond properly. That's the worst of the sunshine; it brings them all out like flies."

They wandered into the yard at the back of the Hydro. Mr. Marston's Daimler was standing there, looking invitingly at them. They got in, and Bobby turned the switches at the dashboard and held the wheel, while Grace gave orders as if he were her chauffeur.

"When you get into Excester, Dawson." she said, "stop at the milliner's –"

A muscular, hairy hand came through the open window and took Bobby by the ear.

"Now then, you two, hop it!" said Matthews. "You'll be doing some damage to the car and I shall get blamed for it. And mind how you get out. I've just cleaned it."

They walked away soberly, but their high spirits got the better of them and they began a game of tag. Bobby raced along, yelling at the top of his voice, straight into the arms of Admiral Urwin.

"What the devil are you kids doing here, making a noise like that?" he asked irritably. "I've come out for a bit of peace and quiet." (He had really come out in the hope of seeing Nurse Hawkins.) "Now clear out! Pipe down!"

They moved on out of his hearing and continued their play near the tennis-court. But they met with no greater success here. Colonel Simcox was strolling along there with Mr. Winkley.

"I'm glad that you agree with me about gilt-edged stock," he was saying. "I could never get that fellow Chervil... the one who murdered Miss Blake, you know... to believe in them. He said that he always liked to see his money earning money..." He broke off abruptly. "What *is* that boy creeping round us for? It's enough to get on anyone's nerves. Here, you! Bobby! Go away! Dismiss!"

"Never mind," said Grace. "Let's play hide-and-seek in the shrubbery. They won't mind that because it's a quiet game, and no one'll notice us."

"All right," agreed Bobby. "Bags I seeker!"

Bobby stood in the intimate dimness of the little leafy room within the thick laurel leaves of the shrubbery, and, covering his face with his hands, began to count up to a hundred.

For some time Grace waited in her place of concealment, uttering occasional derisive "coo-ee's," but when she heard no sound from Bobby she began to stalk the shrubbery, slipping carefully from one clipped yew to another until she was within easy reach of it. She stood still for a moment, then made a dash into the thick-leaved shade. She stared in front of her with horror-stricken eyes, then ran out again, pale as a ghost, and screaming, screaming, screaming...

CHAPTER XXXIII

Mr. Winkley was the first to reach the laurel shrubbery, with Colonel Simcox a close second. As they stood looking down at Bobby's little crumpled body, the Colonel thought he heard his companion say, "I ought to have expected it."

The rest of the Hydro residents, attracted by Grace's screams, emerged from different parts of the grounds and converged on the shrubbery.

"Oh, my God! Another..." screamed Mrs. Marston, stumbling towards her husband, who essayed to give her clumsy comfort as he turned her away from the laurels, breathing heavily and swearing almost inaudibly under his breath.

Mr. Winkley took it upon himself to prevent anyone touching the slight, murdered body of the child, and warned them to keep their distance, while he himself peered at the ground immediately around as if searching for some clue. He sent Colonel Simcox for the doctor, and the others soon regained the composure which had been so badly shaken by the sight of a new murder, and grew suspicious of Mr. Winkley.

"How do we know that you didn't do it yourself, and are keeping us away while you destroy some evidence?" demanded

Lady Warme, who previously had been one of Mr. Winkley's greatest admirers.

"Yes," said the Admiral, hobbling restlessly on his sticks, his voice irascible with emotion, "you'd better be careful not to touch anything yourself. There might be footprints where you're standing. Sleuthing when there's nothing to sleuth, and sleuthing when there's an actual murder, are two different things. This is no job for an amateur."

But the shrubbery was open to the skies, and on the edge of the pine wood. The wind had flung generations of pine-needles over the clipped laurels, and had piled them up into a soft, resilient carpet on which even the heaviest footprints could not be retained. Mr. Winkley continued to prowl round, and the others watched, fascinated.

They were disturbed by a piercing shriek from the terrace as Mrs. Dawson came half running, half stumbling towards them.

"My darling! My baby! I killed him, I killed him!" she cried, and before anyone could put out a hand to stop her she had rushed into the shrubbery and flung herself on her knees on the spiny carpet. She picked Bobby up in her arms, smoothing his hair and speaking to him in an agony of dis-belief that he could be dead. And all the time the cruel length of steel, looking like some fantastic feather that a child might stick in his hair, protruded from the back of his head and gave her the lie.

Mr. Winkley shrugged his shoulders as if calling them all to witness that he had done his best to fulfil the prescribed police regulations under such circumstances, and turned away.

Mrs. Dawson was rocking Bobby backwards and forwards in her arms, as if to reawaken life in his still heart; her eyes were dulled, and she seemed faced with something which her brain could not understand.

Nurse Hawkins stepped forward and touched her shoulder. Mrs. Dawson looked up blankly, then her face puckered in an agony of grief.

"It's my fault!" she cried again. "I killed him! I said there ought to be another murder to make it more interesting. It's a judgment on me. Oh, my God! I said it would be good publicity!"

She allowed the nurse to take Bobby from her arms and place him gently back again on the ground, but it was Mrs. Marston who helped her to stand up, and coaxed her with infinite sympathy and understanding to move away on reluctant feet.

Dr. Williams, grave and pale, joined the little group in the shrubbery, and, going on one knee, examined the body perfunctorily, and shook his head. As he rose to his feet, Miss Astill stepped forward, and dropped to her knees in an attitude of prayer.

"He is safe," she whispered. "Safe in the arms of Jesus."

So they remained, each within earshot and sight of each other, until Inspector Palk came; a very agitated Inspector, who flung his arms about when he spoke to them, and swore when he found that the body had been moved. He was filled with the feeling that he could have averted this third tragedy, yet at the same time he knew that he still lacked the knowledge which would have enabled him to do so. He felt, also, that if he did not speedily gain that knowledge, a fourth tragedy, and then a fifth, might occur. He was pestered in his sleep by a nightmare in which murder followed murder in the Hydro until only the murderer was left alive, and he would awake in a sweat from a hand-to-hand fight with this murderer, whose face he could never see.

"Who found him?" he snapped.

"My little girl, Grace," replied the doctor.

Palk's annoyance increased a hundredfold. He was devoted to children, and to his mind the murder of one and the cross-questioning of another was the worst thing which his profession could hold for him.

"It's quite impossible to question her today," the doctor went on, reading the Inspector's thoughts, which was not a difficult task. "They were playing hide-and-seek and she found him like that. The shock was enough to drive her insane. I've given her a strong sedative and put her to bed. It might be a month before you can question her."

Palk's muttered oath was one which he had learned from the Admiral.

"Does anyone know how it happened?" he asked.

Mr. Winkley stepped forward.

"I was just coming round the bend of the laurel thicket when the doctor's little girl ran out screaming. I naturally went inside to see what was the matter, and found Bobby lying on the ground. I stayed here till the others came, then sent Colonel Simcox for the doctor."

"Oh, naturally!" said Palk with heavy sarcasm. "You happened to be there, and you naturally slipped in to take a look. I should have thought that the most natural thing to do would have been to think that the girl had been hurt and to go and ask her what was the matter."

Mr. Winkley's face bore a look of amazement. He blinked rapidly at the Inspector.

"I... I think," he stammered, "that with all these murders in the Hydro it was quite natural to suspect another one. I didn't mean any harm."

"Harm!" roared Palk, venting his full feelings on Mr. Winkley. "I should hope not, but do you mean any good? Of course you don't! You come here poking your nose into this place and generally upsetting everybody. I suppose you go snooping round examining the wainscoting through a magnifying-glass!" A murmur from the others, and Mr. Winkley's air of embarrassment, told him that he had scored a hit. "That sort of stuff's no good to anyone. I suppose you get your ideas from detective stories. Most people seem to think they're written by detectives. Such rubbish! Most of them are written by women, let me tell you, and what do women know about detective-work? Nothing!"

Having worked off some of his resentment against the murderer on his favourite theme, Palk continued in a more normal tone:

"You take my advice and stick to your detective stories, Mr. Winkley, but don't try to put them into practice; you're sure to get into trouble if you do. Why, for all you know it might have been your detective-work that caused this murder."

Mr. Winkley blinked harder than ever.

"Yes, Inspector, that's what I'm afraid of," was his astonishing reply.

Palk snorted, and turned his attention to the others. He found that, with the exception of Mrs. Dawson and Dr. Williams and his secretary, they had all been at some point in the grounds within easy reach of the shrubbery, and that, with the exception of Colonel Simcox and Mr. Winkley, none of them had been in sight of the others while the children were playing hide-and-seek. They had all heard Grace's screams and her incoherent words about the shrubbery, and had come to see what was the matter.

Palk ordered them to wait for him outside the laurel thicket under Sergeant Jago's eye, while he searched the ground inside, without much hope of finding a clue. The police doctor and photographer had soon finished their routine work, and Palk gave orders for Bobby's body to be removed.

As he emerged again into the thin November sunshine, the white overall of Nurse Hawkins caught his eye, and he questioned her more closely.

"I thought you had to give treatment in the mornings, Nurse," he remarked. "What are you doing out here?"

Nurse Hawkins looked embarrassed.

"Not... not since the murder of Miss Marston," she replied. "The patients won't go into the baths now; they're all afraid. I came out to bring Mrs. Napier into the sunshine."

"But Mrs. Napier isn't here now."

"No, I left her on the terrace about half an hour ago."

"Then what are you doing down here? If I remember, you said that you were on the path behind the laurel shrubbery when the little girl screamed."

Nurse Hawkins looked quickly at the doctor, who appeared not to notice her, then at Palk, then looked down, moving her hands restlessly.

"Well?" snapped Palk.

"I... I came down for a short walk before going back on duty."

"Are you supposed to take walks in the morning?"

Again the nurse glanced at the doctor.

"No... I... no."

Palk decided that there was nothing to be gained by immediate questioning, and indicated that they were all to proceed to the house and to remain within the drawing-room, despite the sunshine, till he needed them. They formed a procession, with the nurse, Lady Warme, Miss Astill, the Admiral and the. Colonel at the head, followed by Mr. Marston and Millie. Then came Dr. Williams and Mr. Winkley in earnest conversation, followed by Jago and Palk, with a constable carrying Bobby.

As they reached the terrace, Mrs. Napier stumbled heavily towards them.

"Have any of you seen a knitting-needle?" she asked. "I've lost one somewhere!"

CHAPTER XXXIV

Once inside the Hydro, Inspector Palk put everyone through an examination bordering on second – if not third – degree. Evidently his suspicions of Mr. Winkley and of Matthews were increased by this cross-questioning, for when at last he returned to Newton St. Mary, he took the former in his car with him, while the latter followed in the police car with Sergeant Jago. There seemed no doubt that Matthews was guilty of the murder both of Winnie and of Bobby, and the general opinion of the Hydro residents was that Mr. Winkley, who had an alibi through being with Colonel Simcox, was being made a bit of a scapegoat by Palk.

After they had recovered somewhat from the first shock of this third murder, they would merely find it a new subject for scandal, and would discuss it in these terms: "I didn't wish the poor child to be murdered, but really it does rather serve Mrs. Dawson right for boasting about putting us all in her new book, doesn't it? As for Mr. Winkley, no doubt the Inspector took him to the station to administer an official reprimand. He's a very nice little man, and I know we all *like* him, but he did rather take too much on himself, ordering us all about as if he were the Commissioner of Police at the very least. No wonder Inspector Palk wouldn't stand for that kind of behaviour."

If they could have been present at the interview between Palk and Mr. Winkley, they would have received a great surprise. It took place, not at the police-station, but at that very luxurious hotel in Market St. known as "The Angel and Child," and started over the best luncheon which the hotel cuisine could provide.

Neither the Inspector nor Mr. Winkley had spoken during the drive to the hotel, but when the first few spoonfuls of soup had been disposed of, Palk looked inquiringly at his companion.

"Perhaps you'll be good enough to make your position clear, Mr. – er – Winkley," he said in a reluctant manner. "It puts me in an awkward position in this affair."

"Winkley is my real name, I assure you, Inspector. I presume that Dr. Williams has told you that I am a friend of his whom he met on Special Intelligence work during the War; that since then I have been attached to Scotland Yard, and that he naturally wrote to me for advice when he became involved in the two murders at the Hydro. As some leave was due to me, I came down on a busman's holiday. It was nothing to do with the advertisement nor with journalism which brought me down here."

"Quite so, sir," replied Palk, "but you mustn't take offence if you find me over-cautious. It's my job to be suspicious of people, and in a triple murder case..."

"Oh, I don't expect you to believe me without proof," said Mr. Winkley, taking out his wallet and handing some papers across the table. "I prefer tackling a case in my own way, but I naturally came down prepared to get into touch with the local police. I think you'll find those in order."

Palk glanced through the papers, then returned them. "That's all right, sir," he said, smiling. "As a matter of fact I got Scotland Yard on the long-distance 'phone as soon as the doctor spoke to me about you."

Mr. Winkley looked keenly across the table at the Inspector, and Palk noticed that he did not blink. Nor, when he spoke, was there a trace of a stammer in his voice.

"The devil you did!" he exclaimed, thinking that the Inspector of the Newton St. Mary constabulary was not so sleepy as the name of the little Devonshire town indicated.

"I have orders to co-operate with you in every way," went on Palk. "They didn't tell me to hand over the case to you, sir, but I imagine that instructions to that effect will come by post later. Well, in any case we should have had to report to them after this last affair, I'm afraid. It's my first experience of murder, and I've failed miserably."

"Now for heaven's sake don't start talking like that," said Mr. Winkley. "I'm down here on holiday, remember, and my standing here is unofficial at present. If they want me to take up the case, they'll have to write and tell me so, and if I know anything about the Yard, they won't write for a few days. I'm untouchable for two days at least, and if we play our cards properly, you ought to have the criminal locked up safely by tomorrow or the next day. Yes, you, I said. Scotland Yard's got as much work to do as it wants at the moment, without coming in on a new murder case. If you manage to get these three murders cleaned up, you'll be a popular man, Inspector." He brushed aside all Palk's protests with, "Nonsense! It always seems unfair to me that the routine man gets no credit when the man with a fresh eye jumps in and interprets his information for him. In any case, I'm a nonentity at the Yard. I've no official rank or standing, and am simply known as 'Mr. Winkley,' or even as 'Our Mr. Winkley,' which makes me sound like a head salesman or a second-rate commercial traveller. I've an unadvertised department with special duties and a certain number of privileges, one of which is to remain unknown and unseen, so I shouldn't thank you for any publicity over this case."

"Hence the term 'free-lance,' I suppose," laughed Palk. "You must have had a great kick out of pulling my leg all the time. I must say you played your part well, sir. You'd make a fortune on the stage. My spine feels like a porcupine's when I remember some of the things I said to you this morning, but I was fairly worked up at the sight of that child."

"I know," replied Mr. Winkley, looking so much younger and more alert out of the surroundings of the Hydro. "You needn't worry about that. You did exactly what I wanted, and established me as a harmless, interfering amateur in the eyes of the Hydro residents and staff. It dispelled any little undercurrent of suspicion there might have been attached to me as a newcomer." He stretched his thin legs out under the table as the waiter removed his plate. "Now, Inspector," he said, "let's start at the end and work backwards. What do you think of the last murder?"

"I think," said Palk slowly, "there's a homicidal maniac loose in the Hydro, but who it is, God knows."

"You think that the three murders are related to each other?"

"I think that the last two are," replied Palk. "It was stretching it a little to suspect two men for two different murders on two different people for two different motives. I can't suspect three: it doesn't make sense, not unless they're all mad in the Hydro."

Mr. Winkley leaned back in his chair and put the tips of his forefingers and thumbs accurately together.

"I have heard Dr. Williams express that opinion more than once," he smiled. "As I see it now, there are several possible solutions to the three murders. Either one man was responsible for the three murders, or this fellow Sir Humphrey was responsible for Miss Blake's murder and someone else did the other two. Or three people are equally responsible, which, as you say, doesn't make sense. I suppose that you suspect Matthews of the murder of Miss Marston and Bobby Dawson?"

Palk hesitated.

"I've pulled Matthews in on suspicion," he said, "because I think he knows more than he has told us about Winnie Marston's murder, but I've no real evidence against him, and I really suspect them all again. I still believe that I've a fool-proof case against Sir Humphrey Chervil, and I certainly half believed that Matthews murdered the Marston girl. But I know Matthews didn't murder Bobby Dawson, because the man I put on to shadow him says that Matthews didn't leave the garage yard during the time when we know the murder must have been committed. If Matthews is out of it, and one murderer is still responsible for the last two crimes, then I strongly suspect Mrs. Dawson. She had the opportunity in both cases, and was actually in the baths when Winnie Marston was murdered. We may find a money motive against her for Bobby's murder... if her husband left his money to his son, and to his wife on his son's death, I mean."

Mr. Winkley nodded.

"Quite feasible," he agreed. "Personally I'm of the opinion that there's only one murderer for the three murders, but that doesn't mean that Mrs. Dawson is innocent."

"It lets Sir Humphrey out, though," reflected Palk, "and I've a cast-iron case against him. On that theory, where will you

find a motive? Miss Blake, Miss Marston, Bobby Dawson...
there's nothing to connect them unless someone is stark,
staring mad."

"As I imagine someone is," put in Mr. Winkley quietly,
taking out a cigarette and lighting it. "Mad in the worst
possible way, for he –"

"Or she," suggested Palk.

"Certainly, Inspector. He or she is sufficiently sane to be
able to maintain an appearance of sanity so cleverly as to
deceive the other guests in the Hydro, 'one of whom, I am
which,' as I might say."

"That's a damnably hard kind of insanity to prove," said
Palk. "Take a woman who is a secret drunkard, for instance.
I've known one go to any lengths to prove that she never
touches alcohol in any shape or form. She'll feign illness, hide
the evidence, and do anything to give the lie to anyone who
accuses her of taking a drink." He noticed that Mr. Winkley did
not seem to be listening, and his voice trailed away. "Perhaps
it's an unfortunate example..." he concluded lamely.

"On the contrary, my dear Palk, said he, talking like
Sherlock Holmes! It's an excellent example, for the woman is
sane in her attitude to everything except drink, and my theory
is that this murderer is sane except in his attitude to one
particular thing, in which these three murdered people
somehow became involved. Suppose that the murderer has an
antipathy towards drink, and that he found Miss Blake, Miss
Marston, and Bobby all at different times under the influence
of strong drink, then we have a connecting link and..."

"But Bobby Dawson," protested Palk. "An innocent boy of
seven."

"Perhaps it's an unfortunate example," repeated Mr.
Winkley slyly, "but I am convinced that there is some such
motive connecting the three murders."

Palk glanced round the hotel dining-room and, finding it
empty except for themselves, packed and lighted his pipe, and
the two men smoked in silence for a few minutes.

"The trouble is that it's such a hell of a background for someone who's not quite normal," remarked Palk at length.

"They're all a bit touched in one way or another, in my opinion, and no one of them shows up very clearly against the others. I sometimes wonder whether I'm sane myself when I'm talking to them. If we could consider each one separately amongst normal, healthy people, it would be so much easier to find their individual kinks. Would you like me to run through the information I've accumulated on the case since the beginning?"

"I don't think there's anything to be gained by it," replied Mr. Winkley, lighting another cigarette from the stub of the first. "I've a pretty comprehensive view of things through talking them over so much with the people in the Hydro. You get to know people pretty well, you know, when you live with them, though I thought at first that they'd never begin to talk about the murders at all. I'll take your papers and read them through, and we shall have to think of some plan of action. It's no use waiting for the doctor's little girl to be fit for questioning because she might tell us nothing of value then. In any case, she will probably not recover from the shock for several weeks, and there may be another murder by then unless we can stop it."

Palk sighed.

"If we could only find the weapon-holder," he said. "Mrs. Dawson said she guessed that it would be in some obvious place, but I can't think of any we haven't searched thoroughly. I've had every room in the Hydro turned upside down, and even the gutters and roofs inspected. No one could possibly be carrying it around with him, for we've examined even their fountain-pens."

"What puzzles me is where Sir Humphrey fits in," remarked Mr. Winkley. "You say he's definitely guilty of Miss Blake's murder?"

"Oh yes," replied Palk decisively, "there's no doubt in my mind about that. The evidence is strongly against him and he doesn't deny that he was the last person to see Miss Blake upstairs. He started the trouble, of course. Stage a murder among a collection of people who are a little abnormal, and you're almost sure to get an imitative crime. The peculiar thing about the first murder is that I haven't been able to get any information about the Blake girl. She doesn't appear to have any home or relations, for no one who knows her has come forward, and there's no letter or scrap of paper with any address or personal writing whatever among her belongings. It doesn't seem to fit in with her general appearance somehow; she ought to have a background somewhere. We're trying America now. But that won't help the baronet."

"His name's Chervil, isn't it?" asked Mr. Winkley, frowning.

"Yes, Sir Humphrey Chervil. I've been rather backward in getting information about him; these other murders rather obscured the first one, and three murders within two weeks doesn't give one a chance."

"Sir Humphrey Chervil," said Mr. Winkley slowly. "It sounds familiar to me somehow. I'd like to see your baronet."

Palk heaved his bulk from his chair.

"We'll go along to the station now, if you like," he said, with the air of a strong man humouring an obstinate child.

CHAPTER XXXV

The Newton St. Mary Police-Station was not far from "The Angel and Child" and Palk and Mr. Winkley strolled along in its direction in the sunny, chilly weather which November had brought to supplant the rain of the last days of the previous month.

"Better visit him in his cell." said Palk apologetically, as they entered the station. "He's quiet enough, but after all, he is a murderer."

Mr. Winkley nodded briefly and they made their way along the thick stone passages to an end cell where the warder on duty rose from his uncomfortable wooden seat on their approach. He glanced through the grille, then unlocked the iron door and preceded them into the cell.

The imprisoned man got up heavily from his narrow plank with a resigned air.

"Well, Sir Humphrey, we've come to ask you a few more questions," began Palk.

"I've nothing to add to what I've already told you, Inspector," said Sir Humphrey. "I'm not guilty of murder and I know you can't prove that I am." He barely glanced at Palk, and again the Inspector had the impression that the man was not unused to police questionings.

Palk looked across at Mr. Winkley with an expression which said "I told you so," which faded as he saw a slow smile spreading over the other's face. Mr. Winkley obviously recognized the prisoner.

"Well, well, well!" he exclaimed heartily, moving forward towards Sir Humphrey. "If it isn't an old friend! The Lancashire police will be pleased to see you, my lad."

"You know him, then?" asked Palk, looking tremendously pleased.

"Oh yes, I know him all right," replied Mr. Winkley.

Sir Humphrey sprang to his feet, looking the picture of injured anger and indignation.

"What's the idea, Inspector?" he shouted. "I've never seen this man before in my life and he knows it. If you're trying to pin anything on to me with your American third-degree methods, I'll have you made a public example to every police inspector in the force. I know something about the laws of this country…"

"You do, Harry," agreed Mr. Winkley. "If you didn't, we'd have had you in gaol long before this. I've often thought that you must have been a law student before you took up your present line of work."

"Look here!" protested Sir Humphrey. "This man –"

"It's not a bit of use pretending, if Mr. Winkley recognizes you," put in Palk. "You might just as well save your breath to answer all the questions I'm going to put to you."

"But I tell you that this man has never seen me before," insisted Sir Humphrey. "Have you?" He turned to Mr. Winkley.

"He's quite right," said Mr. Winkley. "I never have seen him before."

"You see," said Sir Humphrey triumphantly. "It's no use trying these traps on me." But his gaze dropped before the quizzical expression in Mr. Winkley's mild blue eyes.

"No, I've never seen you before," repeated Mr. Winkley, "but what I don't know about you isn't worth knowing. I've a neat folder in my room at the Yard with lots of pretty pictures of you, to say nothing of 'ten little finger-prints, ten little toes,' as the song puts it. You made a mistake on that Lancashire job, Harry. Your psychology wasn't as good as usual, or perhaps the girl wasn't used to it. Anyway, you put a bit too much screw on one of those Lancashire lasses, a Mrs. George Entwistle from Blackborough Hydro she was, if I remember."

The prisoner sat down suddenly and buried his face in his hands.

"He's wanted, then, is he?" asked Palk.

"Yes, he's wanted right enough," replied Mr. Winkley, "but not for murder. He's known at the Yard as Harry the Punter, and obtaining money under false pretences is his particular crime. You must have seen paragraphs about him in Truth: this kind of thing, you know:

The number of share-pushers is still on the increase, and even comparatively astute people can be, and often are, taken in by their plausible methods of attack. Small trial investments, for instance, will often yield handsome dividends at first, but when, tempted by the prospect of vastly increased incomes, the unfortunate victims are gulled into risking more and more of their capital, something seems to go wrong with the companies in which their savings are invested, and both incomes and capital vanish overnight. Some people probably still have painful recollections of the exploits of our old friend Henry Topham, or Harry the Punter, who operated in these islands some five years ago. This ingenious sharepusher, masquerading as Sir Humphrey Chervil, Baronet, worked the residential hotels of Ireland with marked success and seemed to have singularly little difficulty in persuading the residents, particularly retired members of the professional classes, to entrust their investments to his tender care.

"Oh, they're very down on Harry in *Truth*."

"Then he isn't really Sir Humphrey Chervil?"

Mr. Winkley laughed.

"Not he," he said. "I might have known who he was when I first heard the name. I told you it sounded familiar. He was Sir Hilary Chives when I last heard of him. He'll be a whole blinking salad before he's finished!"

"That's an offence to begin with," said Palk. "Why does he always invent a title for himself? He must know he's running the risk of being charged under 'false pretences.' I should have found it out for myself if I hadn't been so busy on the other murder."

"Because most people in this world are snobs," explained Mr. Winkley, "and he trades on snobbery. He knows that he's safe enough. This is a stroke of bad luck for him which might never happen in a life-time. Of course, he wouldn't exist amongst the aristocracy for a day, because the aristocracy themselves are snobs and wouldn't hesitate to look him up in Debrett. But the middle-class people are good game. The very thought of rubbing shoulders with a title is good enough for most of them. I believe they would hardly care if the title were a genuine one or not, so long as they remained in ignorance. They'd rather take it at its face value."

"Yes," nodded Palk. "I suppose that a title acts as a passport among such people."

"That's it," replied Mr. Winkley. "All Harry has to do is to put up at a hotel which caters for retired people with private

incomes – Army and Navy and the clergy are all fair game –
who are invariably dissatisfied with the steady interest they get
on their capital. He gives them the impression that he is made
of money, and sooner or later they approach him to ask his
advice on investments."

"I remember Colonel Simcox saying that he could never get
this fellow to take any interest in gilt-edged stock because he
always boasted that he made his money earn money, but I
thought nothing of it at the time," said Palk. "I suppose he'd
advise them to sell out some of their gilt-edged securities and
put the money into some company whose name he'd give them
in strict confidence."

Mr. Winkley nodded.

"Yes," he agreed, "and, of course, they'd get about ten
percent interest plus a bonus at the end of the first quarter,
and would be so pleased that they'd sell out more capital and
invest it in his company, and wait for the second quarter's
cheque."

"And then wake up," said Palk.

"And then wake up," repeated Mr. Winkley.

Palk snorted.

"'Lord, what fools these mortals be!'" he exclaimed. "How
long has he been at this game?"

"Oh, for years. I've known of him myself ever since I started
at the Yard after the War."

"And you say he's never been convicted yet? It sounds
incredible."

Mr. Winkley pushed back the lock of hair which, at the
Hydro, he wore brushed down over his forehead, and at once
looked ten years younger.

"We've never been able to get any evidence before," he
explained, "and it was pretty tough work getting it from the
Entwistle woman, though she is frae Lancasheer and powerful
fond o' t' brass. Have you ever tried to make a grown man or
woman admit that he or she is a fool? Well, that's what it
amounts to if people who have been stung by sharepushers

give us the evidence we'd require to convict them. They kid themselves that they're such good business men and women, and make a bit of a splash on their first bonus so that their neighbours will envy them, and when they realize that they have been badly bitten, they'll do anything except admit the truth, like that drunken woman of yours."

"Of mine!" exclaimed Palk. "I like that! It's a good thing I'm not married."

Winkley laughed.

"Well," he said, "I don't suppose you've got a case against Harry the Punter if he was only at the Hydro for three months. He's a slow worker, and doesn't get to the share-pushing stage till he's been at a place he's working, for longer than that. In any case, I can't see Admiral Urwin or Mrs. Dawson admitting that they are damn' fools."

"But I can't let him go. He's in for murder," protested Palk.

"He didn't do it. He's a share-pusher, not a murderer. He's in the game for money."

"You're forgetting the motive for the murder, aren't you? The jewels. They would have been as good as money to him."

"No," said Mr. Winkley decisively. "The leopard doesn't change his spots, nor the Ethiopian, poor devil, his skin, though I bet he wished he could when the Italians started dropping bombs on him. Harry would twist money out of the few crowned heads left in Europe if he had the chance, but he hasn't the guts to commit murder. Have him brought along to your room and get a stenographer. He'll talk now, you'll find."

CHAPTER XXXVI

Inspector Falk gave orders for Harry the Punter to be brought up to his room, and, not yet so sure as Mr. Winkley that his prisoner was incapable of murder, he had a double guard placed outside the door, and two police constables to stand on either side of him. When the pseudo-baronet was brought in,

Palk motioned him towards the straight hard chair facing the large office desk, and began turning over the official records of his previous interviews with the man.

"You'd better handle him, sir," he said. "You know him better than I do."

Mr. Winkley addressed the badly shaken prisoner as if he were indeed an old friend.

"Now then, Harry," he said, "you've got yourself into a nice fix. If you tell the truth, I'll do all I can to help you in the charge which the Blackborough police will bring against you. If you don't, you'll go up on trial for murder. Which is it going to be?"

The prisoner looked up with something like relief in his dark eyes.

"I'll tell you the truth," he said earnestly enough, "but I don't admit that the Blackborough police have anything against me, mind. I had nothing to do with Tony's murder."

"Tony?" exclaimed Palk. "Is he confessing to another murder? He'd better be cautioned."

But Mr. Winkley remarked quietly:

"You mean the girl, Miss Blake?"

"Yes," replied Harry the Punter. "Her real name was Antonia, but what other name she ever had, if any, I don't know because I never asked."

Mr. Winkley nodded as if quite satisfied.

"She was your partner, I suppose."

"His partner?' shouted Palk.

"Yes, Harry always works with a girl friend," Mr. Winkley explained again, "or 'operates with a young and charming accomplice' as *Truth* would put it. A pretty woman is invaluable in his kind of job. She can find out a great deal about the financial possibilities of men like Colonel Simcox, in a very short time. She arrived at Presteignton Hydro first to spy out the land, and she must have thought that it had possibilities, or Harry would never have followed her."

"By Jove!" exclaimed the Inspector. "She told Colonel Simcox that she spent her life going from one Hydro to another, and aroused his sympathy because he thought she was in ill health and had to have constant treatment. I thought it rather strange, because Nurse Hawkins told me she never gave treatment of any kind to Miss Blake, but I wasn't sure whether the nurse was telling me the truth or not. Then you did know Miss Blake before you came to the Hydro?" he asked Harry.

"Of course I did," he replied. "I shouldn't have come otherwise. He" – indicating Mr. Winkley – "has told you that I never work alone."

"But why didn't you say so before?"

Harry sniffed.

"A lot of good that would have done, wouldn't it?" he said. "You would only have stuck another motive on me – jealousy, or something. Fancy me being guilty of a *crime passionel*." He laughed at the absurdity of the idea, and went on, "I knew that I'd nothing to do with Tony's murder, and was always expecting you to find a clue to the murderer one day. I knew that I should be set free then, and I meant to go back to the Hydro for another few months to clean up." He glanced at Mr. Winkley. "You promised to help me. You won't hold this against me, will you?" he asked.

Palk grunted in disgust, but Mr. Winkley replied:

"I always keep my promises." He consulted the papers which the Inspector had slipped in front of him and referred to them before continuing his questions. "To go back to the murder of Miss Blake," he said. "At what time did you leave the drawing-room after the concert?"

"About one o'clock," replied Harry the Punter without any hesitation.

"You said that Miss Blake went straight out of the drawing-room and that you went through the writing-room on your way upstairs. Is this true?"

"No. We both went straight upstairs together through the drawing-room door."

"You went upstairs and into Miss Blake's bedroom?"

"Yes."

"How long did you stay there with her?"

"Not more than twenty minutes or half an hour."

"Why did you go inside her room?"

"For no special reason. We were just talking about – er – business, and I naturally walked in with her to finish the conversation."

Palk snorted, and Mr. Winkley looked round at him with a smile.

"It's quite all right, Inspector," he said. "I believe him. You must remember that it was purely a business arrangement between them. You might not think it, but Harry's a respectable married man with a decent wife who's far too good for him. He's really fond of her, and she hasn't an idea what his real business is. She thinks he's a commercial traveller – God help her! – and in a way, I suppose his way of earning a livelihood might pass as that. There wouldn't be any love-making between Harry and the girl, if that's what you're thinking."

"If he's married to a good woman, why doesn't he get a decent job and run straight?" asked Palk sententiously.

Mr. Winkley smiled again.

Just habit, Inspector, just habit," he said indulgently.

It won't be just habit when he goes up for a stretch for this Lancashire business, will it?" persisted Palk. "How will he prevent his wife knowing what he is then?"

"You needn't worry, Inspector," replied Mr. Winkley, "she won't know. You'll be 'sent abroad on a special job,' won't you, Harry?"

Harry nodded.

"I should make it America then," suggested Palk. "It'll be a long trip."

"Well," said Mr. Winkley, returning to his questioning, "when you came out of the bedroom, did you see anyone along the corridor, or standing just inside one of the rooms you passed?"

"No. I looked pretty carefully, too, because I knew what they were in the Hydro for gossip, and it didn't suit me to make them talk too much about us. That's why I hadn't taken much notice of Tony at first, but of course we had plans to make after three months, and I wanted to get some information from her about the men; I got it myself from the old ladies."

"What did you do after you left Miss Blake?"

"I went straight to bed, just as I told the Inspector."

"And did you see her again?"

"No. That's God's truth!"

Mr. Winkley paused for a moment, then said:

"Why did she give you the jewelry that night? Did you usually keep it for her?"

"No. She didn't give it to me at all. The maid told me about Tony's murder when she brought my cup of tea in the morning. As soon as she had gone out of my room, I slipped along to Tony's bedroom and got the jewel-case. The jewels were part of my stock-in-trade, and I wasn't going to lose them if I could help it. I'd paid for them, hadn't I? A pretty penny they cost me, too."

"Do you mean to tell me," said Palk, leaning forward in his chair, "that you went into her bedroom while the police were in the house, and stole the jewels?"

The prisoner closed his eyes for a second, in weariness.

"Yes. You were all downstairs. I had to risk it. And I don't call it stealing to take something which belongs to me."

"And no one saw you?"

"They would hardly have kept quiet about it if they had, would they?" returned Harry the Punter, and Palk had to admit that, in his experience, they would not.

"You swear that you didn't murder Miss Blake, Harry?" asked Mr. Winkley.

Harry ran exasperated fingers through hair, which, lacking brilliantine, was no longer shining like that of a painted wooden doll.

"I swear it. I'm telling you the truth."

"You didn't quarrel with her?" put in Inspector Palk.

"No. Even if I had quarrelled with her, why should I have murdered her? I'd just have paid her off and hired someone else to do her work. She was a good pal, but there are plenty more like her who would be only too glad to work for me."

"But if she threatened to tell the truth about you in the Hydro?"

Harry shrugged his shoulders.

"Who would have believed her?" he asked lightly. "No one had anything on me. As Mr. Winkley says, I work slowly. Even if they had cut up rough I should just have paid my bill and left. I never yet met a sucker who squealed out to tell folks what kind of a fool he'd been."

Palk was convinced by this argument.

"Not till you met Mrs. Entwistle," he gloated. "Do you know who murdered Miss Blake?"

"Good God, no! Do you think I'd have kept quiet if I had? Of course, the women in the Hydro didn't like her clothes and lipstick, but you'd want a stronger motive than that for murder, wouldn't you?"

"Could any of the people in the Hydro have known her before, and had some old grudge to pay?" asked Palk.

The prisoner shook his head.

"No. She'd have told me. It's the first thing she'd look for in a new hotel. That's partly why we never arrived together."

"Can you think of anything, however trifling, which might help us?" asked Mr. Winkley.

"No," he said emphatically. "I've been trying to think since I've been locked up here, and I can't see any sense in it."

"That'll be all for the present, Harry," said Mr. Winkley, rising, "and you might be glad to know that the Blackborough police haven't got a case against you, in my opinion."

Harry jumped to his feet.

"But... Mrs. Entwistle...?"

"Another sucker," replied Mr. Winkley. "So long."

Palk whistled softly.

"My God," exclaimed Harry the Punter, "you've got a nerve!"

"You've nothing to squeal about, my lad," remarked the Inspector. "You can think yourself lucky not to be standing your trial for murder."

"But can't I go, then?" asked the late Sir Humphrey. "You promised you wouldn't use what I've just told you against me. I wouldn't leave Presteignton."

"You must go back for a bit," said Mr. Winkley. "There's a killer at large, and we don't want to complicate matters by having you around."

CHAPTER XXXVII

"Well, what do you think about it now?" asked Palk, as a burly constable brought in thick buttered toast and strong tea on a tray, after Harry the Punter had returned to his cell.

"He's innocent," said Mr. Winkley, "and he's told the truth."

"But if he didn't murder Miss Blake, who did?"

Mr. Winkley waved his hands in the air like a stage money lender.

"It might be anyone. We must go through the evidence again and see if we can find some kind of clue, or we shall have another murder on our hands before we know where we are."

Palk thought for a minute.

"If Sir Humphrey's innocent – I shall never remember to call him by any other name – and Matthews is guilty of Miss Marston's death, perhaps he killed Miss Blake as well," he suggested.

Mr. Winkley added another lump of sugar to his cup.

"Perhaps," he admitted, "but it isn't very satisfactory. He's connected to Miss Marston by gossip, but not to Miss Blake nor to Bobby. Even if we could attach a motive to him for Miss Blake's murder, we know he wasn't responsible for Bobby's, that is, if that man of yours who shadowed him is to be believed."

"He's one of my best men," said Palk.

"Well, then..."

The Inspector fidgeted a little.

"I've been wondering whether I was a bit too hasty in bringing Matthews here," he said. "I don't mind confessing that I was rattled at the time. I've never seen a kid murdered before, and well... I'm fond of kids. I've nothing on Matthews at all except circumstantial evidence; the fact that he had been seen about in the car a lot with the Marston girl, and Cox's evidence that he saw him in the treatment-rooms asking for her..."

"Don't worry," Mr. Winkley reassured him. "There are times when it's good to be a bit hasty, and this might be one of them. Has he made a statement yet?"

Palk sighed.

"No. Jago can't get a word out of him. I never knew a dumber pair than he and Sir – er – Harry."

"Let's assume that he isn't guilty, for a moment," suggested Mr. Winkley. "I don't think that he is, myself."

Palk could hardly have looked more surprised if Mr. Winkley had produced a rattlesnake from his mouth.

"That's all very fine," he said, "but when I say I was hasty in detaining him, I don't mean that I think there's any doubt of his guilt, but just that I haven't enough evidence for a conviction. If he isn't guilty, why won't he talk?"

"I think I might guess," was the reply. "I'd rather like to ask him a few questions."

The Inspector jabbed at the bell.

Matthews was brought into the room between two policemen, and Palk was struck by the change which had taken place in the man's appearance since his first interview with him immediately after Winnie Marston's murder. Then, he had looked smart and immaculately turned out. Now, he looked haggard and unkempt, as if he had slept in his chocolate-coloured uniform for several days. He twisted the gold ring on his little finger and looked at the Inspector with wild eyes. He did not appear to notice Mr. Winkley.

"Sit down," said Palk. "I want to ask you a few more questions."

Matthews sat down.

"I've nothing to tell you," he said sullenly.

Mr. Winkley leaned forward.

"Don't you want us to find your wife's murderer?" he asked in his clear, quiet voice.

Matthews sprang to his feet, as the previous prisoner had done not long before.

"My...? How do you know?" He tried to recapture the sullen look. "What do you mean? I don't know what you mean," he said.

Mr. Winkley smiled wisely.

"Oh yes, you do," he said, as though Matthews were a naughty child and he were an indulgent father. "You've forgotten that you have to sign a register to get married. 'Albert Matthews, chauffeur, to Winifred Angela Marston, spinster.' Wasn't that how it went? You must have realized that the police would find out all about it sooner or later. You'll save our time and your neck by talking now, Matthews. Now then, Winnie Marston was your wife, wasn't she?"

"You seem to know," said Matthews, clenching his hands together till the knuckles were dead white.

After Palk's first quickly muffled exclamation of astonishment, the room was quiet. Mr. Winkley did not speak. He stared at Matthews with steady eyes.

"Damn you!" shouted Matthews. "You think I killed her! I didn't, I tell you, I didn't!"

He sat down suddenly in the chair and buried his face in his hands, drawing in his breath in great, sobbing gulps.

"We don't think you killed her," said Mr. Winkley calmly, putting up his hand to check Palk's protest at being included in this belief.

Matthews dropped his hands and looked up through bloodshot eyes.

"You'll try to pin it on to me, though," he said bitterly. "You don't know who did it, and you don't care as long as you can pin it on someone."

"Don't talk rot," put in Palk, no longer able to restrain himself from speech. "If you're really married to Miss Marston you've got no motive. The motive would be if you'd got her into trouble and couldn't marry her."

Matthews looked quite capable of murder for a moment – if the victim were Palk.

"Don't talk like that about her," he shouted. "Miss Marston wasn't that kind of girl. She wouldn't go away with me before we were married, though I'd never have let her down."

"You're sure you haven't got a wife already?" persisted Palk.

"I haven't, damn you!" yelled the chauffeur, and would have hurled himself at the Inspector if the two constables had not held him down on his chair.

"You're making it very difficult for us, you know," said Mr. Winkley in soothing tones which sounded more like those of a patient and often-tried family lawyer. It seemed to the Inspector that he had even begun to blink again... he wasn't at all sure that he liked this play-acting. "Very difficult. We really don't wish to build up a false case against you, but you are almost forcing us to do so because you won't give us the help we need to track down the real murderer. Inspector Palk has no desire whatever to insult the memory of your dead wife. He is merely trying to tell you what a wrong impression you are giving us by concealing the truth."

His voice had the required sedative effect. Matthews took out a handkerchief which, to judge by its colour, served equally as a spare car duster, and wiped the perspiration from his hands and upper lip.

"I'll tell you all I know," he said at length. "I might as well, now that you've found out so much. I'll do all I can to help you hang the dirty swine that killed Miss Marston. She was a nice girl."

Mr. Winkley had a momentary flash of insight into the kind of life Winnie Marston might have led with a husband who called her "Miss," and thought of her as "a nice girl."

"You admit, then, that you were married to Miss Marston?"

"Yes. We got married at the Excester Registry Office the day before she was killed. I was supposed to be giving her a driving-lesson, so that anyone might have known we were in the town, without knowing why. It's a good big town, and no one was likely to see us really."

"Did you spend the night together?" asked Palk.

"Why, you... you..." stuttered Matthews. "Didn't I say she was a nice girl?"

"Surely that's a very natural thing to do after you're married," came Mr. Winkley's soothing voice. "Please answer the Inspector's question."

"I'm... sorry. No, we didn't."

"Didn't you mean to live together afterwards?"

"Yes. We were going away together the next day in the car, but she... she was murdered."

"I see," nodded Mr. Winkley. "But was there any reason why you were going to wait until the next day? Surely the simplest way would have been to go straight away from the registry office to wherever you intended to go eventually."

Matthews looked up wearily.

"That's what I thought too," he explained, "but Miss Marston said the other was a better idea because we could get further away before they found that we'd gone. She was so sure about it that I let her have her own way."

Millie's estimation of her sister's character rang in Palk's ears. "You don't know Winnie. She was one of the clinging sort, and if she wanted a thing badly enough she'd get it, whatever anyone else said."

"Where did you intend to go to if Miss Marston hadn't been murdered?" asked Mr. Winkley.

A slight smile drifted over Matthews' face.

"As far as we could get before the boss found we'd pinched his car," he said. "And now perhaps you'll see why I didn't want to talk. The boss has got a devil of a temper, as I dare say you already know, and if he knew I ever meant to clear off with his daughter and his car, there'd be hell to pay. I didn't mind risking anything if I had her with me, but when that fell through, I thought I might as well keep my job. After all, I've got to live, haven't I? And good jobs don't grow on every gooseberry bush these days."

Palk snorted.

"If you'd thought more about keeping your neck," he said, "you'd have been more helpful to us. Now let's get down to the truth about the morning when Miss Marston was murdered. Cox said he saw you coming out of the ladies' treatment-rooms. What were you doing in there?"

"I never went right in," said Matthews. "I knocked on the door and no one answered, so I just turned the knob and stepped inside."

"You had no business to be anywhere near those rooms. What did you go for?"

"I wanted to see Miss Marston. We had arranged to go away at half past eleven. I waited a quarter of an hour, then went to look for her."

"Because she was fifteen minutes late?" queried Palk. "Isn't that rather far-fetched? I never yet met a woman who was punctual for an appointment, even if she was running away from home."

"Miss Marston was always punctual," said Matthews, "and, you see, the boss had sent word that he wanted the car at half past twelve, so I didn't know what to do. I thought that perhaps we should have to put off going away till the next day. I never meant to go inside the baths and find her. I thought I could send a message she'd understand, by the nurse."

"What time did you get to the baths?"

"About ten past twelve. I didn't go straight there because for a time I'd forgotten that she had said she would be there."

"Did you see or hear anyone inside there?"

"I didn't see anyone, but I heard Miss Marston call out, 'Hello, what are you doing here?' and I thought at first that she could see me from behind a curtain, though I couldn't see her. I was just going to reply when I heard a voice from the same place, and guessed that she was talking to someone else."

"Did you hear any of the conversation?"

"No. Miss Marston had called out a bit loud, or I shouldn't have heard her to begin with. After that, I couldn't hear any more words, only the two voices."

Mr. Winkley leaned eagerly forward.

"You realize, of course, Matthews, that it was almost certainly the murderer whom you heard talking to Miss Marston. Did you recognize the voice at all?" he said.

"No," replied Matthews after a pause. "I didn't recognize it, but I thought at the time that it must be Nurse Hawkins."

"But if you thought that," said Palk, "why didn't you wait and give her the message you'd intended to send to Miss Marston?"

"Because I heard footsteps in the corridor and knew I'd get into a row if the boss or the doctor caught me there, so I slipped across to the men's department and pretended to look for Ted Cox, though I didn't expect to see him there in the morning."

"What happened then?"

"Well, Ted did happen to be there, and he cursed me like blazes when he knew I'd been looking for Miss Marston. Then I went back to the garage, and waited a bit longer. When she didn't turn up, I had to take the car round to pick up the boss and drive him out."

"When did you first hear of the murder?"

"Ted Cox was waiting for me in the garage when I got back. He told me that if you knew I'd actually opened the door of the ladies' baths, I should be for it. He said he'd told you that I'd asked him if Miss Marston was in the baths, and made me promise that I'd stick to the same story, but I thought it would be safer to say nothing at all."

"Well," said Palk, "if this story about you and Miss Marston getting married is true, I suppose you can prove it. You've got the marriage certificate hidden away somewhere, I suppose."

Matthews hesitated for a moment, then said:

"I burned it."

"Burned it?" ejaculated Palk in amazement. "But it was your proof..."

"I didn't want to prove it," said Matthews wearily. "I didn't want you to find out that we were married, and I knew as soon as Ted Cox told me about the murder that you'd suspect me and search my room, so I burned it. I knew I could always get a copy if I wanted it."

Palk was unconvinced.

"We didn't find a wedding-ring," he said. "I suppose you burned that too."

"She had one all right," said Matthews, tugging at the plain gold band which fitted so tightly on the little finger of his right hand. "Here it is. It was her idea that I should wear it for her. She said no one would ever find it then. You see, she was afraid of the boss. She said he'd kill her if he ever found out." He succeeded in pulling the thin, worn circlet from his rough finger, and placed it on the desk between Palk and Mr. Winkley. "It's my mother's wedding-ring," he explained. "I wanted to buy her another one, but she wouldn't let me. She said that what was good enough for my mother was good enough for her. She was..."

...A *nice* girl, and I could never understand,
Why did she fall for the leader of the band,

whistled Palk under his breath.

CHAPTER XXXVIII

Inspector Palk pushed his chair back and, getting up, walked across to the window and stood looking down at the market square of Newton St. Mary, jingling the keys and loose change in his trouser pockets.

"Miss Marston and the car!" he said. "And I shouldn't wonder if the car meant more to him than the girl. I wonder how long it would have taken her to get tired of life with him?" He turned to face Mr. Winkley. "I ought to have found out about their marriage," he went on disconsolately, "though I still don't see what clue I missed, with no ring or certificate in existence."

"You didn't miss anything," replied Mr. Winkley. "It was merely a lucky guess. It seemed the only possible explanation for Matthews' silence, assuming, as I did, that he was not guilty of murder. The only thing he had to lose was his job, and it seemed likely, as he wouldn't talk, that he was afraid of losing it through some connection with Winnie Marston. I don't entirely ignore the scandal which goes on in the Hydro, because I find that scandal is usually woven round a nucleus of truth, however small. The other possibility, that he had already raped her, was knocked on the head by the doctor's examination; her sister, who really knew her far better than anyone else, thought that she had decided to run away with Matthews –"

"And she was a nice girl –" grinned Palk.

"So it seemed likely that they were already married. It was just luck."

"That's what you say," returned Palk, "but the fact remains that I ought to have thought all that out for myself. I've tripped up pretty badly on this case. It's what the journalists would call My Big Chance, and I'm Making a Hash of It."

"Nonsense!" retorted Mr. Winkley. "All your work is sound. You've had the job of gathering all the material together and building up the foundations; it's dead easy for someone like myself to come along and build up the top storey."

But Palk refused to be comforted.

"That depends on what material you're using," he said. "If you're building a card castle, it's the top storey that takes the most putting on."

Mr. Winkley leaned back in his chair and crossed his legs.

"I spend all my time at the Yard putting jigsaw puzzles together," he said.

Palk swung round suddenly.

"Good lord! You don't mean to tell me that you're like old Admiral Urwin and his crossword puzzles, do you?"

Mr. Winkley smiled.

"I thought that would startle you," he said. "No. I admit they're not real jigsaws, but it's a similar kind of practice. If any piece of information comes into the Yard which no one can make head or tail of, it's dumped into my department, and I have the task of sorting it out and making sense of it. It's all stuff which is pretty badly involved, or it doesn't qualify for my department at all, and it means keeping a few thousands of tiny, ill-assorted facts in my mind for years, sometimes. A kind of continuity-girl stunt, if you can understand. An obscure reference to cats in 1919 might remain unintelligible until 1939, when an equally obscure reference to mice might turn it into sense. I'm all the time chiselling down pieces of information into the queerest shapes and then trying to fit them into each other. Plain routine never gets the right results in these cases, and mine is the only department, I suppose, where logic fails, and a wild guess more often hits on the truth."

"All right," said Palk, grinning, "I'll play." He sat down again in his chair and fidgeted with his notes. "We'll say that Matthews is innocent. I've had the marriage at Excester Registry Office verified by 'phone, and it's O.K. We haven't had time to find out whether it's bigamous or not yet, but we'll assume that it isn't, and that Matthews is now telling us the truth. Where does that get us?"

Mr. Winkley took out his cigarettes and offered them to Palk.

"It gets us to a point where we can eliminate Dr. Williams, Mr. Marston, Colonel Simcox, and Admiral Urwin," replied Mr. Winkley, striking a match and lighting Palk's cigarette and his own. "There's no doubt in my mind that Matthews stepped inside the door of the ladies' treatment-rooms at the very moment when Winnie Marston caught sight of the murderer. He says that he thought at the time that it was Nurse Hawkins who spoke, and no man in his senses could mistake her voice for a man's."

"The doctor's voice isn't very deep," said Palk, "and Matthews couldn't hear very clearly. Of course, I know that the doctor is your friend, but..." He sounded embarrassed.

"Don't worry about that, Inspector," replied Mr. Winkley. "I quite realize that the doctor is a suspect, and so does he; but I think that the very nature of Winnie's words lets him out. She might have called out, 'What are you doing here?' to the Colonel or the Admiral, but she certainly wouldn't have said it to the doctor, even if she hadn't expected to see him at that moment. She was his patient, and it was part of his job to visit the treatment-rooms at some time during the treatment. He'd be a rotten doctor if he didn't. Do you agree?"

Palk nodded, and they were both silent for a minute while their thoughts seemed to wreathe upwards with the erratic blue spirals from their cigarettes.

"If the three murders are the work of one hand," the Inspector remarked at last, "I strongly suspect Nurse Hawkins. She has the necessary training to know what kind of blow to strike to effect instantaneous death; she had as much opportunity for murder as anyone in the Hydro in the first and third crimes, and more than most in the second; there was a knitting-needle among the instruments in the men's baths;

Matthews thought it was her voice he heard, and Winnie Marston's remarks might have expressed surprise because the nurse had returned so soon after saying she would be away for half an hour."

Mr. Winkley nodded.

"I see your point, Inspector," he said, "but in my opinion you're stretching the facts a little, and that always leads to a distorted conclusion. Collect your facts and make a mighty guess if you like, but never stretch them in order to maintain a logical sequence of reasoning. You say that Nurse Hawkins had as much opportunity as anyone to commit the murders, but you forget that she has an alibi for that very important half-hour during which Winnie Marston was killed. I'm by no means of the opinion of Mr. Weller Senior that there's "nothing like a alleybi'; but the fact remains that Lady Warme cannot be shaken on her certainty that the nurse was with her when she said she was. I don't think that Lady Warme is sufficiently fond of Nurse Hawkins to perjure herself on her behalf; indeed, she rather gave me the impression that she wished the nurse hadn't got an alibi. I don't place any significance on Matthews' saying that he thought he heard the nurse's voice. It was natural for him to assume that it was hers because he was expecting to hear it.

"Again, the argument which applies to the doctor, applies equally to the nurse. Winnie Marston wouldn't have been surprised to see the nurse return to the massage-room, even if she had not been expecting her. All the liniments and bandages and towels are kept in the cupboards there, as you have seen. Miss Marston might have said something like, 'Hello, back again?' but she certainly wouldn't have said, 'What are you doing here?' not even rhetorically. If only we could find the motive!"

Palk jumped up and began to pace restlessly up and down the floor.

"Motive! Motive!" he exclaimed. "What possible motive can there be for murdering a child? The only explanation is that someone at the Hydro is a raving lunatic, and we're trying to find out who it is by reasoning. Why, we're beaten at the starting-post!"

He checked himself as Sergeant Jago came into the room, after an apologetic knock.

"I came to report, sir," he said. "I'm just back from the Hydro."

"Find anything?"

The sergeant pursed his lips and shook his head.

"Not a sign of anything, sir. I've had all the men searching the hotel and grounds all day."

Palk turned, with a hopeless gesture, to which Mr. Winkley replied with a nod of encouragement.

"Come and sit down, Sergeant," he said. "If two heads are better than one, three heads should be better than two." He proceeded to give the sergeant a brief outline of the day's work and the conclusions to which they had come about the two prisoners. "We're at a dead end," he continued, "and only a brilliant guess can help us. Let's see what you can do in that line. If you had to pin the three murders on to one of the women in the Hydro, whom would you choose?"

Sergeant Jago looked carefully at Mr. Winkley to see whether he was serious, decided that he wasn't, and started to chuckle.

"Blow me if I wouldn't put it on to Miss Brendon," he said. "That nurse-companion of hers, Rogers, probably pushed her along in the bath-chair, guided her hand to the victim's skull, and carried her upstairs to her room again!"

Even Palk could not help smiling at this idea.

"I'm afraid I haven't much hope of that," he said. "But it would certainly relieve the monotony for the old lady. It must be pretty awful for her to be almost blind and lying upstairs all day, knowing that there are all these murders about the place. I don't know that I ever thought about it before."

"Bless your soul, she doesn't mind," replied Jago. "That nurse of hers guards her like a trooper."

"You seem to have managed to get on the right side of her," remarked the Inspector. "When I went to interview her, I thought her a cantankerous old – er – lady."

Jago grinned in delight.

"Oh, I got to know her when we were searching her room," he said. "You never saw anything like the amount of stuff she keeps in it. She must have been collecting it ever since she was a child, and that wasn't yesterday, by a long chalk. The companion followed me about the room all the time, and told the old lady everything which I picked up, and Miss Brendon gave me its life history. We got on very well together. She told me that she used to be considered quite a lad when she was a girl because she used to wear bloomers when she went out cycling."

"Oh, kiss me, Sergeant!" exclaimed the Inspector, and Jago grinned again.

"What on earth does she do all day?" asked Mr. Winkley.

"Tats," said the sergeant.

"What?" his superiors shouted together.

"Tats," repeated Jago. "Yes. It's a proper word. Tats. Makes lace on a cushion covered with bobbins. They make a noise like false teeth clicking together."

"Good lord! I haven't seen one of those since I was a boy," said Mr. Winkley. "I never noticed it when I was having tea in her room."

"You wouldn't, sir," replied Sergeant Jago, "not unless she was using it, and I suppose she wanted to talk while you were there. She'd feel quite emancipated again to entertain a gentleman in her bedroom. Talk! She never stops. It's my belief that all the scandal of the Hydro starts in her bed-room."

Palk regarded the sergeant with a tolerant air, but Mr. Winkley leaned forward a little, as if he found the sergeant's remarks of greater import.

"That's very interesting, Sergeant," he said.

Sergeant Jago, not used to praise, tossed his head from one side to the other as if to counteract any tendency it might develop of becoming swollen.

"Well, that's just my idea, sir," he said. "You'd think that these murders would have put an end to the scandal for a bit, wouldn't you? But they haven't, though. They're all at it again now."

"Oh!" said Mr. Winkley. "Who are the victims this time?"

"Dr. Williams and that quiet mouse of a secretary, Miss Lewis," replied Sergeant Jago, "and as for being victims, sir, all I can say is that all the ones who've been murdered so far were young and better-looking than the others, so perhaps Miss Lewis *will* be the next one!"

To their amazement, Mr. Winkley suddenly jerked up his arm and pointed a forefinger at a spot between the sergeant's eyes.

"That's it!" he cried. "I'm beginning to see the truth now. We should have seen it before if we hadn't got each case tucked away in a compartment of its own. It's the first murder which should have given us the clue. We've been concentrating on the wrong ones. Motive? There's plenty of motive, and it's still there, but we've no evidence, and we shall never be able to prove it unless –" He got up abruptly, and, picking up his overcoat from a chair in the corner, began to struggle into it. "I'm going to make an experiment," he said, turning to Palk. "I'm going back to the Hydro now. You and Jago are to follow me there. I shall be in the doctor's rooms. Come in by his private door, and mind no one sees you."

He picked up his hat and made for the door.

"But – what arrangements...?" asked Palk. "Don't you want any men?"

"No. Just you and the sergeant. I'm not going to make an arrest. I'm only going to arrange an experiment. So long!"

And before the Inspector could protest, he had crammed his hat on his head and had swung out of the room, leaving Sergeant Jago gaping in utter bewilderment.

CHAPTER XXXIX

The following evening at eight minutes past ten, Ada Rogers tiptoed into Miss Brendon's room to make sure that her mistress was asleep, closed the door softly, and went to pay her nightly visit to Mrs. Dukes, the housekeeper. The hour rarely varied by so much as two minutes, for a cup of tea and a gossip in the housekeeper's sitting-room was Rogers' only recreation in the Hydro. Regarding herself as superior to the housemaids, and herself regarded as an inferior by Nurse Hawkins and the doctor's secretary, Rogers had a considerably limited participation in the social amenities enjoyed by the rest of the staff. The housekeeper was the one being in the Hydro by whom she was accepted as a friend, and with whom she could relax.

She found Mrs. Dukes sitting in a worn arm-chair, with an old blade from a safety razor in her hand, and one bare foot resting on a hassock.

"Come in quick, Ada, and shut the door," she said. "I'm sorry, I'm sure, that you've found me like this, but I just couldn't bear my foot any longer. I know you don't mind."

"You poor thing," sympathized Rogers. "You do suffer something cruel with your corns. It's a shame that you have to stand on your poor feet the way you do all day."

"Well, I have had rather a day of it today, I don't mind telling you. Just when I thought I'd finished, the doctor sent for me and told me to have Miss Blake's bedroom that was, cleaned out so that Miss Lewis can sleep there. It's been under lock and key since the police arrested Sir Humphrey, who was always so nice to us, and I'm sure I don't believe he ever murdered the girl though they do say seeing's believing; so you can just imagine the state it was in and me with my feet aching like this. I should have thought to-morrow would be time enough to turn it out, but no, he must have it ready tonight. So I said to him, 'Well, Doctor, if Miss Lewis doesn't mind, I'm sure I don't,' and I just got hold of two of the girls and now it's finished."

"I should think Miss Lewis didn't mind, neither," remarked Rogers. "Why, it's one of the prettiest bedrooms in the house. What does he want to give it to her for, I'd like to know. Putting ideas into her head, I call it, as if she isn't stuck up enough already and me always as nice as pie to her. I don't see why anyone should mind sleeping there; after all, it isn't as if that poor Miss Blake had been done to death in her bedroom."

Mrs. Dukes suppressed a shudder.

"That's as may be, Ada," she said, "but I wouldn't sleep in there, no, not if you were to crown me with a golden crown. That room's haunted, you mark my words. Not but what it's a good idea of the doctor's, though." She gave a final pick at the offending corn and drew on her stocking. "There, that's better. Now I'll make you a nice strong cup of tea."

Ten minutes later, Ada Rogers was cosily ensconced in a creaking wicker chair in front of the fire, her black alpaca skirt folded back over her bony knees, and a cup of thick Indian tea within reach of her right hand.

Mrs. Dukes' sitting-room was drab-looking and over-furnished, for here the odd knick-knacks of furniture banished from other parts of the building by the doctor found a resting-place. But to Ada Rogers it was easily the nicest room in the Hydro, and if she had ever had the chance of furnishing a sitting-room herself, she would have made it an exact replica of this.

"That's new, isn't it, Emmie?" she asked, pointing to a tripod of bamboo, with three swinging ferns, supporting an aspidistra in a garish green pot.

Mrs. Dukes popped the last piece of buttered toast into her mouth and nodded, licking her fingers.

"Um. The doctor found it somewhere in the Hydro and I shouldn't like to say what he called it. He told me to throw it out on to the rubbish-heap, but I couldn't do that. Waste not, want not, is what I say, though I'm sure I get no thanks for it."

"You'll get your reward in heaven, dear," replied Rogers. "We all know that this place could never last a minute without you. Just you try giving them notice and see what they say. If the doctor doesn't like plants about the place I'm sure it's his loss, and they look very pretty in here. But then, this is such a tasteful room. I must say that I'm surprised at the doctor using language about things. It isn't like him, from all accounts."

Mrs. Dukes ran her tongue noisily over her top teeth (in the privacy of her room she allowed herself natural manners which the maids had never seen), and pursed her lips.

"Well, it is and it isn't, in a manner of speaking," she replied. "He used to be the perfect gentleman to me and to everyone else. Indeed, I've often thought he overdid the genteelness. It's quite correct when he's talking to you or me, of course; but when it comes to saying 'please' to a lazy good-for-nothing like that Amy Ford whose mother was no better than she ought to be, well, it's too much, if you take my meaning."

Rogers nodded sleepily, for Mrs. Dukes had added "a little drop of something" to her tea, and its effect was soothing.

"But that was before young Bobby Dawson was murdered," Mrs. Dukes continued. "Ever since that day, the doctor's been a different man, snapping at you when you ask a straightforward question, and swearing at a bit of dust which he'd never have noticed before. Well, I won't say that it isn't natural for him to be that upset and him thinking that his own daughter might be the next to be murdered, but I was all upset myself and no one could say I wasn't, and I never took on like that. No, you take it from me, Ada, there's another reason."

Rogers reacted in true Hydro form to this hint, and, blinking the sleep from her eyes, gazed expectantly at her friend.

"Another reason? You mean...?"

Mrs. Dukes nodded heavily.

"Yes, a woman. Oh, I know, Ada. Men are men the world over. They can't throw dust in my eyes. I've buried two husbands—"

"And if they were alive, you wouldn't be here now," Ada supplemented rather ambiguously. "But you don't mean to tell me that the doctor's in love, Emmie?"

Mrs. Dukes nodded again.

"Oh, Emmie, not – not with you?"

Mrs. Dukes drew herself up rigidly.

"Ada Rogers," she said, and her voice was grim, "I may have my ambitions, but I hope I know my place, which is more than some people do that I could mention. I must say that I'm surprised at you saying such a thing to my face. I'm sure I gave you no reason for it. There's talk enough and to spare behind my back, without my best friends insinuating things."

Whether her indignation was really due to this remark or whether the gin in her tea had caused this morose effect, Rogers could not discern; but the housekeeper was genuinely upset, and it was some twenty minutes before she would allow herself to be pacified, and Rogers left at half past eleven without having had her curiosity satisfied.

"No, Ada," were the housekeeper's final words, "I know my place and no one can say that I make mischief. But you're an intelligent woman, just keep your eyes and ears open. That's all I'll say."

Rogers made her way from the housekeeper's room up the back staircase towards the long corridor known to the staff as "Spinsters' Walk." Bedrooms in the Hydro were allotted in strict accordance with propriety, and it was along here that unmarried women guests or widows, real or grass, slept. As she turned the corner, she saw a slim figure, wearing a blue dressing-gown and befeathered bedroom slippers, enter a door on the right. Few of these bedrooms were now in use, and the corridor was only dimly lighted, but Rogers was near enough to see that the figure in front of her was that of Miss Lewis, the doctor s secretary, evidently returning from the bathroom. For a moment she wondered what the secretary was doing in one of the guest-rooms, then remembered what the housekeeper had told her about Miss Blake's bedroom. "A good idea of the doctor's," she had said, but Rogers had her own opinion of that.

As she drew level with the door of the room which would always be known to present and future generations of the staff as "That poor Miss Blake's bedroom," she noticed that it had been left ajar, and at once her unvoiced suspicions came crowding into her mind.

"A good idea of the doctor's!" she thought again. Maybe and maybe not. There was more in most things than met the eye, and you don't leave your bedroom door open at half past eleven at night by accident, she argued, not if you're sleeping for the first time in a room whose last occupant had been murdered. Not you! Not unless – and she almost smacked her lips over the thought – not unless you were expecting a visitor.

The thought startled her, and she tried to justify it to herself. Well, that sort of thing did happen, didn't it? It had happened more than once in this very hotel to everyone's knowledge and it might happen again.

Her thoughts had taken her to the end of the corridor when she heard footsteps, muffled by the thick carpet, approaching along the right-angled turning facing her. She hesitated, then, obeying a sudden impulse, turned, and running softly back, entered a small, dark, maid's closet with a conveniently open door which stood almost exactly opposite the room Miss Lewis had entered. Barely avoiding contact with the enamel pails and jugs which practically filled the confined space, she held her breath as the footsteps drew near and halted at the open bedroom door. Without hesitation the newcomer pushed the door still further open, saying, "Are you there, darling?" and was greeted by a flurry of pale-blue satin and bare arms as Miss Lewis greeted him and drew him into the bedroom. The door closed and the key clicked in the lock, but not before Rogers' quick eyes had seen the familiar face and recognized the voice. A grim smile came to her lips as a low murmur of voices came from the room, and she stood still in a riot of triumphant thought.

The doctor! The doctor and his secretary! The dirty pair! Oh my, what a scandal! Well, Mrs. Dukes had told her to keep her eyes and ears open and she had done it to some purpose. So that was what Emmie had meant, was it? No wonder Miss Sly-puss Lewis hadn't wanted to make any friends in the Hydro: she had been afraid that her little game would be spoiled, of course. Fancy now! The cheek of the doctor to bring his bit of skirt openly into one of the best bedrooms so that he could visit her at night. Perhaps she wasn't the first one either. After all, a doctor could go so openly into a woman's bedroom, and Miss Lewis wasn't the first attractive woman to have stayed in the place. There had been Miss Blake and Winnie Marston, and look what had happened to them!

Oh, she knew what she knew, but she wouldn't keep silent any longer. She'd spoil their little game for them. They'd been clever, too clever altogether for most people, but not clever enough for Ada Rogers. Oh no!

She extricated herself noiselessly from the closet, and with heightened colour and belligerent step, strode round the corner on her interrupted way to her own bedroom.

CHAPTER XL

Half an hour afterwards, Dr. Williams came out of his secretary's bedroom, his thoughts in a turmoil.

Until tonight he had not realized that he regarded Gwynneth Lewis with any feeling deeper than the normal liking which any man possesses for an efficient secretary who helps to ease the difficult round of his daily work. He had thought of her as sweet-tempered, clever, and good to look at, but she had always lacked any definite personal attraction for him. She was always in the background of his life and he had come to regard her as something of a nonentity. As a very useful and necessary nonentity, be it said, but still, as a nonentity.

Not until tonight had he realized that all this apparent lack of personality had been part of her pose as the perfect secretary, as part of her official make-up. Not that she used real make-up, he thought, somewhat inconsequently. He had always been glad of that. He sympathized every morning with the men in the newspaper advertisements who were eternally doomed to take out girls with cosmetic complexions, or lips that had that painted look. Not that it was really any business of his, of course, but still he was glad that he had had the sense to choose such a girl as his secretary. The thought held a subtle flattery.

But tonight he had realized that she was not really a nonentity but a most attractive, flesh-and-blood woman, the kind of woman he would choose to marry if he ever wanted to marry again, which, of course, he didn't. The very idea was absurd, although a wife did help to make a doctor's life a happier and more social affair, of course.

He puzzled over this change of attitude which had been so sudden and rather alarming. Perhaps, he thought, it had been her swift embrace and the perfume from her hair, or the pressure of her cool, bare arms. Perhaps it had been the sight of her, dressed in that blue silk thing with her hair brushed over her shoulders, and her bare ankles gleaming softly pink in the light from the fire. He had never seen her before dressed in anything but a neat costume or severe afternoon frock, for the staff were never encouraged to wear evening dress even at social functions like Lady Warme's concerts. The residents did not approve of such things.

Sitting there, in the intimacy of the bedroom, he had felt most sharply attracted towards her; so much so that he had begun to wonder whether, after all, it was an entirely new sensation, or whether it had not always been there, whether he had been aware of it before and had deliberately stifled it. If he had belonged to any other profession, he might have put it all down to the natural reaction of a man who sees a pretty woman in the intimate warmth of her bedroom. But that was so much a part of a doctor's routine that he dismissed the idea, although, to be sure, the women he visited professionally at Presteignton Hydro were usually anything but pretty – except Miss Blake and Winnie Marston, those poor unfortunate creatures; but they were different...

The thought of them brought back to his mind the reason why he was walking along the upper corridor at this time of night. No doubt Winkley had some reason for this play-acting, though what it was was quite beyond him. For the hundredth time, he wondered if it was possible that the police suspected Gwynneth Lewis of murder. She had seemed so remote from all the crimes that he had never even considered it until today; but the police must have thought it possible that she might have been in some way involved in them, or surely they would never have staged this night's performance.

It was quite ridiculous to think of Gwynneth – such a pretty name, and how glad he was that she had never cut her hair short! – as a murderess; yet, strangely enough, it had been the thought of this possibility which had first made him aware of her as a woman.

He descended the stairs and paced the twisting corridors to his private rooms like a man walking in his sleep. He barely acknowledged the presence of Mr. Winkley, Inspector Palk, and Sergeant Jago, as he entered his study and sat down heavily in one of his leather chairs.

"Well." he said with an effort, "I suppose it went off all right."

"Yes," replied Mr. Winkley. "It couldn't have been better."

Sergeant Jago, who had restrained himself with difficulty from making any remark that evening, could no longer contain himself.

"Ada Rogers!" he exclaimed. "Ada Rogers, of all the...! Well, blow me if I wasn't right all along. When do we get an arrest?"

"You said it was Miss Brendon," growled Palk, "and as for arresting anyone, don't worry, it may never happen! We still haven't got a stitch of evidence for arresting anyone, as far as I can see. I tell you frankly, Mr. Winkley, I still don't see any sense in it. Yet you say that what's happened tonight was what happened on the night that Miss Blake was murdered."

Mr. Winkley regarded him with tolerant eyes.

"Something like that," he said.

CHAPTER XLI

The following night a watcher might have seen the same thing repeat itself. Dr. Williams walked along corridors, which were apparently deserted, to the same bedroom. But this time he remained behind its locked door for an hour before leaving, and this time Ada Rogers was not hiding in the maid's closet.

Another hour passed.

Inside the bedroom, Gwynneth Lewis, wrapped in the blue satin dressing-gown, sat beside the few embers glowing in the old-fashioned barred grate. She felt partly excited, partly nervous, partly incredulous, and wholly conscious of another deeper and more overwhelming emotion underlying all others. She played nervously with a few strands of hair which fell in a soft, thick cloud over her shoulders, and listened to the faint creakings which are familiar to old houses at night. As always when alone, she thought of the doctor.

Was it possible that the police suspected him? If so, they were wasting their time. She knew him to be incapable of hurting a mouse: he could never destroy a human life, especially the life of a child like Bobby Dawson. Other people saw the doctor when he was on duty, his manner calm and reassuring: she saw him when he was irritable or tired or worried or angry, and she loved him all the more for these weak, unguarded moments. Other people might believe him to be capable of murder: she knew he was not.

She started, listening, conscious of the wild thumping of her heart, but any sound she may have heard was not repeated, and she returned to her errant thoughts.

The events of the last two evenings had shaken her out of the studied composure which everyone in the Hydro accepted so much as a matter of course. It was not easy for her to believe that the doctor really cared for her, and yet... She blushed at the remembrance of their last embrace at the doorway of her bedroom tonight, and at the recollection of the look in his eyes. A deep, startled look as if he was reluctant to believe what he knew to be the truth.

They had been very indiscreet. Could anyone have seen them, and if so...

A sudden alien noise broke across the night creaking of the hotel; a subdued but insistent knock, knock, on the door of her room. She started up, and by the dryness of her throat and the dampness of her forehead she knew that she was afraid.

Her thoughts became wild.

Knock, knock. Who's there? Dawson, Dawson who? Daw's son was murdered, murdered, murdered. Knock, knock. Palk. Pork and beans for breakfast. As if anyone would ever eat them for breakfast. Americans perhaps, you never knew with Americans. Knock, knock. Who's there? Dukes. Duke's son, cook's son, son of a belted earl. Why were earls belted? Was it something to do with wearing a sword? Must look it up in the encyclopaedia tomorrow. If she was alive tomorrow, that was. Knock, knock. What a silly game! Who on earth had invented it? Someone on the Stock Exchange perhaps. But who is it at the Stock Exchange who does all this inventing? And why?... Knock, knock. The knocking on the gate in Macbeth. How did Shakespeare know about all the feelings the human mind was capable of? Had he ever lain awake at night with a murderer knocking on his door? A murderer! Knock, knock...

This was foolishness. She summoned all her courage and, as if in obedience to an unheard command, moved towards the door, and turning back the key, flung it open.

The corridor lights were out and the figure outside was dim and shadowy in the distant, friendly haze from the lamp on the table beside the bed.

"I'm so sorry to disturb you," said a gentle voice, "but I have such a dreadful headache. I thought you might let me have some aspirins. I haven't any left."

A shaky little laugh expressed Miss Lewis's relief.

"Why, of course. Come in," she said.

"I am so glad you're not asleep. It's quite an act of Providence that you were moved so near to me. I do so much dislike disturbing you, but I suffer so much with headaches. I've had them ever since I was a girl, but lately they have grown so much worse. I took coffee again tonight. It was very foolish of me. Coffee always upsets me."

Miss Lewis went over to the table beside the bed and took up a small, transparent bottle. Her visitor closed the door softly, and came across to take it from her.

"Thank you so much. I'll just take two out of the bottle, if you don't mind, then I shall know how many to return to you tomorrow."

Miss Lewis looked carefully at the thin figure in its unbecoming, shapeless dressing-gown and boudoir cap, and exclaimed in surprise:

"Why, you've brought your work-bag with you!"

"So I have. How stupid of me! I'm so used to carrying it about everywhere with me that I suppose... force of habit... very stupid, but when you've such a terrible headache..."

"Oh, it's quite easily done," replied Miss Lewis, simulating a cheerfulness she was far from feeling. "Perhaps you'd like to take the aspirins while you're here."

Her visitor smiled.

"How kind you are! I believe I will. No, please don't trouble. I'll pour out the water myself." She stretched out a hand to take the glass from Miss Lewis, and as she did so, the two aspirins fell from her hand on to the floor. "Oh, how very stupid of me! How very clumsy!"

"You'd better have two more," said Miss Lewis, putting the glass on the table.

"No, no, please, no. Such a waste. I can see them quite clearly just under the table. If you wouldn't mind getting them for me... I'm so sorry to be such a nuisance, but... my head..."

Miss Lewis bent down and peered under the table.

"They must have rolled right underneath," she said, pressing her chin down on her chest to see better.

She heard a slight click behind her, and in the next instant a shout, "Stop her!" As she stood up, she had a confused impression of flailing arms, and the chair in front of the fire overturned with a crash. The door burst open, and Dr. Williams rushed in, followed by several police constables.

The doctor came straight across the room and put his arms round his secretary.

"Are you safe?" he asked anxiously. "She didn't...?"

"I'm all right," said Miss Lewis with a tremulous little smile, "only terribly scared."

The constables relieved Palk and Jago of the struggling fury they could scarcely master, and held her in their midst. Inspector Palk laid his hand on the prisoner's shoulder and she ceased struggling.

"Ada Rogers," he said, "I..." He hesitated and peered closely into her face. "Good God!" he exclaimed. "It's... it's..."

"Miss Astill," finished Mr. Winkley, "and here" – stooping to pick up something from the floor – "here is the weapon and the handle."

"How could I be expected to recognize anyone in that get-up?" asked Palk, indicating the shapeless garment which Miss Astill was endeavouring to wrap round herself, "and how the hell can I be expected to see anything without lights?"

The sergeant stepped across the room and pressed down the switch, illuminating a light in the centre of the large, airy room and one over the dressing-table.

The object which Mr. Winkley was holding out to Palk was a steel knitting-needle of a pattern with which they were all familiar. It was fixed firmly into a handle made from a small, corrugated horn, such as is used to form the handle of a carving knife, coloured in mixed shades of yellow, blue and gold.

"What the...?" ejaculated Palk, pulling the needle out and inspecting the handle.

Sergeant Jago pounced upon Miss Astill's work-bag which lay on the floor, and held it towards the Inspector.

"Here you are, sir," he said. "Her bag! However did we come to miss it?"

Inspector Palk looked down and recognized the same bag which he had searched so carefully during his first interview with Miss Astill.

It was a large, soft bag, made of heavy tapestry material gathered on to a double steel frame. On one side the steel frame was bent upwards and the two ends fitted into each end of a coloured horn handle; on the other side the steel ends were bare and the horn handle was missing. Palk fitted the handle he held in his hands in place, and the two hooked ends of steel clipped into position, on the principle of a toilet-roll holder. He slipped it out again and inspected it.

"Very ingenious," said Mr. Winkley. "The steel frame of the bag must be exactly the same size as the knitting-needles. The hole probably decreases very slightly towards the end to give the grip. But if the hole runs right through..."

"It doesn't," said Palk, holding the end of the handle up to the light. "There must be a thick wall of steel towards the end so that there is plenty of resistance when a blow is struck with the needle."

He fitted the handle on the bag again and handed it to Sergeant Jago. "To think," he added savagely, "that that blasted woman thriller-writer, Mrs. Dawson, was right all the time! She said it was Miss Astill, and she said we should find the handle right under our noses. Why, I actually had that bag in my hands!" He again went up to Miss Astill, who had made no further attempt to struggle, and put his hand on her shoulder.

'Ephemia Mary Astill," he said, "I arrest you for the attempted murder of Gwynneth Lewis. Also for the murders of Antonia Blake, Winifred Mary Marston, and Robert Henry Dawson, and I have to warn you that anything you say may be taken down and used in evidence against you."

"That doesn't apply to me: I'm the daughter of a cavalry officer," said Miss Astill calmly. Then her dull-brown eyes blazed as if lighted by a deep-white flame, and her face became suffused with colour. "Why did you come?" she cried, spitting through her broken, yellowed teeth in sudden excitement. "In another minute she would have been dead. Another harlot removed from the paths of the righteous. She would have tempted the doctor, but he shall never lie on her breast. The Master speaks to his hand-maiden. He calleth her to service. The paths of the chosen people must be cleansed from the stains of sin. Naked women and bawdy men shall go no more a-whoring. Foul-mouthed children, aping lechery in their play, shall play no more. The first-born of Egypt shall be slain. You must let me go or I cannot answer for the consequences. Mine is the task, mine the labour. The Hydro has become a brothel; it must be made white as driven snow. The task of cleaning the Augean stables is a responsible one: I and Hercules together..." Her voice ran into fancies so foul that Gwynneth put her hands to her ears and hid her face against the doctor's shoulder.

Sergeant Jago made a step forward, thinking to try and stop the filthy stream of words, but Dr. Williams shook his head, and with a motion of his free hand, signalled to him to remain where he was.

At last the profanities died away into indistinguishable mutterings. Dr. Williams put Gwynneth away from him and walked slowly over to Miss Astill.

"Now, Miss Astill," he said in clear, professional tones, "you have had a lot of worry lately, and you're very run down. I'm going to send you away for a holiday, and these people are going to take care of you. Your work is finished now, and you must go where you will be safe."

"My enemies encompass me around," she said, drooping dejectedly. Then she raised her head and stared at the doctor with her old, dull expression. "You understand," she said. "You always did. I am loyal to the doctor and I have the King's shoe. They want to kill me for it, but Heaven will guard me. I am ready."

The doctor nodded to Palk, who gave whispered instructions to Sergeant Jago. The constables urged their prisoner forward. Miss Astill drew up her thin shoulders, marked time with an elaborate goose-step, and marched along in their midst without a backward glance.

The four people left in the bedroom stood still until all sound of the little procession had died away. Then they relaxed, their hands fumbling for cigarettes and matches.

"Thank the Lord that's over!" exclaimed Palk, wiping his brow. "Mad as a hatter, of course. She'll never hang. Well, I always knew she was a suspect, but it beats me how you found her out unless you discovered more evidence than I did, Mr. Winkley, and I still don't know how she managed to murder Winnie Marston. I hate to drag you over to Newton St. Mary at this hour of the morning" – he glanced at his watch – "but I flatly refuse to allow you to go to bed until you've told me all about it. If you insist on my having all the kudos in this affair, the least you can do is to tell me how I solved it so brilliantly!"

"Them's my sentiments too," said the doctor. "What about coming down to my sitting-room? There's a big fire there, and I told them to put out the whisky –"

He broke off abruptly, for Mr. Winkley and Inspector Palk were already outside the door.

CHAPTER XLII

Twenty minutes later, they were all sitting round a blazing fire in the doctor's private sitting-room, and even Miss Lewis held a glass of whisky-and-soda in one hand and a cigarette in the other. Inspector Palk held his heavy, broad-shouldered body almost upright, as though he still felt himself to be on duty; Mr. Winkley's long, thin figure was so stretched out that it scarcely seemed to touch the chair at all; the doctor leaned back with the unstudied ease of a man in his own home, looking slightly less immaculate and less dignified than usual; and Miss Lewis propped herself contentedly against the arm of her arm-chair, with her slim, bare legs drawn up beneath her, in a position in which every man present found it impossible to believe she could be comfortable. She laughingly waved away the offers of their three chairs, and for several minutes they smoked in silence.

'If you don't begin," said Palk at length, "I shall fall asleep in this very comfortable chair and lay myself open to a charge of neglect of duty while under the influence of drink. At least I have drink taken, as they put it in Ireland."

Mr. Winkley breathed a stream of reflective smoke down his nostrils.

"I'm quite willing to tell you all that I know," he said, "but I warn you that you mustn't expect an exposition of brilliant deduction or sparkling humour. I'm not an Ellery Queen, nor a Peter Wimsey, nor do I possess the Gallic wit of Poirot. We derided Sergeant Jago's tendency to model his deductions on those of the latest thriller he had read, but to a certain extent we allowed ourselves to be misled in the same way."

"Why?" exclaimed Palk. "I never read thrillers."

"I know," replied Mr. Winkley. "What I mean is that we disregarded the obvious. We spoke of trying to take each individual suspect away from the Hydro in order to judge him better against a saner background. What we should have done was to concentrate on the background and evolve the most likely solution from it. When I first arrived at the Hydro, it struck me as strange that such a thing as a crime of passion or greed, such as we took Miss Blake's murder to be, could have taken place against a background of such respectability. I could have understood it if Miss Blake's murder had been an outside job, but it did not seem to fit otherwise. The ruling characteristics of the Hydro were scandal and old ladies, and it seemed to me that only by fitting both of these factors into the murders should we ever reach the truth. That is why I adopted the pose of a rather foolish man who dabbles in detection, so that I could absorb the atmosphere of the place. When at last I got a clue to the murderer, it seemed so obvious that the Hydro should produce what might well be called 'The Case of the Suppressed Spinster,' that I felt justified in playing my hunch. The trouble is, as I say, that writers of detective fiction have become so ingenious in evolving newer and better solutions to crimes, that we are apt to consider the suppression theory old-fashioned, whereas in reality it is far more common in real life than the family curse or the cousin from Australia."

"That's true enough, I suppose," agreed Palk, "but after all, we knew Miss Astill was a suspect. I still can't imagine how you came to work it all out."

"You'd have worked it out for yourself in time," replied Mr. Winkley. "I had a hunch that showed me a short cut, that's all, and living as I did amongst the residents, I had a better chance to get the feeling of the place. As I told you, Inspector, I have to solve problems in my department at the Yard by hunches, because they aren't sent to me at all until they have been exposed to the X-ray of official investigation without showing any result. I had a start on you because I had no preconceived ideas to get rid of."

"Sir H– er – Harry the Punter being my preconceived idea," grunted Palk.

"That's it," grinned Mr. Winkley.

"I didn't mean to interrupt you by asking questions," said Miss Lewis, "but... Harry the Punter... who is he?"

Palk explained, then asked Mr. Winkley to continue.

"Yes," went on Mr. Winkley, "you already had fixed solutions to the first two crimes with plenty of evidence to justify yourself. But I was so sure that both murders were the work of one hand that I at once dismissed 'Sir Humphrey,' because he was in gaol at the time of the second murder, and I dismissed Matthews because I couldn't connect him to the first murder. Having washed out your two chief suspects, I had a whippet's start. The doctor is my friend and so I didn't suspect him" – Palk moved uneasily in his chair – "though officially, no doubt, I ought to have done. Also, it was he who asked me to come down to investigate and he would hardly have done that if he'd been guilty."

"Not I," laughed the doctor. "I have far too great a respect for your reputation."

"Well, I suspected everyone else, although from the beginning I didn't really think it was a man's murder. Men are habitually suspicious of instruments such as knitting-needles and hatpins, and though Colonel Simcox used knitting-needles for his socks, I thought he was telling the truth when he said he'd use his Service revolver if he'd wanted to kill anyone. I didn't seriously suspect the staff, apart from Nurse Hawkins, nor the Marstons, and that again narrowed things down to about half a dozen of the female of the species."

"I always had a feeling that it was Mrs. Napier," put in Miss Lewis, "when I wasn't too busy to think about it at all. After all, she is the most abnormal one of the lot."

"Well, of course, I examined the case against her very carefully," replied Mr. Winkley, "but I decided that although she might quite conceivably commit a murder, she was not cunning enough to have kept quiet about it. She was jealous if anyone but herself was in the limelight. Her presence at all the scenes of the crimes was an attempt to take our attention off everyone else and focus it upon her: witness, for instance, her appearance on the scene of each crime to create an impression as dramatic as possible upon us all. This was so in the baths, and again after Bobby's murder, and even at the scene of my reconstruction of Miss Blake's murder. But there was no sign of her immediately after Miss Blake's actual murder, simply because she hadn't heard about it. She was even willing to confess to a crime she knew she hadn't done just for the sake of what Mrs. Dawson would call 'publicity.'"

"That woman!" muttered Inspector Palk under his breath.

"Mrs. Napier's actions were queer and abnormal," continued Mr. Winkley, ignoring the interruption, "but they were impulsive rather than planned, while the murders gave the impression that they were well thought out and planned."

"You never seemed to suspect Lady Warme or the Admiral," remarked the doctor.

"Palk eliminated them for me," returned Mr. Winkley. "The Admiral couldn't stand without holding on to something, and the person who struck such a blow must have had the good timing dependent on a perfect balance, or the one vital spot would have been missed. As for Lady Warme, she was having treatment for her shoulder which was so stiff that she could not have raised her arm high enough to lend sufficient force to the blow. She had no knowledge of anatomy either, as far as I could discover. It is not a necessary attribute for the sale of grocery except in so far as it is needed for dissecting a side of bacon."

"A fine hydropathic remark," laughed Dr. Williams. "Well, I quite frankly suspected Nurse Hawkins." he went on, "and that's partly why I sent for you. She had the knowledge and strength to strike the blows; she had the best opportunity of anyone to kill Winnie Marston; she acted in a suspicious and almost furtive manner when anyone questioned her, and I was really afraid to let her attend the patients for fear of another tragedy, but, of course, after the second murder, wild horses wouldn't have dragged them into the baths any more."

"I considered her," said Mr. Winkley, "but I kept an open mind. Her furtive manner when answering questions showed that she had something to hide, but it was always possible that it was something of great importance to herself rather than to the case. I watched her carefully, and I noticed that she broke a number of rules which would have got her into trouble if you had found her out. She smoked pretty frequently when on duty, for instance, and there was quite a lot of truth in Mrs. Napier's assertion that the nurse neglected her, for she slipped away whenever she had a chance. However, I decided that it was nothing more than the desire to keep herself in Admiral Urwin's eye. You see, I didn't turn a deaf ear to all the scandal in the Hydro. It is my experience that scandal is generally based on a bit of truth which becomes distorted as it travels."

"As a matter of fact," said Miss Lewis, "Nurse Hawkins told me yesterday that she is officially engaged to the Admiral, but she asked me to say nothing about it until this affair was cleared up. All the nurses are the same. People talk about them being keen on their jobs, but they would all rather be married. They come here to try and get off with some rich bachelor or widower, and usually begin by setting their caps at the doctor." The whisky gave her the courage to smile roguishly at him.

"That's the first I've heard about it," he returned.

Palk took out his pipe and, having asked permission, began to pack it with tobacco.

"I must say I suspected Mrs. Dawson," he said, "and I'm almost sorry it wasn't her, for it would have made a very pretty case. It seemed too much of a coincidence that she should have actually planned the murder of Miss Blake with a knitting-needle, on paper only. You can never be sure of women; they're all a little unbalanced, if you'll forgive my saying so, Miss Lewis. Mrs. Dawson might have got so taken up with all her murder-story writing that she wanted to get her information at first hand. It might have turned her brain so that she got her identity mixed and actually committed a murder when she thought she had only written about it."

"As you say, Inspector," smiled Mr. Winkley, "it would have made a pretty case and she certainly seemed a most suspicious character. But I borrowed the manuscripts of her two previous books from the agents, and they convinced me that she couldn't even plan a murder, let alone carry it out. She would have left a complete paper-chase of clues behind her. Her books are robust affairs with plenty of blood and a great sense of the dramatic. All the same, I understand that her brilliant first novel, *Murder in the Hydro*, has already been accepted on the strength of the publicity she obtained by being at the Hydro during the murders. And she wanted the money to educate her son, poor soul!"

'Then you suspected Ada Rogers," said the doctor.

"No," replied Mr. Winkley.

"No?" repeated Dr. Williams in amazement. "Then what was the point of staging that open scandal between Miss Lewis and myself so that Ada could see us?"

"Haven't you tumbled to that yet?" asked Mr. Winkley. "Perhaps I'd better give you the case against Miss Astill from the beginning."

"Wait a minute," said the doctor, getting up from his chair. "Let me fill your glass first."

CHAPTER XLIII

"I first noticed Miss Astill," began Mr. Winkley, after the amber liquid in the glasses of the three men had been adjusted to a satisfactory level, "on the first day of my visit to the Hydro, because she was the only one who seemed to suspect that I was from Scotland Yard. That was nothing in itself, but it did just strike me that it might be a case of the fear being father to the thought. Then I staged the reconstruction scene in the drawing-room..."

"I could never make out why you concentrated on that murder instead of the one in the baths," interrupted Palk. "To all intents and purposes you were going over a crime which had already been solved."

"You must remember that I never believed 'Sir Humphrey' guilty of the murder, and I had a feeling that all the clues lay in that first crime. However, I admit that I partly staged it in the drawing-room because I realized that, as Dr. Williams says, wild horses would never have dragged them into the baths, and I hoped that the murderer would be induced to come forward in some way."

"Then I was in danger on that settee," remarked Miss Lewis. "I certainly felt that I was at the time."

"No. You see, I had taken the precaution to turn out the lights and no one could have found the exact spot to stab your head in the dark."

"I was furious with you about that reconstruction," smiled Palk. "I really believed that you were one of these well-intentioned amateurs who do so much to hamper the police. You said at the time that you had gained some valuable information out of it. I always wondered whether you meant that or not."

"I got another piece of information which tended to strengthen my suspicion of Miss Astill," returned Mr. Winkley, "but of course I exaggerated it all to blazes when I told you it was valuable. You see, the drawing-room furniture had been changed round as much as possible since the murder; that was the doctor's idea to try and persuade people to make use of the room again; and the settee had been pulled crosswise to the one side of the hearth. I had been shown all over the Hydro by Dr. Williams, and knew that the settee had been standing directly in front of the hearth when Miss Blake's body was found, but, as a new arrival, I had to pretend not to know this, and so asked how it was that Miss Lewis was so clearly visible to the whole room when she sat on the settee. It was Miss Astill who volunteered the information that the settee must have been moved since the murder, but I didn't place too much importance on this at the time because it was quite possible that the maid who found the body had described the whole scene thoroughly to her. I just docketed the fact until after Bobby's murder. Then I did get a definite line on Miss Astill, but it was just luck. As you know, when Grace screamed I 'happened' to be nearest to the shrubbery, and naturally 'slipped' in to have a look!"

He cast an expressive glance at the Inspector, and Palk wriggled unhappily in his chair.

"All right, don't rub it in," he growled.

"Well," laughed Mr. Winkley, "I sent Colonel Simcox up to the house for the doctor because I had only that minute parted from the old boy and knew that he hadn't had time to kill a beetle let alone to kill a child. I was able to get a good look at everyone as he or she came into the shrubbery, but it didn't tell me much until after Mrs. Dawson was taken away. Then Miss Astill knelt down beside the body with her back to all the others, and said, 'He is safe in the arms of Jesus.' Her voice sounded reverent enough, but when I looked down at her face I saw that it looked excited and suffused, just as it did half an hour ago, and her expression was... well... gloating is the only word that expresses it. It was the look you might expect to see on the face of a priest who has just made a human sacrifice to Moloch, and it set me thinking backwards, in the way that one is taught to tackle geometry problems at school. I at once assumed that she was the murderess and, as she didn't look normal, I assumed that her motive was abnormal too. I went back to Newton St. Mary with the Inspector and we talked the case over together. I was lucky to recognize Harry the Punter and to make a good guess about Matthews, but it was really Sergeant Jago who solved the case for me. He put forward two suggestions which, I admit, he would never have done if he'd thought we were discussing the murders seriously. He said that all the victims had been young and good-looking, and that all the scandal of the Hydro was manufactured in Miss Brendon's room. He also said that someone had just started a new scandal involving the names of Miss Lewis and the doctor."

The two people he mentioned exchanged glances, and Miss Lewis blushed unaccountably.

"Inspector Palk gave me his records of the case," continued Mr. Winkley, noting the blush without appearing to do so, "and I went very carefully over his notes relating to Miss Astill. I felt that I was on the right track when I dis-covered that she had become violently excited, almost frenzied indeed, when speaking of Miss Blake's morals and clothes, or her lack of them. It occurred to me that a possible motive might be the removal of some form of immorality from the Hydro, which seemed to fit even better when I remembered that Miss Astill was always talking about her loyalty' to it.

"You may think this isn't motive enough for murder nowadays, when most young people wear evening undress, and drink and say 'My God,' but you can't judge Miss Astill by normal standards. She is a product of an age which is fast dying out, and is quite incapable of adapting herself to modern ideas and fashions. She is a spinster who has reached what is vaguely spoken of as 'The Dangerous Age' (if you can call any one age of woman more dangerous than another, which I doubt), who gave up all her youth to nursing an invalid mother and an irascible father. You heard her say that her father was a cavalry officer, and I bet he gave her hell. If it doesn't convey much to you, let me remind you that an officer in those days was the product of a discipline which demanded that dying men should stand to attention and salute when visited by their superior officer in hospital. Brought up strictly as a prude, Miss Astill was kept out of contact with the outside world, and when she came to Presteignton Hydro after her parents' death she lived amongst the same kind of people who still dressed in the fashions of their parents. The appearance of Miss Blake must have been a severe shock to her sense of propriety and modesty. I am told that Miss Blake came down for dinner the first time in a skin-tight, cerise evening gown with no back and very little front, with shoes and lipstick to match, and that she at once made a bee-line for Colonel Simcox, who, up to that time, had been Miss Astill's recognized champion."

"She was got up to kill that night," remarked Miss Lewis. "She would have been noticeable even at a night-club, so you can imagine what she looked like at the Hydro, where the women sport bottle-green or black velveteen dresses with high necks and elbow-sleeves in the evening. The men couldn't take their eyes off her."

"Of course, it was all part of her work to dress like that," said Mr. Winkley. "She attracted the men while Harry the Punter attracted the women."

Palk tapped his chin with the middle finger of his left hand.

"But if Miss Astill felt that she was divinely inspired to clear the Hydro of all immorality, I don't see why she left Nurse Hawkins alone," he said. "Surely she and the Admiral were the obvious pair to start on. The place was seething about them all the time."

"In her own way Miss Astill was very fair," replied Mr. Winkley. She never acted on hearsay alone. Miss Blake would never have been killed unless she had been seen going into the woods and into a bedroom with Sir Humphrey, and Winnie Marston would never have been killed unless she had been seen in the car with Matthews' arms around her. Nurse Hawkins was all the time out for marriage; she was very careful, for her own sake, not to allow the Admiral to take the slightest liberty with her. It was only oglings and tender words between those two."

"But where does Ada Rogers fit in?" asked the doctor.

"That's where Sergeant Jago helped me," said Mr. Winkley. "The Hydro scandals actually did originate in Miss Brendon's room. Ada Rogers' ruling characteristic was an overwhelming devotion to her mistress. When Miss Brendon's sight began to fail, Rogers kept her own eyes and ears open more widely, so that she could gather as many scraps of information as possible to tell her. After that, she developed a tendency to give news value to each incident in order to entertain her mistress... after all, it is a method adopted extensively by all journalists today. Rogers was in a particularly advantageous position for getting news because she was the connecting link between the staff and the residents. She learned the gossip of the day from the housekeeper and retailed it to the residents through her mistress, and she also obtained it from the visitors to Miss Brendon's room and retailed it to the housekeeper. Miss Brendon's chief friend was Miss Astill. When Rogers had found some extra juicy piece of scandal, Miss Astill would be asked up to Miss Brendon's room to tea on the following day. I knew that if we started a rumour about the doctor and Miss Lewis, and followed it up by staging the little bedroom scene right under Ada Rogers' nose, that Miss Astill would be invited to tea by the old lady on the next day, just as she had been invited on the day after Winnie Marston had been seen making love to her father s chauffeur."

"Yes, that's all very clear," interpolated Miss Lewis, "but why did she act so quickly in my case? It was only twenty-four hours ago that Dr. Williams and I acted your little drama at the bedroom door, when we were sure that Ada Rogers would see us and pass the information of our "intrigue' to Miss Astill through Miss Brendon. What made her act so quickly?"

"She always acted quickly," replied Mr. Winkley. "She had her own distorted idea of fair play. She never acted on suspicion only, but once she had real evidence of some supposed immorality, she acted at once. Miss Blake was killed the same evening that Miss Astill saw Sir Humphrey go into her bedroom; Winnie Marston was killed the morning after Miss Astill had visited Miss Brendon and learned of her *affaire* with Matthews; Bobby Dawson was killed probably within ten minutes of his doing or saying the thing which offended her. The attempt on you, Miss Lewis, was made an hour after she had seen Dr. Williams leave your bedroom. And again she was scrupulously fair to you in her queer way, for she would not have killed you on Ada Rogers' evidence. She hid herself in the maids' closet, just as she did before Miss Blake's murder. You were convicted on the evidence of her own eyes. She acted swiftly because her method of murdering her victims was swift and simple. It did not need any elaborate preparation. But even if she had not moved quickly to kill her other victims, I knew she would be in a hurry to murder you, because for years she had cherished a secret passion for the doctor and she hoped that one day he'd look her way."

"Good lord!" exclaimed Dr. Williams with great feeling. "As if I'd look twice at an old hag like her!" He endeavoured to prove his statement by looking several times at Miss Lewis.

"Once would have been enough," replied Mr. Winkley.

"Go on," urged Palk, looking cross-eyed at the bowl of his pipe.

"Well, as soon as Miss Astill heard of this new scandal, all she had to do was to take another knitting-needle out of Miss Brendon's tatting cushion..."

"What?" roared Palk, nearly knocking a front tooth out with his pipe.

"Didn't I tell you that?" asked Mr. Winkley with aggravating composure. "Yes, she kept the knitting-needles there. I suspected it as soon as Jago started talking about it. It was the obvious place and about the only one which was likely to be overlooked."

"It may be obvious to you, Mr. Winkley," put in Miss Lewis before Inspector Palk could recover his breath sufficiently to ask the questions trembling on his lips, "but how did the knitting-needles get into the cushion in the first place, and how did Miss Astill get them out when she wanted them without anyone seeing her?"

"I thought that part of it so clear," replied Mr. Winkley. "Miss Astill put a supply... half a dozen, I should imagine... we can check up on that tomorrow... into the cushion, after she had decided to begin murdering certain people. It was quite easy for her to push them into the cushion when Miss Brendon was making her lace, if she chose a time when Rogers was absent for a few minutes. Miss Brendon's hearing was acute, but any sound they made would mingle with the clicking of the bobbins. When Miss Astill wanted to obtain possession of what the newspaper reporters call 'the murder weapon' she could easily work one out of the cushion with her hands if she stood over it when the old lady wasn't using it. It was easy enough, because Miss Brendon so rarely did any tatting within recent years, and all she had to do then was to slip the needle into the work-bag which she always carried around with her. It didn't require much sleight of hand, and it was the obvious place because, although it was in everyone's sight and thus allayed suspicion, it would never be likely to be moved from Miss Brendon's room. I made sure that the needles were hidden inside the cushion, but didn't have it moved because our only chance of proving that Miss Astill was the murderess was to catch her in the act of attacking someone."

"You wouldn't think that a thin little woman like her would be strong enough to murder anyone," said Miss Lewis.

"She was very wiry," said the doctor. "I've seen her lift Mrs. Napier to her feet more easily than Nurse Hawkins could do in spite of her extra weight, and, of course, anyone insane becomes possessed of almost superhuman strength, as the body feeds at the expense of the brain. You all saw how strong she was tonight."

Miss Lewis frowned.

"I still don't see why she murdered Bobby Dawson. He was such an innocent child."

"Are children innocent in these days?" asked Mr. Winkley. "We shall never know what immorality he was guilty of in Miss Astill's sight, until the doctor's little girl is fit to talk about it, and perhaps not even then. I can only guess that he did or said something which she considered immoral. He may have unbuttoned his trousers in front of her – you know how supremely unconscious of themselves little boys of that age are. To a woman with such a mania, only a tiny thing would be needed to make her decide to remove him."

"How horrible!" exclaimed Miss Lewis, her eyes filling with tears. "Just think of him standing there with his little hands held up to his face, counting up to a hundred before he could look round, and that... that fiend creeping up behind him!"

They were all silent for a moment, then Palk said:

"You haven't told us how she did it, yet."

CHAPTER XLIV

Mr. Winkley helped himself to another cigarette from the doctor's silver box.

"I imagine that Miss Astill had already planned to murder Miss Blake on the night of the concert," he began, "and was waiting with her door unlatched to hear when her intended victim came up to bed. The fact that 'Sir Humphrey' actually went into her bedroom that night only served to justify the murder more completely to Miss Astill. She was, of course, just as incensed against 'Sir Humphrey' as against Miss Blake, but was cunning enough to realize that if she played her part well she would implicate him in the murder and so rid the Hydro of both of them at once. With this idea, her evidence was partly true and partly false. She very cleverly led you, Palk, to believe that she was going along to the lavatory when Sir Humphrey and Miss Blake came upstairs; but actually, as soon as she heard them, she slipped into the maids' closet opposite Miss Blake's bedroom and watched from there, just as Ada Rogers watched the doctor last night. She may have returned to her room then, but she didn't wait long before knocking on the door, because Miss Blake was still fully dressed when she was murdered; so we can take it, I think, that she hadn't had time to undress, since she would think nothing of going downstairs in a dressing-gown, or in her pyjamas, for that matter.

"Miss Astill must have got her to go downstairs by saying that she had left her purse or some such thing in the drawing-room and was afraid to go down alone. You heard tonight how plausible she can be. When they got down to the drawing-room, she probably pretended that she could see her purse under the settee, and when Miss Blake stooped down to look, she stabbed her in that vital spot at the back of her head with the needle. Then she lifted the body on to the settee where it was found."

"But how did she know about that vital spot?" asked Miss Lewis. "It must have required some special knowledge... I mean, I should never have dreamed that you could kill anyone through the skull with a knitting-needle. Oh, I know that there are plenty of medical books about the Hydro, but I still don't see how Miss Astill could have got the idea of killing anyone in that way from them, unless she knew what to look for."

"She did know," replied Mr. Winkley. "Mrs. Dawson told her."

"That woman again!" groaned the Inspector.

Mr. Winkley smiled.

"Yes, Inspector. Our lady novelist had been studying all the medical books she could find, with the object of discovering some new and striking – if you will forgive the pun – method of murder for her new book. As you know, she is not the type of woman to keep any new idea to herself, and she promptly told the first person she saw all about it. Perhaps you remember that she was almost sure she'd explained this idea to someone, but couldn't recollect to whom. I saw her again this morning and she was very helpful. She had recovered from the first stunning shock of Bobby's murder, and her only thought was to find the murderer and see him hanged. I made her take her mind back to the time when she was planning her new book, and at last she remembered that it was Miss Astill with whom she had discussed the idea of killing anyone through the medulla with a knitting-needle. She had the book with her and had pointed out the exact position of the vital spot on a diagram of a skull. We know that Miss Astill had taken a course of nursing in her young days, so that she could attend her father, so she had a rudimentary understanding of anatomy, and she had plenty of opportunity for studying the backs of her victims' heads."

"That all sounds okay to me," agreed Palk, "but it wasn't so easy for her to get to Winnie Marston in the treatment-rooms without being seen. She could get out all right, but how could she get in without running the risk of bumping into Nurse Hawkins or Mrs. Dawson?"

"She was in there before Nurse Hawkins came, in the morning," explained Mr. Winkley, "and hid inside the lavatory all the time Winnie was having treatment."

"Then it was moth-balls!" exclaimed the Inspector. "No, I've not gone mad too," he laughed as he saw the surprise on their three faces. "You must have noticed that Miss Astill's clothes always smell as if she has just taken them out of summer storage, and I thought I smelt mothballs in that lavatory, but Sergeant Jago said it was the disinfectant tablet. If I'd been Mr. Winkley, now, I should have gone about the Hydro sniffing, until my nose led me to Miss Astill."

"It's just as well that you didn't," laughed Miss Lewis. "They all use moth-balls here, even the Colonel, and I think that the ones Lady Warme uses are the strongest."

"But if Miss Astill hid in the lavatory," remarked the doctor, "she certainly did run the risk of being seen either by the nurse or by Miss Marston."

"She did, of course," agreed Mr. Winkley, "but that would only have put off the murder for a time, and to Miss Astill, one day was as good as another, for she didn't know that by the next day Winnie would no longer be in the Hydro. But as it happened, luck – or you may prefer to call it the law of probability – favoured her. She remained unobserved, and slipped out of the lavatory when Winnie was resting. It was to her that Winnie said, 'Hello, what are you doing here?' Winnie probably didn't see Miss Astill come out of the lavatory, as her head was turned the other way; but even if she did, the usual long dull story so prevalent in the Hydro about cascara versus senna pods, or liquorice versus vegetable pills, would have explained her presence quite satisfactorily. She was entitled to be there, and Winnie wouldn't have any cause to be suspicious.

"The doctor says that she was almost certain to be feeling sleepy after the treatment, and Mrs. Marston told me that Winnie always curled herself up to sleep with her head pressed forward like a kitten's, and death was instantaneous. Miss Astill ran very little risk of being seen when she came out of the rooms, because Mrs. Dawson was in the electric-room having treatment, and Nurse Hawkins was still upstairs with Lady Warme. If Matthews had come right into the ladies' room, she would have slipped back into the lavatory again, and found the opportunity to escape after he left."

"What about Mrs. Napier?" asked Dr. Williams.

"She didn't go into the baths until much later. She probably saw the police arriving and followed them. She slipped into the cubicle when the Inspector was in the men's department and the police doctor and photographer in the massage-room. She undressed in Winnie's cubicle and waited to be discovered."

"Then when Nurse Hawkins said that she saw the curtain swaying and thought Miss Marston was dressing in the cubicle, the baths were really empty except for herself and Mrs. Dawson?" asked Palk.

"Yes," replied Mr. Winkley. "The curtains do sway in the draught, and it was only because she expected Winnie to be there that she assumed it was her movements which were causing the swaying. If she had not expected anyone to be there, she wouldn't have noticed the curtains moving."

"Do you think she would still have murdered Winnie Marston if she had known she was already married to Matthews?" asked Miss Lewis.

"No, I don't," said Mr. Winkley. "That's the pity of it. Marriage is a sacred state to Miss Astill... the great enemy of the sins of the flesh... and as such she would have respected it."

"And poor Bobby's murder?" asked the doctor.

"That was the simplest of the lot. Miss Astill merely had to wait till Grace was out of sight and then slip quickly into the shrubbery. He was standing with his head bowed between his hands, as all children do when counting in Hide-and-Seek.

"Oh, 'twas the foulest deed to slay that babe,
And the most merciless that e'er was heard of!"

Palk's voice was deep and impressive.

Mr. Winkley nodded his appreciation of the aptness of the quotation, and concluded:

"I don't need to explain about the handle we couldn't find. You all saw it tonight."

"I ought to have found it at the very beginning," growled Palk. "Why, she even brought that bag to the interview with her, and I turned the whole bag upside down on my table without suspecting it. The trouble was that although I was looking for a handle, I expected to find a superfluous one, and not one which was already serving as a handle." He got up rather abruptly from his chair and knocked his pipe out against the side of the grate. "Well, Mr. Winkley, you seem to have cleared up every point," he said. "I should like to come along and have a look at that department of yours at the Yard one day. I'm sorry to break up the party, but I must be getting back. I've a busy day in front of me today." He made further movements indicative of leaving, and Mr. Winkley, glancing at Miss Lewis, got up, stretching his long legs.

"I'll come as far as the main door with you, Inspector," he said, "then I'll go up to bed. No, don't you bother, old chap," as the doctor moved forward to accompany them; but his protest did not prevent the doctor from walking with them along his private corridor as far as the double baize doors, where they stood chatting for a few minutes.

When Dr. Williams returned he found his secretary curled up in an arm-chair, face in hands, sobbing broken-heartedly.

"Why, Gwynneth!" he exclaimed, without realizing that it was the first time he had openly made use of her Christian name. "What's the matter?"

Miss Lewis lifted her head and fumbled for a handkerchief in the pocket of her dressing-gown. She turned away from him for a moment, then blew her nose, wiped her eyes, and stood up. The doctor thought that she looked very little like an efficient secretary, and very much like his daughter, Grace, at the end of a disappointing day.

He moved close to her.

"Won't you tell me what it is?" he asked.

Miss Lewis looked round, startled at his tone, smiled a little at what she saw in his eyes, and said:

"Are you asking me as my employer or as my medical adviser?"

Dr. Williams gave a snort – a blatant and finished snort which would have done credit to any one of the Hydro residents – and strode to the door. For one agonizing minute Miss Lewis thought that he had gone, but he strode back again. She did not raise her eyes.

'Tm asking as a man, Gwynneth. I love you. I've loved you for a long time, but I didn't realize it till Winkley's foolhardy scheme put you into such danger tonight. I'm not attractive, I know. I'm over forty and I've been married before. I don't fancy my chances, but I love you. Do you think you could ever care for me?"

This time Miss Lewis looked straight into his eyes.

"I am in love with you," she said a little breathlessly. "I always have loved you, and everyone in the Hydro but yourself knows it."

For some time after that, neither of them spoke, and at the end of it, Miss Lewis looked less like an efficient secretary than ever. When they did speak again, their conversation was not very coherent, and it was not until some time afterwards that Miss Lewis ran to the mirror set in the overmantel and uttered little exclamations of dismay at her reflection.

The doctor laughed at her.

"You know that you look adorable," he said. "I wonder what Grace will think about this."

Miss Lewis swung round.

"Oh, Doctor!" she exclaimed. "I'd forgotten you have a daughter. Won't she hate the idea of your marrying me?" She smiled provocatively at him and looked, as he had said, adorable, with her hair ruffled over the blue silk dressing-gown. "I suppose you do mean to marry me?"

"I suppose I shall have to after having you alone in my rooms at two o'clock in the morning, insufficiently clad by all Hydro standards. Think of the scandal about us already! And you'll have to learn not to call me Doctor."

"Darling!" she exclaimed. "Whatever will the 'inmates' say about us now?"

"That's easy," laughed Dr. Williams. "They'll say, 'What did I tell you? I always knew there was something between the doctor and his secretary!' And, as usual, they'll be right!"

THE END

Mystery
Rutland

146 5773

Lightning Source UK Ltd.
Milton Keynes UK
UKOW01f0822200617
303733UK00008B/171/P